Monsoon Rainbow
IN CANADA

Jayashree Thatte Bhat

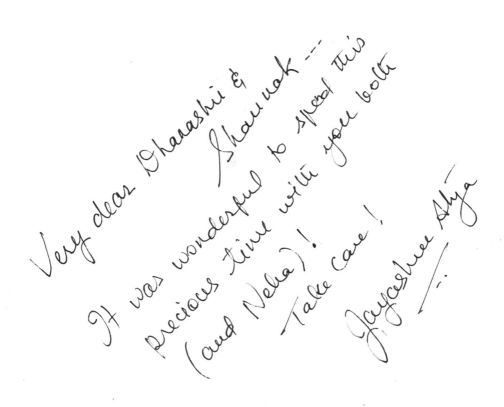

Very dear Dharashie &
Shaunak --
It was wonderful to spend this
precious time with you both
(and Neha)!.
Take care !.
Jayashree Ahya
:)

Produced by:

FriesenPress
Suite 300 – 852 Fort Street
Victoria, BC, Canada V8W 1H8

www.friesenpress.com

Distributed to the trade by The Ingram Book Company

Also By Jayashree Thatte Bhat

Books in English Language

Hindustani Vocal Music as seen outside India – A Comprehensive book on Classical Vocal Music of North India

Journey through Breast Cancer – A Scientific Knowledge Based Novel on Breast Cancer

Books in Marathi Language

Mawalthichi Zadey – A Collection of Stories

Manawache Varadaan – A Collection of Scientific Stories

Samna Breast Cancershi – A Scientific-Knowledge-Based Novel on Breast Cancer

Matrutwachi Aas – A Scientific-Knowledge-Based Novel on Human Fertility

In my New Dream,
A garden of roses I see,
Never the thorns do I fear,
For, nothing but hope fills in me.

With hard work and pride,
I begin to chase the dream,
A new life has begun,
In the promising Canadian stream.

I run and fall, and float and sink,
But never lose heart,
For, the sweet nectar of Canadian life,
With gratitude, I drink.

... An Immigrant of Canada.

Acknowledgment

In the first and the foremost place, I pray the Almighty God for the eternal blessings and Grace upon me, without which nothing would be possible.

I extend my sincere Thanks

To my husband for his good wishes and complete support in writing this book;

To my daughters and all my friends who encouraged me to write this book;

To all the people in the Immigrant Services Agencies in Ontario and Alberta for sharing their personal stories and thus enlightening me;

To the Editors who edited my manuscript with helpful suggestions;

To the FriesenPress, without whose help, this book would not be published

And reach my readers!

Dedicated to...
All immigrants who come to Canada with the very same dream –
A better life;
And have a common thread that transcends geography,
time, religion, color or creed.

Introduction

I emigrated to Canada at a time when the concept of immigration was still new to the people in India—a time when people from India were making their journey across the Atlantic Ocean to come to Canada for better prospects, and not just for political refuge. Opportunities seemed much better, and the pastures looked much greener in Canada compared to those in their homeland. For some people, especially those coming from the educated middle class, the situation was favorable for advanced education; obtaining higher degrees was a major attraction in Canada. These people carried with them a stack of official papers, such as a passport, medical certificates validating their health, documentation of their academic credentials, and most importantly, a Canadian visa issued by the Canadian embassies in India, permitting them to settle in Canada. Absence of any of these papers was never excused. These were the *immigrants,* a new wave of people coming from India; they were setting up their homes in Canada with dreams in their hearts and ambitions and aspirations for a better life.

I was one such immigrant (from the typical, educated middle-class of India) who had set her foot on Canadian soil with her heart full of hopes and dreams for further education and a better life. For people like me, getting advanced degrees from the Canadian universities was set as the goal of life by family members. The expectation was equally clear that one would return to India after the achievement of the goal, which was not necessarily a goal of one's own. Therefore, most talked about going back to India after the completion of the intended degrees; seldom did anyone openly declare plans of settling in Canada *permanently*, secretly holding that thought close to their hearts. Such a statement carried some stigma among Indians. My own situation was not any different; my family and friends back in India expected me to return there eventually, so I never dared to talk openly of settling in Canada permanently until much later.

After landing in Canada, I found a job through Manpower (in a small medical lab that paid me minimum wage) to support myself and to save some funds for my studies later. Over a period of time, I saved enough money, and after passing the qualifying exams, I was accepted into university. I quit my daytime job and gained entry into the graduate school of a reputable university in Ontario, studying towards a graduate degree in science. I was finally on the *right* track, and my family members back in India felt relaxed.

The financial assistance that was given to the students was so meager that I had to take up a part-time job to supplement my poor finances. I managed to get a teaching job as an English teacher at the Immigrant Aid Society. This job was initially meant only to support my finances, but since it proved to be very enjoyable, I continued for many years beyond the years of my studentship.

During these years, both at the university as well as at the Immigrant Aid Society, I had a wonderful opportunity to meet new immigrants from India, and I developed close relationships with a few of them. I am eternally grateful for this opportunity as it provided me a perfect tool with which to assimilate into Canadian society; it also helped me to understand the perceptions of many Indian immigrants about Canada. I learnt that a few among them had very striking experiences as they journeyed through their lives. Although they *seemed quite average* outwardly, they were, in reality, quite extraordinary! Each one of them represented a singular human experience, and as such, each one of them assumed a special place in my heart. I always had a craving for new experiences and, whenever possible, kept notes about them—sometimes on paper, and sometimes just mentally.

It was the culmination of all these notes that inspired me to write stories about these people.

It gives me a great pleasure to present to you a collection of stories based on the experiences of those wonderful people whom I had the privilege to meet, and who have been in my heart for a long time. Compiling these stories is the realization of a significant personal goal—and it is my way of saluting those wonderful people.

Nothing is as exhilarating as the process of creating characters on paper and making an attempt to share your experiences with the world; letting the world see through those special eyes and being filled with some dramatic highs can prove to be quite addictive. Those extraordinary people were already in my heart. In presenting them to you (in the form of characters assuming the primary roles in these stories), I feel confident that they will enter your heart as well, filling it with passion and compassion.

The characters in these stories serve one more purpose: they provide an opportunity to reveal the commonality of all the people who have emigrated to Canada from all over the world. At the same time, they bring about an understanding of the impact of culture and traditions on each and every one of them. Although they represent people of *Indian* traditions only, the power of tradition in any land is the common thread of all humanity. This common thread transcends geography, time, religion, color, or creed; it inevitably draws upon shared human experiences, such as love, hate, work, worry, birth, death, marriage, and dreams. Whatever the details that give concrete form to an experience of these characters, they testify to the common experiences of everyday life around the world, to the humanity of individuals, and to the predicaments of mankind.

Having said this, I realize that attitudes differ from society to society and also from generation to generation. It is of equal importance to recognize that different traditions carry different overtones. They could be set in one way in a rigid society while being different from those in a society committed to newness and change. With the tremendous growth in transportation and communication, the world is becoming smaller and smaller; what would have once been considered regional can now carry international significance—hence the different overtones!

The readers will notice that all stories are written in the first-person singular. That could be a literary convention to achieve credibility and authenticity. However, in these stories, the intent is not to stick to the literary convention—it is to tell the readers that these are stories of people I actually met, and how I happened to be the audience to the experiences that they shared with me. The *I* who narrates these stories is not just a character developed for the purpose of telling these stories in the first-person singular— it is based on a real person: *me!* In the same way, all the characters are based on real people…yet just as all the characters are developed for some dramatic effect and impact, so is the *I* character, for I am not as inquisitive, shrewd, witty, wise, and brave as the *I* in these stories.

Most of the stories in this collection may seem to be more on the tragic side, displaying victimization of the main characters by the Indian traditions; however, the incidents narrated here are *rare* occurrences. A vast majority of immigrants from India ordinarily are satisfied with their stations in life. They seem happy in their married lives and do the jobs they are paid to do, more or less competently. All of them have their tiffs, their jealousies, and their celebrations, religious or otherwise. They are good, decent, normal people who have made their homes on Canadian soil. The majority of them seem to go through life without ever changing their once-established view, making only a few minor adjustments to suit the lifestyles of their newly-adopted country. I have always respected them, even admired them at times, but they are not the people about whom I could write stories. The stories in this collection are about people who have had some kind of *singular and defining* life experience, either prior to or immediately after moving to Canada.

There is one more point I wish to make: these stories, although about real people in the real world with real-life experiences, reflect my own personal sense of cultural tension between the two worlds, old and new. The synthesis of thoughts at the end of each story, views expressed during the narration, or questions posed throughout the stories are merely to present my own opinions and my own views and beliefs. After observing and listening to these people and thinking of their experiences, I have come to the belief that age-old traditions and customs do have a powerful hold on all of us; this is especially true for Indian traditions. There is neither criticism nor any glorification intended for the old Indian traditions.

The scene of all these stories is the province of Ontario, where most of the immigrants from India made their debut as immigrants to Canada at the time I emigrated to Canada. I was one among them. With the advent of Internet and telecommunications, people wanting to move away from their homelands could access information about the most remote areas of the world in minutes. However, in those times, people from India, myself included, had limited information about Canada, most of us having a little knowledge of only two or three major cities of this land.

As described earlier, all the characters in these stories, including *I*, originate in India, a land of the torrential monsoon rains. Most of them are closely associated with the academic environment of the university in Ontario, since that was considered to be the primary destination when coming to Canada, especially those from the typical educated middle class.

I, and the character of *I*, have enjoyed being with these people, for they have filled us *both* with their joy and suffering equally. They have gone through the thick and thin of life without leaving any trails behind, unless otherwise captured by someone like me. Their stories illuminate a veritable rainbow through the wide, colorful spectrum of human emotions—anger, anxiety, frustration, confusion, despair, disgust, love, romance, hope, and peace—displaying, in the truest sense, a *Monsoon Rainbow* in the Canadian sky!

Bride of a Monster

Rita is in her late forties—a relatively young person by today's standards. Her luxuriant head of prematurely gray hair, coupled with a young-looking face and body, makes her a strange sight. It catches the eye immediately. Quite tall for an Indian woman, she has a perfect, olive-brown complexion that is adored by her Western friends, she says. In my eyes, she is a picture of elegance.

Rita grew up in the suburbs of Hyderabad, a city in South India. She was a rebellious eldest child with two younger sisters in a typically bourgeois family, and consequently went through a lot of stress in her youth. That was what made her gray so fast, she has always claimed. Her real name is Sarita, but she prefers the short form, Rita, a name that is more fitting in the Western world, she thinks.

She has a few funny and unusual mannerisms. When she wants to express strong aversions, she closes her eyes, raises her slightly thick eyebrows, and turns the corners of her mouth downwards. And when she is impressed with something, she adds a slow rhythmic nod to it. I don't know what magic she does with that slow nod, but she makes the same face seem very pleasant, as though her good impression filters through her closed eyes with the addition of her characteristic nod.

Her regard is really unusual, too. Whatever she looks at, she looks at with one eye at a time. "I'm an alternator," she jokes, "because I see with alternate eyes!" She has strong opinions on just about everything, even trivialities that she sees, hears, or reads about. When an article about the nutritious and medicinal nature of dandelions appeared in the newspaper, I remember her turning her head with a deep-throated, "Ha! Medicinal, my foot…" She went on for almost an hour, telling me how someone she knew got a bad case of diarrhea because of chewing dandelions, and how a pregnant friend who ate them lost her baby.

I met Rita very early in my days as an immigrant to Canada. Meeting someone like her was a boon to me. She provided me with numerous opportunities to meet even more admirable people. Our meeting was a strange coincidence, and developing it into a friendship was even stranger. The series of events that happened after our chance meeting assured us that we were destined to meet at some point in our lives.

After I quit my daytime job and became a full-time graduate student, I soon found out that money and time both became scarce, and any kind of entertainment was out of the question. I had no life outside the campus, and I was slowly reaching a point of burnout. Even the modern laboratory equipment, which had impressed me initially, failed to divert my emerging feelings of homesickness. I came to the conclusion that homesickness is not just physical—it must be emotional, psychological, and spiritual, too. I remember reading once that birds have a strong homing instinct. I could relate to that easily. I knew I had to do something about it, something that would help me get out of this quagmire of homesickness, and be within my means of affordability as well.

I thought of inexpensive Indian entertainment, perhaps a Hindi show or a Bollywood movie, nostalgic old favorite, which would be nothing but some erratic fantasy of pure entertainment value. In India, I never cared for this kind of entertainment, but now, I was longing to grab a few moments of 'home'! I decided to go to the Indian Immigrant Aid Society, a place that would generate some solace to my homesick heart.

Fortunately, the building was within walking distance from my graduate residence. I decided to walk there one afternoon, after my lectures were over. It was an old building that must have seen better days. Four stories high and cemented in red brick, it looked abandoned and forlorn. It had two huge doors at the entrance, with only one locked. I opened the unlocked door and stepped inside.

A narrow, dimly-lit hallway, with a huge hot water heater occupying almost half of the space, greeted me. The hallway led to a huge aristocratic-looking staircase that was quite large, wide, and ancient. I climbed up, and upon inquiry, came to know that the Indian Immigrant Aid Society occupied the top two floors of the building, with its office located on the third floor. I had not seen any sign for an elevator, so I started climbing up the staircase again. Just as I reached the third floor, I saw a huge bulletin board on the wall facing the staircase, with a few posters of Hindi movies stapled to it. Familiar faces of actors and singers stared back at me. I could feel my homesick heart starting to beat a little faster. I darted towards the board and touched those life-saving posters. My eyes scanned the notices pinned on the bulletin board; the information swam before me.

A few feet away from the bulletin board, a small table held an old rotary dial telephone. A tall brown woman wearing a long black skirt, a burgundy-colored silk blouse, and a matching silk scarf with the typical Indian paisley design was standing with her one hand resting over the table and the other holding the receiver to her ear. Although quite clear to comprehend, this woman had a heavy accent that sounded very Indian. I could not avoid overhearing the conversation. She was giving directions to someone on how to get to the Indian Immigrant Aid Society.

"Turn left under the overpass and go straight through the traffic light—if it's green, of course," she said.

I chuckled inadvertently. The woman turned, and I looked away quickly, embarrassed.

"You liked that, eh?" she asked me, after she put the receiver down.

I pretended to ignore her question, and read the notices on the bulletin board. When I saw her approaching me, I looked at her and nodded with a guilty look on my face.

"Don't worry about it," she said as she smiled.

Her disarming smile dismissed my guilt immediately, and gave me the courage to tell her what had amused me. "I liked the generous specificity of your instructions," I said.

She must have liked my honesty because she didn't say anything further. She extended her hand towards me for a handshake and said, "I am Rita Reddy. And you are..."

"Neila Singh." I briefed her about my intention for visiting the Society.

"Where do you work, Neila?" she asked.

"I'm a graduate student at the university."

"Are you interested in teaching here?"

"Huh?" She caught me off guard.

"I said, are you interested in teaching here?"

"Teaching what?"

"English, of course. Teaching English to new immigrants from India who don't know the language."

"I've never taught English before."

"So what? As a graduate student, you must know English quite well. Canada wants her people to be functionally fluent in at least one of her two official languages, English and French. The government encourages it. They give us a small grant to conduct such classes," she explained further, briefly and crisply.

I must have looked confused while listening to her, because she looked at me with the same surprise that I saw earlier.

"God, we're not teaching Shakespeare or Milton here. Our purpose is to help our government meet their goal. We teach new people how to converse and comprehend simple English in general, that's all. And my experience is that when these new immigrants see an Indian teacher from India, they feel a lot more comfortable. It's only natural, I suppose. So, interested?" she asked me again. I stayed quiet, as this whole incident was most unexpected.

"Fortunately, we have many volunteers here at the Society," she continued. "We cannot offer any money for their services as the Society just can't afford to pay for any volunteer services. However, the language teaching staff does get a small pay, an honorarium as we call it. I can arrange that for you, too, if you can teach English here."

Her offer was tempting, especially knowing that this work would offer me some kind of ties with India, thus reducing my homesickness; of course, it would provide me with some money, too. But then, what made her offer this when she hardly knew me?

Full of doubt and a bit confused, I mumbled, "Well, that sounds really good."

"So, do you wish to accept my offer or not?" she asked. She was direct.

"Well, yes, I suppose," I managed to reply to her authoritative question. I was feeling a bit amused at this strange incident.

"Good!" she said, looking pleased. "You will be very happy to join here and meet other teaching staff members, I assure you." She looked at me intently and continued. "Come now, come to my office. We'll sit and talk a bit about what your new job entails." She led me to her office while explaining what she did at the Society; I followed her quietly, listening to her every word, mildly impressed with her confidence. Even her gait impressed me. She pointed to a hard plastic chair and asked me to sit down. I did, obediently.

Rita was the Society's Executive Director, and worked in the office full time. Her responsibilities included, among many other things, assigning specific duties to people who volunteered at the Society. Assigning people to teach English to the new Canadians was one of her main responsibilities. She opened a folder that was on her desk, which held a few papers and some chart-like schedules, and started reading to herself in a soft voice. "Geeta is doing the classes on Mondays and Wednesdays, and Tuesdays and Thursdays, Vanita was assigned, but she has babysitting problems on Thursday afternoons, she just told me this morning. Hmm…" She looked up. "How would you like to teach Thursday afternoon classes? It's for two hours. Can you do that?"

"Uh, let me check my class schedule at the school first," I said.

"Thursday's class is an introductory class. There are seven people registered, all women, recently immigrated from India. The classes will run for twelve weeks, at the end of which the students will be assessed for their knowledge of English language. There's no credit or anything given for these courses; the aim is only to impart some basic knowledge of the English language. The students are encouraged to re-register if they feel they're gaining something from these classes. That's all. If you can teach on this day and in this time, my offer is there for you, okay?"

I nodded quietly.

"See, getting teachers for evening classes is not a problem for us; that works out all right. Many are willing to teach even voluntarily for these classes. And most of our volunteer teachers have full-time day jobs. But getting people for afternoon sessions poses a big problem. If you're available, that would be lovely." She looked hopeful. Once again, I quietly nodded.

She closed the folder after making a note in it with her pencil, then reached towards the upper shelf to put it away. I was watching her gestures and mannerisms all the while. Every time she emphasized some point, her right hand would give a small jerk to her wrist as though she was about to propel a small object or toss a Ping-Pong ball. At the same time, her left hand would check her hair bun, creating an impression that was evocative of a dancing pose for that brief moment. All this seemed quite interesting and quite amusing, too. She was different from most of the people I had met thus far, and was quite genuine too, without a trace of fakeness about her.

"Where are you from—in India, that is?" I asked her casually.

"From Hyderabad," she replied.

"Hyderabad?" I felt a bit excited. "Were you born there?"

"Yes. Why?"

"And brought up there too?" I asked again, with a little excitement.

"Yes. I was born, brought up, and educated in Hyderabad. Why do you ask?" I sensed a faint curiosity with a bit of annoyance in her voice.

"Because, I'm..."

"You are what?" she interrupted.

"I am from Hyderabad, too. Born, brought up, and let's say, half-educated..."

"Oh, my good God, really?" Now she sounded quite excited.

"Yes. What a small world!"

"Yes, yes indeed! No wonder I felt drawn towards you." She laughed loudly, which would have startled some people.

"Me too." I admitted, and joined her laugh. "We both have walked on the same soil as youngsters."

"Oh, but you must have still been in diapers when I left Hyderabad, though," she said, and laughed again.

The meeting was over and we both came out of her office. She walked me down the staircase to the front doors, telling me how wonderful it would be for me to join the teaching crew at the Society. After saying a friendly goodbye to her at the front door, I walked back to my residence in total silence, all the while contemplating what had transpired in that simple attempt of finding some casual Indian entertainment for myself. I had returned home with an offer to teach English to the new immigrants from India, and the offer was from an Indian who was born and raised in the same city as I was! What a strange coincidence! It was very tempting to accept this offer, as it would not only break the monotony of studies and exams, but take me every week for a couple of hours into an Indian environment, something that I felt I was badly in need of. Getting a little bit of money was an additional benefit, and meeting Rita, a person from my hometown, was a big boon. The very next day, after checking my class schedule, I telephoned Rita and gave her my positive answer.

I started teaching on Thursday afternoons regularly, hoping to see Rita every time I was there. If I didn't see her, I would inquire about her in the administration office. The feeling must have been mutual, for she would regularly drop in to my class, although this was not required of her; if she came before the class was over, she would wait for me outside the room. Before we realized what was happening, Rita and I became friends. Our age difference of more than twenty years or our career differences didn't matter. We enjoyed a good *tête-à-tête* with each other.

Over time, we started visiting each other outside the Society for coffee or for an occasional dinner. The dinner would normally be her treat. The time we spent together became special for both of us. It was during these times that I was privileged to peek into her thoughts and convictions.

"There's nobody better than I am, and I'm no better than anybody else," she would say very passionately. While saying this, she would put her right hand on my shoulder, look straight into my eyes and say, "I hope you will always respect the fact that you are just one of the multitudes. I know I am." Rita truly believed that everyone was created equal.

"Yes ma'am," I would say. Occasionally, I would be tempted to stand at attention with my hand in a mock salute while saying this; when I did this, she would laugh heartily. She was obviously enjoying my company, too. Once in a while, she would open her life to me like a wide-screen TV, with no reservations.

"My ex-husband never thought this way. He never respected anyone, especially women," she said once. She was looking into space when she uttered this.

"Your *husband*? So, you were *married* once…" I said, a bit shocked; she had not shared this information with me until now. She did mention her mother a few times in some context or other, but never her husband.

"Yes, I was married once. The guy was well-educated and supposedly very bright."

"Sounds great," I said.

"Great, but…"

"But…?"

"Things are never what they seem, Neila. The man proved to be such a son of a bitch."

Shocked by her swearing—a rare occurrence with Rita—I stared at her. But strangely, there wasn't even a trace of anger on her face. Instead, she looked lost in thought, as though taken to a world of her own, a world I did not know. I waited for a few minutes, wondering if I should ask or not, but then I saw her shaking her head rather violently, as if to shake off her thoughts. Afterwards, she gave me her usual sweet smile.

I had begun enjoying teaching English at the Society, and started looking forward to Thursday afternoons. I was getting more and more confident in this new venture. Fortunately, no one had dropped out of the class, which was unusual, according to the previous records. Since all my students were women, I always referred to them as *the women* rather than *the students*. Even Rita knew about it. "How are *the women* doing?" she would ask periodically.

I was slowly getting to know all those women, which added to the joy of teaching. My job was enhanced by using a wonderful tool that I had: I was fluent in Hindi, the national language of India, which most of the women in this class were quite familiar with. I would explain most of the material in Hindi, and then try to translate everything slowly in English. I used this useful tool for many other purposes besides teaching English, such as explaining a few general things about Canadian life or Canadian politics, and sometimes even to inquire about their lives in Canada. It created a congenial environment for them to learn and practice English, and sometimes for discussing their personal lives or unloading their tensions about their folks openly in the class. The barriers between us were slowly evaporating.

In such discussions, I learned a lot about their personal lives, especially since their settling in Canada. Many of them had never gone outside their homes without their husbands accompanying them, not even to a grocery store, or a shopping mall, or their children's schools. Many of them were completely homebound for days at a time. They were left all alone, with no one to talk to or visit every single day after their husbands and children left in the mornings to go to work and school. Their sole outing, unaccompanied by their husbands, was coming to these classes. I was surprised and equally saddened by this information.

"In India, I would go to a friend's or a neighbor's house after my husband left for work," one woman told me.

"You can do the same here, too," I said.

"No, we can't. No friends because no English!"

"Oh, surely you know some people here."

"Yes, but how do we go? Friends live far."

"By bus or subway or…"

"No."

"How do you all come here, then?"

"Walk. Close from my house," one of them said.

"No, not me. My husband does shift work; he drops me and picks me up."

"Me too."

Many of them responded this way.

"And what if your husbands can't drive you here?" I asked.

"Then we miss the class," they responded almost simultaneously.

Were they prisoners in their homes? Were they lonely and miserable? They all seemed like intelligent women, so why were they so dependent on their husbands? Why couldn't they at least go somewhere in the city independently? Did knowing the local language play such an important role in one's life? No matter what anyone thought, and despite any criticism, the Canadian government was right for encouraging new immigrants to learn the language of their adopted land.

One day, my confidence in my abilities to teach this class led me to propose a daring experiment. I decided to arrange a field trip with the class. We would go to a shopping mall by public transportation and return to the Society. I discussed this idea first with Rita, and then I announced it to the class. The women were very happy, clapping and cheering. So, together, we made a plan. We would first gather in the class, then set out to a shopping mall. To do so, we would take the subway first, then the connecting bus that would take us to the shopping mall. We would go into a boutique in the mall and look at a variety of clothes and accessories. Each woman would make a small purchase, a scarf or a hairpin or something inexpensive, but prior to buying, she would ask about different clothes, discuss colors and sizes, and inquire about different accessories to the salesperson. We would then return together to the Society before the class time would be over. They all agreed gladly and a day was set for our trip. They unanimously decided that they need not tell their husbands about it, since this trip was going to take place during their usual class time. I didn't interfere in their decision.

Our field trip started with the anticipated excitement. We all got on the subway, then the bus, and arrived at the mall as per the plan.

Everything went smoothly as planned in the class. Most of them bought something small and inexpensive. One of them bought a blouse and a silk scarf, with a request to return both the items should she change her mind. I was impressed with her bravery. She asked me if I could go with her if she needed to return the items to which I gladly agreed. We arrived at the Society exactly two hours later. I could see that they all felt as though they had conquered something in life. So did I, actually, for this type of venture was new to me. In our excitement, we all decided to have one more field trip before the semester came to an end.

"Why not next Thursday?" many women asked with enthusiasm.

"No, no, that is too frequent," I said.

"Oh, please! I want to return this blouse and scarf next Thursday," the woman who had purchased the items said. They all started pleading, so I had no choice but to give in. The very following Thursday we decided to go to the mall again.

The following day proved to be very busy for me. Two assignments were due for submission on the following Monday, so I spent my entire day in the library researching and gathering relevant information for my paper. By the end of the day, I picked up my stuff and started walking towards the exit of the library. I was very tired and was thinking of just resting or watching some TV shows in the graduates' lounge. As I came out of the library, I was surprised to see Rita, accompanied by two men, rushing towards me.

"Where have you been?" Rita asked. She sounded breathless.

"In the library. Why?" I asked, still trying to understand what she was doing there.

"I have been looking for you all over your department for the last couple of hours."

"I was in the library for the whole day working towards my assignments. But why were you looking for me here on the campus, Rita?" Although the question was directed at Rita, I looked at the two men who were with her, wondering who they were.

"You see these men? They are husbands of..." she named two women from my English class. "They claim that their wives have disappeared."

"What?" I practically shouted.

"Disappeared."

"How?"

"I don't know how."

"But they were with us for our field trip just yesterday."

"What trip?"

"The field trip. Surely you remember?"

"Oh, the field trip."

"Rita, I took your permission and you not only permitted but encouraged it. As a matter of fact, the Society funded our transportation cost. You knew we were going to a shopping mall." I was beginning to get a little defensive.

"Yes, I remember the field trip, but..."

"What is this trip she is talking about?" One of the two men interrupted Rita with an annoyed look on his face. I had momentarily forgotten that the women had kept this field trip as a secret from their husbands.

"It is a part of our English class," Rita told him. "You needn't worry about it, it was okay as per our class schedule." She covered it beautifully. "What did you teach them in this trip?" Rita turned to me and asked.

"I showed them how to take the subway and a bus, then go to a shopping mall and talk to the salespeople in the shop. That way, they got some practical experience with English speaking."

"And..."

"And, after we purchased some stuff from a shop, we took the train and bus back from the mall to the Society."

"Aha! That's how my wife has disappeared," one of the two men exclaimed.

"What?" Rita and I said simultaneously.

"And mine, too. I demand an explanation," the other man added.

"Wait a minute. Can someone please tell me what really is going on here? What is all this commotion about?" By now I was getting a little irritated and quite honestly, a little scared, too.

"These two men claim that while they were at work, their wives left home some time during the day and have not returned. They suspect that their wives either ran away from home or that something has happened to them," Rita told me.

"I never allow my wife to go outside by herself. I take her out myself once a week to your Society for learning English. That's all," the first man said, sounding quite angry.

"So do I," the other man said. He sounded even angrier than the first. "My wife is forbidden to go anywhere on her own." He was now yelling, looking alternately at Rita and me. The first man started yelling, too.

"Wait, just a minute, please! Your wife is a very decent and honest woman," I said to the first yeller, "and so is yours," I said to the other. "These women love their children too. They would never, I mean *never* run away from home or disappear just like that, as you claim. Take my word, I know them quite well by now. And nothing has happened to them either, they are not stupid." I gathered my courage and talked authoritatively. Rita looked relieved to see me so well collected. Her look of relief boosted my confidence.

"Perhaps these women are genuinely lost somewhere," Rita said, supporting me wholeheartedly.

Suddenly I remembered that one of these two women had bought expensive merchandise, a blouse and a scarf; she was going to return it next Thursday during our field trip. What if she got ambitious and decided to do it by herself with a fellow student from the class?

"Let us call the police," I said.

"That's an excellent idea. Why don't we call the police?" Rita supported me again.

"Police? No, no, no..." Both men started strongly opposing our idea.

Rita and I looked at each other. We knew exactly why they were refusing any police help. We both knew that most people in India are averse to calling the police, as it is taken as a derogation of one's dignity.

"Gentlemen, calm down. Police are very helpful in Canada. They are here to protect and serve! Don't be afraid. Taking help from the police does not carry any taboo in this country, okay?" Rita reassured them, and continued talking until they finally agreed to call the police for help. She immediately contacted the police and found out that the two women were safe at their respective homes. The story turned out to be just as I had guessed. The woman with a major purchase requested one of her classmates to accompany her to the mall and help her return the merchandise. The two women, in order to impress their teacher and all their classmates, went to the shopping mall by themselves. Somewhere during their expedition, they got onto a wrong bus and got lost. They became very nervous and were on the brink of tears. But fortunately, they also remembered the role of police officers in Canada that we had discussed in our class. So one of them mustered her courage, approached a police officer, and explained the whole situation. The police officer helped the two women to return home safely. I was happy to hear this story, and I would get a pat on my back from Rita later in the evening.

In the following class, the two women told the class how they learnt a lot about Canada on their little adventure. The class, including myself, was pleasantly surprised to hear that they could converse with the police officer in English. Although pleased with their story, I decided to never again take a field trip for any of my English classes. This incident made me quite cautious, and, sadly, a little distant from all the students in the class. I became a little aloof from them, which proved to be more to my disadvantage than them, as I was genuinely enjoying their company and our conversations.

This incident, as insignificant as it proved to be later on, also gave me a quick glimpse into the plight of many people, especially women, who came to Canada from various countries. Not knowing the language can create phenomenal challenges, I suddenly realized. How fortunate I was to be fluent in English, one of Canada's two official languages, before I had even set foot on this soil; how advantageous it was for me to aspire to new horizons with relative ease. This incident also helped develop some gratitude within me for the opportunity to help new immigrants overcome their handicap of not knowing English, and to indirectly help them in their desire to build their homes and raise their families in the new country they had chosen.

This incident gave me one more benefit: the friendship between Rita and me deepened. She expressed many times how proud she was of my courage, and I started respecting her even more for the support she had given me during those tense moments. She started inviting me, whenever possible, to her "humble abode" as she would put it, for snacks or dinner.

Her humble abode was a small one-bedroom apartment in an old building downtown. It was very close to the Society's office. She liked its proximity to her workplace. Everything in the apartment seemed as old as the building itself, but it had its charm, especially the old-style bathroom. I remember being a little amused the first time I entered it. There were two separate faucets in the sink: one for cold water and the other one for hot water, not like the one I had in my room, with two faucets but only one outlet.

"How does one get *warm* water to wash hands through two taps?" I once asked her.

"Use a cup and fill it up from both the taps," she answered.

The bathtub was a big oval-shaped ceramic bowl sitting on legs, with an intricate design on its edges, something I had seen only in old movies.

The kitchen was also built in an old style, with appliances that looked like the forefathers of modern appliances. "My fridge has a personality all its own, and a stubborn one at that," she would say. I remembered a funny incident about her fridge once.

Rita opened the refrigerator, grabbed a can of soda for herself, and asked me if I wanted something cool to drink. After I politely declined, she closed the fridge door. Just then, I changed my mind and asked for a cold drink.

"Oh shoot," she exclaimed.

"Oh, if you are out of it, it's okay…" I said. I thought that she had run out of the pop.

"I have got plenty of stuff, but we will have to wait," she said, further adding, "this damn fridge has an attitude."

"What do you mean?" I asked, feeling rather amused.

She explained that her refrigerator was the kind that closed with a hiss as the rubber vacuum seal around the door sucked it shut. Then it wouldn't let go for a good thirty seconds. Naturally this made it impossible to immediately reopen it. She stood by the refrigerator impatiently waiting for the door to complete its vacuum-sealing process. The passing seconds were almost visible to me, expiring in the air around her.

"Isn't there some kind of a device that would solve this problem?" I asked.

"No, nothing at all. Just buy a new fridge, I guess." She sounded resigned. After thirty seconds, she opened the refrigerator door and handed a can of pop to me. I laughed and teased her for such a profound incompatibility between her own efficiency and that of her old appliances.

Rita invited me one Saturday afternoon for coffee. She was going to try out a new recipe and needed me as a guinea pig. I gladly went. She called me into the kitchen when I arrived. I was about to sit at her kitchen table when I saw a beautiful dress on the back of one of the chairs.

"Oh, what a lovely dress. New one?" I asked. I really liked its bright blue color, boat-shaped neck, and long sleeves neatly tapered at the end with matching decorative buttons.

"Try it on," she said.

"It would be too long for me. You are so much taller than I am."

"Just try one arm in the sleeve, and see." Rita was busy setting up the table.

"Why?"

"Just do it, see how you feel."

I inserted my arm into one of the sleeves, wondering why she had insisted. Just as I put my arm in it, I hurriedly took it out. The material was very itchy. I didn't like it at all.

"Well?" she asked me, pouring some coffee into a mug.

"Honestly, the dress looks beautiful, but I didn't feel comfortable at all. It's itchy and rough on the skin. Why don't you return it?" I said.

"Return it? It must be at least twenty years old. I wore it just once for a couple of hours, and when I took it off, my whole body was covered with rash. That damn thing's been hanging in my closet ever since. I don't know why I am keeping it still. I should have thrown it out a long time ago. It is definitely going in the trash now."

She handed me a mug of freshly-brewed coffee and took one for herself. She then laid out on a plate a few pieces of what looked like small pancakes. I didn't know what they were made of, but I could see pieces of green onions in them. She put a small bowl of muddy-looking sauce beside the plate of pancakes. She served a couple of pancakes on a small plate for me and asked me to try the sauce. I hesitated. The brown-colored sauce didn't look appetizing at all.

"Try it. It doesn't taste so bad, believe me."

I served a small spoonful of that sauce on my plate. "Umm, you are right, it is pretty tasty," I said, after tasting it. "But it doesn't look very inviting, does it?"

"You are right, it doesn't look appetizing. This is an old traditional recipe my friend gave me a few weeks ago," she said. She scooped a large spoonful onto her own plate. "You know, it is so funny how shallow we are sometimes. We go for the looks, good or bad, and judge something without really looking deeper."

She sounded philosophical. I nodded in agreement while munching on a pancake. Rita got up from the table and walked slowly towards the window. She stood in front of the open window and started talking as if to the world.

"Have you ever been in a beautiful park that is completely enclosed by huge stone walls that are cold and totally colorless?" Although she was looking out through the window, I knew that the question was directed at me; I also knew that it did not require any response from me. I had learned, after meeting her a few times, that when she spoke like this, it was like a prefix to emphasize her next statement.

"I have, many times. Growing up in a city like Hyderabad, I most definitely have," Rita responded to her own question, looking absorbed in her thoughts.

"Oh yes, Hyderabad, that beautiful city, *our* hometown," I said, realizing immediately that she was not in the mood to hear anything from me about our hometown. I kept quiet.

"Yes, yes, my dear, *our* beautiful city," she said. She momentarily turned her head towards me and then looked outside again. "Hyderabad boasts to have enormous gardens and lush green parks," she continued, "but unfortunately each and every garden is surrounded by huge stone walls that look so frigid and passionless. They are constructed as if to purposely hide the beauty of the gardens. Did you notice that?" She turned her head and looked at me. "I have been to these parks a hundred times at least. You look at any of these parks, and they are simply marvelous. But then you look at those huge stone walls, and they are so repulsive. Aren't they?"

I nodded. I had been to those lush green parks many times when I was growing up in Hyderabad. The parks were simply beautiful, but as she had put it, they did have huge stone walls around them, each and every one of them. However, it had never registered this way in my mind.

"Every time I have looked at those walls, I have felt this strange knot rising in my stomach, making me feel as if those walls are crying, literally *crying* for something, for some beauty, some adornment, something, anything that would make them desirable and sensuous like the parks, not cold or dead." She paused for a brief moment, and then with her gaze fixed on me, she added, "And you know what? Those walls are like me. Oh yes, they are *me!*" she said intensely.

I could feel that her attention was somewhere else. I slowly let out my breath, not breaking eye contact with her.

"Neila, do you think I speak harshly?"

I didn't know what to say. But then, I didn't have to say anything because I could feel that this was just a dialogue with herself, in my presence.

"I speak harshly because I want to portray myself as a cold, frigid bitch to the world," she said.

"But you are not cold and frigid, Rita. You are a very warm and friendly person," I said; I meant every word.

"I am like those stone walls," Rita said, interrupting me. "No beauty, no adornment, and I keep all my emotions closeted inside. With my harsh speaking, I portray myself to be dry and emotionally dead, like those walls, but I keep my true self, all those things you said about me, enclosed within me."

"Hmm..." I said. I didn't know how to respond to Rita.

"And I sincerely believe that by making myself repulsive, I make myself seem interesting."

"That's a strange way to look interesting."

"Yes, it is strange, isn't it?" She gave me her characteristic look with her eyes closed, eyebrows raised, mouth turned down, and she added a slow rhythmic nod.

"Well, right now you look more like a mischievous child than a repulsive woman to me, Rita," I said. She really did look like a naughty child at that moment.

"Do you think I am too outspoken? To the point of being almost rude?" she asked.

What was I to say? I remembered calling her on her forthright-ness a few times in the past. "Frankly, I prefer the word *forthright*, not *rude*," I said.

"I am known to exhibit no sympathy whatsoever, so I am told. At times, people have called me downright insensitive. Do you think so, too?"

"Rita, why are you asking me all these questions? I like you—I like you a lot, period. It really doesn't matter to me how people read you or what you are thought of by others, forthright or rude or whatever." I didn't quite get the direction of our conversation.

"But it matters to *me*. I know exactly how I am and I find it necessary to explain."

"You don't have to explain to me, and you don't owe any explanation to anyone Rita. Honestly, you don't."

"But *I personally* need to explain a few of my personal attributes, Neila. I need some validation, some reassurance."

"Validation? Reassurance? You? A strong person like you is in need of validation?" It was jolting news to me.

"I have become so outspoken, or so rude, or so forthright, as you have called me, or emotionless or frigid or..."

"Okay, so you are all of that. So what?" I interjected, a little impatiently.

"Neila, I am all of those because I am a person who was rid of all her emotions a long, long time ago. I am like those cold stone walls that only provide an enclosure to the beautiful gardens. Whenever I think of those gardens, the only thing that comes to my mind are those stone walls; I feel nothing for the lush greens, the flowers, the children playing, or young couples necking behind the shrubs..."

For the life of me, I couldn't figure out what she was saying.

"But I am also someone who needs to be adorned. So what do I do? I purposely become outspoken or forthright, or sometimes even rude. I feel all these qualities add some kind of shiny luster to my personality. This is, let us say, my own special adornment." She looked at me with anticipation.

"Harshness and rudeness are never for anyone's adornment," I said in confusion.

"Yes, they are, my dear—for me, they are. That's how I decided to decorate my *persona*, and I eventually became good at it." She had a beaming smile on her face. Was it of victory or defeat? I couldn't tell.

"You don't have to tell me any of that, Rita. Really."

"Neila, people develop all kinds of impressions about me, because they don't know my background. Actually, no one does. Even you don't know it," she said with an emphasis on the word *background*.

This is going to be another monologue in my presence, I thought. "Rita, you need not tell me your background either," I said, but she ignored me completely, and continued.

"No one knows my complete story, except my father of course! And, oh yes, that bastard, my ex-husband, knows it, too." I could see a layer of faint anger on her face. "Well, let me tell you..." she began. With one look at my face, she could see my curiosity. She had my total attention from then onwards. She inhaled deeply, and fixed her gaze on my face. She started narrating her past. "I was the eldest of three girls, raised in a decent, educated family in Hyderabad. My father was a high school teacher—not a rich man by any standards, just a simple, middle-class one. He was a history teacher who was very good in his profession, and was a very gentle man, too. People respected him. My mother was a proud homemaker. I would say she was a perfect homemaker, caring for the finest details. 'Homemakers form the precious backbone of the world,' she would always say with pride and passion. She saw significance in the smallest detail of a homemaker's life. If someone asked her for a recipe that required kneading the dough with bare hands, I remember her instruction being, 'First, remove your rings, bangles, bracelets, and whatever you are wearing from your fingers and arms.' That's how she would start telling the recipe. I guess I inherited that quality from her. I do that with everything, I suppose."

She gave me a meaningful smile. I instantly recalled her overly-detailed instructions to someone on the telephone when I had seen her for the first time at the Society.

"I would take the liberty of teasing my mother about this habit of hers, but she would just laugh at it. Although she never complained and seemed perfectly happy and content with her own life, she was quite ambitious for her three precious girls. She wanted us to live in big bungalows with garages for the cars. And in her picture, these bungalows had to have servants to do all the housework.

"'Amma'—that's what we called our mother—'servants won't pay as much attention to detail as you have trained us to do,' we girls would tease her. Then she would say, 'In that case, I would train your servants before they start working in your bungalows.' We would all laugh. There was a lot of teasing and playfulness in my family when I was growing up. Such a sweet, warm family it was! Such a good, innocent childhood I had." She sighed deeply.

"What about your father?"

"Daddy was a gentleman to the core."

"You called your father, 'Daddy?'" I knew of many Indian families where it was normal for the children to address their mothers in their mother tongue, but their fathers in English, or in the British way, as it was called in those days. Rita's family was obviously one of them.

"Yes. I think being a history teacher in an English school must have influenced him to teach us to address him that way. Anyway, Daddy would always sit at the table in the kitchen and participate in our 'girl talk' and say something funny or sometimes just sit silently and observe and listen to all of us. We had only one table in the house and Daddy had a fixed place, 'his' place, at this table. From his place, he could see the whole house, all three rooms, of which one was a living room. The table was used for everything: eating our meals, doing our homework, and even as a place for Amma and Daddy to play cards sometimes in the late evenings. Amma's apron would come off her waist and hang on the hook late in the evenings—a visual declaration that the kitchen was closed and all the house work was done for the day.

"Invariably, she would win the card game. I didn't know what that game was called, but I never saw Daddy win, even once. When I was very young, I expressed my surprise about this to Daddy; he was a strong man, so I felt he should win. But then Daddy said, with a smirk on his face, 'Your mother cheats big time, that's why she wins.' My young innocent mind was intrigued at this. 'That mother of yours, she is an alternator,' Daddy would add. 'What does that mean, Daddy?' I asked. He said, 'It means that she sees her own cards with one eye and my cards with the other. And that's how she wins.' For a long time, I didn't get Daddy's joke, and couldn't figure out how Amma managed to do this."

So *that's* where Rita got the term *alternator*.

I looked at her. She was completely silent, absorbed in her thoughts, as if the clock had been turned back and she was in that house, enjoying being a little girl again. After a few moments, she shook her head as if coming out of a trance.

"At the age of nineteen years, I became a girl of marriageable age, according to everybody in the community, especially my mother. She invited this well-known matchmaker to our home. The matchmaker was a woman in her sixties, quite short and plump, with eyes like a hawk. She eyed me for a few minutes and then gave some information to my mother about a suitable boy.

"My father wanted me to finish my undergraduate degree before marriage. He did not like the idea of Amma inviting the matchmaker and discussing my marriage before I finished my studies. I still remember a long, heated argument between my parents that night. This was a rare occurrence in my family. Daddy sounded quite angry. I had never heard or seen him get this angry in my nineteen years, but slowly, he calmed down. We girls were pretending to be sleeping in the adjacent room, when in reality we were standing outside their closed bedroom door listening to their argument. Amma must have finally convinced him, because his angry voice had quieted down and they were talking in a low voice. We couldn't hear anything clearly. The next morning, Daddy called me into his bedroom.

"'Sarita, we have found a very good boy for you,' he said in his usual gentle voice. In my family, young men were always referred to as 'boys' until they were married, no matter how old they were. Funny, isn't it?

"I was not ready for marriage yet; I wanted to finish my college degree. Daddy told me not to worry. He assured me that he and Amma would talk to this boy to allow me to continue my college studies even after marriage."

She looked at me with a plain face and said, "In today's times, this phrase *allowing the wife* sounds so archaic, doesn't it? But in Hyderabad, during my times, it was normal for people to use such phrases. My father convinced me to meet the boy first and then decide. My darling father! How considerate he was. I was grateful to him and agreed to meet the boy. An official meeting was arranged between the boy and me, and I liked the boy. I actually did. His face had a gentle expression, just like my father's. He was older than me by ten years, but not too old according to my mother. He lived in a nice house, a bungalow with a garage, as Amma told me, and owned a car, a baby Austin. Amma seemed very happy."

Rita stopped for a moment, took a few deep breaths and then continued. "What impressed me the most was that he looked gentle like my Daddy and he was willing to let me continue my studies at the college. I was happy about this, and so was Daddy. I immediately said 'yes' and got engaged to be married soon. The whole family was happy. We got married after a few weeks and I moved into my own bungalow with a car in the garage, just what my mother wanted for me! Just what I was led to dream of, by my ambitious mother."

Rita stopped for a moment again, and after talking a long breath, looked at me with her mannerism of closing one eye and looking with the other. Then she said, "In my family, and I am sure in thousands and thousands of other families like mine in Hyderabad, we girls were led to long for the security of hearth and home. We were required to have a lifetime commitment from the altar to the grave. We imagined perfection, stability, and a mate for life. We girls were brought up to believe the standard litany of childhood, then education until marriage, followed by marriage and children, and then living happily ever after until death. The order was never changed or questioned..."

"It is not just in Hyderabad, Rita—I think that was the custom for all girls in India, especially in the days when you were growing up. I remember my mother telling me about herself, and innumerable stories about many of her friends who had gone through life in the exact manner that you just described, and in almost identical order, too." I tried to support Rita by mentioning my mother and her friends because I wanted to make her feel that she was not the only one going through such a tedious routine in life, although I knew very well, and had seen in many instances, that these customs were changing, and were getting better. My own parents had gladly supported my decision of coming to Canada *alone,* and pursuing advanced education without being forced into marriage first.

"But look at me!" Rita blurted out angrily. "What happened in my case? The bastard proved to be a swine, really a bloody swine." I was stunned and saw her becoming absolutely livid. "Even a swine would be gentler than that son of a bitch!" she added. She alternated her eyes.

"Why? What happened?" I stammered.

"What happened? I will tell you what happened!" Now she had both her eyes wide open, and quite frankly, she looked a bit scary.

"That bastard, that no good son of a swine wanted me to, wanted me to do..."

"Wanted you to do...what?" I asked impatiently.

"To do prostitution..." Rita had bent down her head completely. I couldn't even see her face.

"Pro...sti...tu...tion..." I said each syllable clearly as though I was practicing the word. I was in total disbelief. I felt as though my heart had missed a beat or two.

"Yes, prostitution."

"Oh my! Oh Rama, Rama! Oh... "

A few seconds passed in total silence, Rita with her face red with extreme anger, and my mouth being wide open in disbelief.

"I thought…you said he was…he was a good, gentle man..." Still in complete disbelief and totally flustered, I managed somehow to break the silence.

"Ha! Gentle, my foot! That fucking son of a bitch wanted me to sleep around with other men!"

I didn't dare to look at Rita. I was scared to hear this most unusual swearing which she was expressing in such a high pitch of voice. It was enough to indicate to me that flames of anger must be oozing out of her eyes. I myself needed a few deep breaths. I tried to calm and collect myself. I wanted to ask her *why?* for it was my firm belief that there was always a reason behind every action, even an immoral one. But this was not the time to ask her why, nor was the action she was forced to take a moral one.

"Do you know why? I will tell you how it all happened. Remember that I once said I would tell you the whole story of my past? Well, I do need to pour my heart to someone today. I really need that today." Rita emphasized the word *today*, but I didn't ask her about that, either. Instead, I just quietly let her continue.

"The story of my life, really, my wretched life, it goes like this: my ex-husband was a diploma holder in civil engineering from a local technical institute and was working at the Hyderabad Municipal Corporation—or the HMC, as it was called then. He was an overseer. The bungalow and car and all those riches he had flashed in front of my parents were all on borrowed money. I realized much too late that it was a bait to trap me. That cunning asshole must have concocted a plan with the help of that matchmaker—who knows?"

Rita walked to the sink, filled up a glass with water, took a few large sips, and continued. "He was working at the HMC for many years before my marriage. He was very ambitious, but was not getting any promotions, so he was feeling frustrated. One day, soon after our wedding, he came home from work. New bride that I was, I was cooking a nice dinner for my new husband, his favorite *aloo-matar parathas and dahi-raitha*. He came behind me and gently laid his hands on my shoulders. I shivered, goosebumps rising on my whole body. How lovely his gentle touch was! I turned around and looked at him. He started rubbing my shoulders and I almost swooned. His gentle face made him look like an angel from heaven. I loved his face, I really did. 'What's cooking today?' he asked me in his gentle voice.

"'Your favorite,' I answered, telling him what it was. He held my face in both his palms and started caressing it. We were married barely for six or seven days at the time. The bridal henna designs on my hands were still visible. I felt shy, and in that shyness, I started denying him the pleasures with the usual stuff an Indian bride is supposed to say. So stupid, I tell you. Every young woman loves to be caressed by her beau, then why pretend to deny it, right? Anyways, he made me turn the stove off and slowly led me to the bedroom. Being a newly-married couple, what else do you expect? We were in heaven.

"I was lying down on the bed in his arms, half-naked still, enjoying the angelic aftermath of our lovemaking when he said, 'Today is going to be a special day for both of us.' I was excited to hear that. 'How so?' I asked him. He looked at me with his loving eyes and gave me a detailed account of his afternoon in the office. He said that he had a long meeting with his boss that afternoon, and in that meeting he expressed his desire for a promotion. I remembered his boss very well. He had attended our wedding reception and had given us a beautiful gift. He looked like a man in his mid-fifties or so.

"'So what did the boss say?' I asked. I was thrilled to hear about the meeting, thinking that my husband had finally received a promotion."

"'Sarita,' my husband said, 'my promotion is definite.'"

"'Oh, that is wonderful,' I said. I embraced him hard and started kissing his face.

"'Only if,' he said, very calmly. I stopped kissing him and looked at him. 'Only if,' he repeated.

"'Only if what?' I was getting quite impatient.

"'I don't know how to tell you, darling, but my promotion is guaranteed only if my boss can have you.'"

"I thought I didn't hear him right, but he shamelessly repeated himself. It felt as though someone was pouring hot oil in my ears.

"'Well, Sarita, you know I have been seeking this promotion for a long time now, right? This big loan I have taken from the bank to pay for this house and a car, I really need that promotion and the money that comes with the promotion.' He went on and on but I could hear nothing. I was stunned, completely frozen and horrified. I felt that I was going to pass urine right there on our bed. I looked at his face, the face that I thought had the same gentle expression like my dad's—the reason why I had married him in the first place. His face didn't look gentle and kind at all. As a matter of fact, he looked like a demon. That face had a devil's eerie smile and expression on it. My look turned into a horrified frozen gaze. I was scared stiff and I was shaking with fear. I honestly don't remember anything, just that there was a big tremor developing in my entire body.

"'So what do you say, Sarita? What do you say? You will do this much for me, right?' he said. Holding my shoulders with both his hands, he started shaking me gently. The same shoulder shake that I had found so romantic just a few minutes ago was hurting me now. I felt as if his fingers had pierced my flesh and I was bleeding profusely. The devil was waiting for an answer, an answer to his ugly, grotesque proposal."

Rita took a sip of water to moisten her throat. Her voice was sounding very dry and shaky.

"God knows how long I was in that state, but the devil was relentless, asking me for an answer over and over again. Finally, I managed to breathe a bit. I took a few long breaths to collect myself and protested, 'I am your *wife*—how can you think like this?'"

"'You *are* my wife—that's *why* I am telling you to do this. Did you forget all those oaths and promises of obedience and wifely duties?'

he asked me. He had not raised his voice, but it sounded completely dry and cruel.

"'And what about your promises of protection and security for me as my husband?' I mustered my courage and asked him angrily.

"'I am not denying any of that. Once I get this promotion, I shall provide for you even more than this. I just need your help to get over the obstacle, that's all,' he said, again sounding very calm, like a devil who knows his game of trapping his prey. At that moment, I realized that there was actually a sadistic Satan within that deceptive gentle look. And I was married to him, with an oath 'for better or worse' for life.

"'What do I do? What *should* I do?' I asked. I was angry, and I was confused.

"He thought that I was asking him instruction for the next step. 'That's my girl!' he said with a pat on my back, as if I had passed his test of loyalty.

"He wanted me to comply with his plan of selling my body to his boss, so that in return he would get that damned promotion which would benefit *both of us*. I turned my gaze from his devilish face to my own hands. My eyes scrolled over the faint henna design that I had done in my wedding. Henna designs on my hands still, a sign of being a bride—yes I was still a bride...a bride to a monster!"

With her hands covering her face, Rita started sobbing profusely. A strong, feisty woman like Rita, sobbing like this? I had never seen her in such emotional imbalance ever before. Perhaps nobody ever did. It was very, very disturbing and distressing. I waited for a few moments and then quietly passed a few tissues to her.

I needed a few for myself too. I wasn't married, so I didn't quite relate to problems between a husband and a wife. But being a young woman and nurtured in a similar cultural environment as Rita, I could very well comprehend her predicament. She was a couple of decades older than me, but the basic value of the virtues of woman-hood and self-respect were universal, and no culture or time was an exception to this fact. I could, therefore, imagine the horror, fear, and grief behind this monstrous and dreadful demand Rita's husband was making on his young bride.

A few minutes went by without either of us saying anything. Finally, I got up, wiped my tears, and, holding her arm, slowly led her to a chair near the table. She sat down. I handed her a few more tissues and helped her wipe her face. She was still crying.

"Finally, you got out of the bedroom and ran away from there, right?" I looked into her eyes with hope of getting a positive answer. She shook her head. "You didn't run away from him right away?" I asked. I was surprised. She shook her head again. "You slapped that *soovar*[1] hard and then ran away far from him, right?"

"No, no, no, no, I didn't slap him, I didn't run away from him, I didn't even leave that *soovar!*" She was still crying and sobbing.

"Then?" I was afraid of what was I going to hear.

"I went to his boss like a whore the very next day and satisfied his sexual desires. I did the same thing again the next day, and the next day, and again and again, God only knows how many times." She was sobbing and talking, talking and sobbing. "His boss loved kissing my arms with those bridal henna designs, and loved my young, unused body—that shameless *soovar* husband of mine told me. And one day, he came home happy, informing me that he got that damn promotion."

I was dead silent.

"It paid off! My being a whore to that man paid off. My husband was ecstatic. He started buying me nice expensive gifts, but I had lost all interest in him, interest in everything and everyone, especially in my husband. After that, I stopped feeling anything at all. Not a single damn time. I had become a robot. The only sane thing remaining in my deplorable life was my college work. I was studying towards a bachelor's degree in social work. I was completely focused on only one thing: my studies and the degree. My husband never posed any obstacle to my studies, nor did I give him any friction in his sadistic plans of utilizing my body for his personal career pursuits...."

"You mean ..."

"The bosses changed. Sometimes there was a quorum of two or more people who took the decision of promotions and raises in their office..."

---

1 Swine, in Hindi

"Oh my sweet God; this is too much..."

"I had become this monster's tool to progress in his career, a sure tool that he could utilize any time to climb up the ladder in his career. I complied with his devious plans every time, and he never interfered with my studies. It was a win-win situation! A sweet, amicable deal, wasn't it?" Rita gave a loud sarcastic laugh and then continued.

"Everything looked so hunky-dory from the surface. No one, I mean *no one*, not even my own parents, could ever suspect that I was hurting from within, that I was burning inside. I would visit them once in a while. They would visit us sometimes, too. My mother just loved visiting me in my *bungalow with a car!* She was very happy and would tell everybody in the community how wonderful it was for me. My continuation of the studies, even after marriage, was like a cherry on top for her. 'And you didn't want to marry this wonderful boy because of your studies, silly you. What did I tell you?' my mother would gloat.

"That monster was very respectable and hospitable to both my parents. My two younger sisters were longing for a man like mine, my mother told me once. You can't imagine how I shuddered with disgust after hearing that from Amma. But I kept quiet and maintained my ugly secret. The façade I had put on outwardly was so perfect that no one could imagine what kind of ugly life I was leading, or what kind of grotesque marriage I was having.

"I finished my studies successfully in three years and received a bachelor's degree in social work. Everybody was happy. They were complimenting me, and even more so, complimenting my husband. It was *he* who had allowed me to study. It was *he* who had shown extreme patience and tolerance to let his wife study even after marriage."

Rita was completely overtaken by intense anger. She stretched her lips to the fullest, and with her jaw clenched together, she flared up both nostrils, made a fist with her right hand, and started punching in the air.

"Did you tell your parents or sister or somebody about all this?" I tried to calm her down with a question.

"No, never. I told no one. Not even Amma. She was waiting for a grandchild now. Waiting for the 'Light of the next generation,' she called it. Can you imagine that? Having a baby with this devil? Bringing another devil in this world, perhaps?" She shuddered with total disgust.

"I didn't want a baby, but neither did *he!* Not in the near future, anyway. That would have been disastrous to his personal career plans, right? The vehicle that moved him up in his career, getting out of shape because of pregnancy? He provided me with all the necessary birth control devices to avoid pregnancy and personally made sure I was carefully using it." Rita then gave a very sad sounding laugh and said, "Having a baby is one of the most desired experiences in a woman's life, so I have been told. Some desired experience! By that time, I didn't *ever* want to have a baby. I didn't even want to have a married life anymore. To hell with the damn marriage, damn baby, or damn that fake story of living happily ever after! To hell with it! My dreams were shattered to pieces. All my desires for a married life or a baby had been cut out of me as if permanently removed by a sharp scalpel." She was quiet for a few minutes, trying to calm down.

"What did you do after graduation?" I asked softly.

"I found a temporary job in the same department with my professor's help and started working, with a promise to myself that I would never, ever again go through anything even remotely dreadful as this in my life."

She got up from the table. Still very much in an infuriated state, she walked to the window. A couple of minutes later, she said, "I wanted to run away from that place, as far away as possible. I requested my professor to find me some work, any type of job or an assignment, that I could do far away from that city—even *outside* the country. Money would not matter at all."

"You did? And?"

"And the professor did find something for me, after some searching."

"What did he find?"

"An assignment with CIDA."

"CIDA? What is that?"

"That is the Canadian International Development Agency. The Agency had a lot of work in various areas of social work, and they were looking for people to work within India as well as outside India. I applied for the job immediately, and with my professor's help, got it right away. The job required some training to be taken before starting. Nobody in my family knew about this. My husband was the last person I wanted to tell. He was under the impression that I was still continuing my temporary job in the department of the university. I was training for six weeks, after which they gave me an option to either work right there somewhere in India or relocate to Canada. Well, you can guess what I chose."

"Wow! You landed a job in Canada. Wow!" I was thrilled to see she was so brave to make that choice independently.

"Yes, it was the right choice and a good decision. And you know what? This time, it was *my* decision for *my* own good! I felt as though I had outwitted fate." Rita said with great pride. After a long time, her usual expressions came back to her face, and I felt good, and a bit relieved, too.

"When it was time to put together all the papers, arrange a flight, and all other things, that's when I decided to tell the whole story. The only person that I wanted to tell was my Daddy. I felt he would be the only one in the family who could fully understand my plight and withstand it."

"What did he say when you told him all that?"

"Well, even he couldn't bear it! He was devastated after hearing what I had gone through for three years. Three years of pure hell! He was crying, crying like a child, and apologizing profusely, for he took the whole responsibility of throwing me in that hell. Can you believe that?"

"Apologizing?"

"Yes, because he was the one who had convinced me to marry this devil. He felt devastated. But I consoled him, assured him that I was tough. He calmed down and gave me his blessings and promised me he would tell Amma and the rest of the family only when the time was right. He also promised to help me serve divorce papers to my husband and see that the divorce proceedings were complete.

My sweet Daddy! Do you know what his parting words were?" She looked at me and I just shook my head.

"He said to me, 'Try to develop scabs now, my child,' and then he added, 'and look ahead! Life is full of wonderful offerings!' My loving father! A man of truly fatherly qualities. I shall never forget his loving advice." Rita became very somber, her tone heavy with melancholy. It was a beautiful advice, and a practical one too.

"Neila, do you know why I am telling you all this *today*?" she asked me. I again shook my head.

"You know we have a small library in our Society, and in the library, we receive most of the Indian newspapers from India, right?" I nodded.

"This morning, when I was browsing through the Indian newspapers, I suddenly came across a small photograph with a brief write-up underneath. It said, 'A dedicated teacher of history with a mastery over teaching the *Mogul* and British periods in India...' I looked at the photograph carefully, and sure enough, it was Daddy's! And it was in the *obituary* section, Neila. My daddy is gone! Daddy is no more! Gone with him forever is the small world of a little girl where she used to dream freely. I had intentionally abandoned that place where my little world was located, a long time ago, but I had every intention to visit that place someday—someday in the future, when my wounds would be healed and I had developed *scabs*, as Daddy had advised me. But now, now I can't go there. His parting words are his last words for me now."

"But you have your mother there..."

"No. I never contacted anyone after I left India, not even my mother. In these last twenty-five years, I received only two letters from India, both from my father. One letter to inform me that my divorce was final, which apparently ruined my mother's health, and the other letter giving me the sad news of my mother's demise."

"Oh my, I am so sorry to hear that..."

"So was I, really. I was very sad to read about her death in Daddy's letter. To this day, I don't know if it was my divorce or my treacherous married life that ruined her health and killed her. Perhaps it was a combination of both those things, but I never did find out. Now my father is also no more!"

Rita started crying silently. This silent weeping was even sadder than before when she was sobbing hard. Rita, a tough woman in every sense, was looking more like a helpless child crying for some comfort now.

Initially, when I saw her indulge in her past, I had some reservations about her intentions. However, now it became clear like the daylight seeping in through the open window. It wasn't her futile indulgence. Rita *was* hurting inside. And what she needed was a compassionate listener. Especially at this moment when she'd accidentally stumbled over the sad news about her father's demise.

What I had heard from her about her ex-husband was so monstrous; it was utterly beyond my imagination. I couldn't fathom that such a perverted human being could be born in a civilization that was more than five thousand years old, or in a society that was founded on a great philosophy and old culture. Was that even a human being, or a devil incarnate?

And there was Rita, a high-spirited, talented, and disciplined young woman, who gave in to the devil's aberrant whims without losing her own human dignity or spirituality. That clearly was an assurance of credibility of the old civilization and its world-renowned philosophy. While quietly suffering through such a grotesque ordeal and excruciating pain, she exhibited complete maturity and utmost respect to her family without losing her own focus. She had, as she said earlier, outwitted her fate.

The whole afternoon was like a poignant drama, unfolding one sad event after another. It had caused a lot of stress on me, too. After all, I had become Rita's *friend*! I got up and started patting her back softly, trying to console her.

While doing so, I casually looked around her kitchen. The so-called beautiful dress that was lying on the back of the kitchen chair caught my eye—the same one that had caused a bad rash on Rita's body when she wore it just for a short time. It was shining even more brilliantly in the afternoon sun.

That dress was like her gentle-looking husband who had caused a horrible permanent rash on her heart, I thought. I felt a strangling panic with this realization. I immediately picked up the dress and threw it in the trash can, trying to shut its lid as tightly as I could, while I continued to gently pat Rita's back and tried to control my own tears.

Epilogue

After my graduate degree, I moved to another province in search for better prospects and settled down there. Over the years, with the usual trappings of a moderately successful employee in the Canadian corporate world, I lost touch with Rita completely. It was almost after three decades that I revisited the Immigrant's Centre in Ontario, only to find, to my grave disappointment and dismay, that Rita was no more. She had left this world, leaving no trace.

It is quite natural that in our ever-changing lives, we periodically lose old pillars of support and find new ones. However, that one old place where we feel unconditionally supported, and completely free to ask millions of tormenting questions about life with some guarantee to get answers, should never be lost.

Rita was one such place for me, and I had lost it permanently.

Haunted by the pi

Raj Panday is a mathematician, a Number Theorist, as he says. He claims to have published more than twenty papers on the number theory in reputable mathematical journals. He often describes them as "big big" journals. Raj's strong prowess in mathematics seems to fail miserably in the area of vocabulary and verbal expression, which I observed in our very first meeting at a small party held by the graduate students of the university.

Raj Panday must have been in his late-forties when I met him some forty years ago. He kept a beard that was already streaked with gray and had a head full of unruly hair. His dark brown skin made his teeth seem a lot whiter than they really were. His wide brown eyes, set on his bony face, seemed to complement his narrow forehead.

I was a new immigrant to Canada then, and was experiencing the novelty and culture of this new country.

"You came out of India?" a bearded man with a glass of white wine in his hand asked me in a very heavy Indian accent.

"Yes. I came from India." With a brown complexion, long brown hair, and an attire that was comprised of a silk sari wrapped around my body, I was exhibiting my identity as one from India without a shadow of doubt.

"I am Dr. Raj Panday, senior scientist in the department of mathematics," Raj said.

"Nice to meet you, sir." I addressed him as *sir* very naturally, with an inherent East Indian attitude of expressing respect towards all teachers.

"And when did you come here?" he asked me.

"I joined the graduate school just a week ago, sir," I answered, again very politely. I didn't volunteer any information about my coming here much earlier than that.

"Ah, fresh off the boat, still."

"Excuse me?" I said. I didn't quite understand his remark, but somewhere within me, I felt displeasure at this expression.

"I received a PhD in mathematics from Bombay University, you see. I came here a long, long time ago, you see. When people in Canada came to know about my theories, they called me immediately to join the department, you see."

I was politely nodding at his every "you see," murmuring "I see" as a response, but actually not understanding anything at all and slowly starting to get a bit annoyed.

"So you are a professor of mathematics here?" I asked him.

"Um, not really."

"Oh?"

"No, there is too much politics here, you see. They don't understand me—they told me, you see."

"They? Who are *they?*"

"They, the students."

"Oh?" I asked as I grew more inquisitive.

"The students complained to the authorities that they couldn't understand my teaching, you see. They complained and complained. So finally the department took away all my classes and gave me a research project, you see. Since then, I am a senior research scientist with the department of mathematics here at the university, you see." The man gave me a complete résumé of his credentials in literally two minutes. Although I was meeting him for the very first time then, I could "see" everything clearly. I could see why the students had a problem in comprehending his teaching. It couldn't have been his heavy Indian accent, as there were a few Indian professors with strong accents in various faculties, but it could have been his clumsiness and irrelevance in his explanation that must have confused the students. That was, of course, my personal guess, since even I—an Indian who was "fresh off the boat"—couldn't understand him well. My first impression of him has lasted all these years, without any change.

Raj remained without any teaching assignments and without receiving any tenured position for all those years at the university. However, he was enjoying an official relationship with the university as a senior research scientist in the department of mathematics. He never taught privately either, unlike a few other faculty members who were teaching regularly on a private basis. Raj was the one who provided me this information about them. He spent more time on his research projects in the basement of his house than at the school itself. He was a lone inventor, he told me once, and claimed to have developed a new technique of conducting research, something he proudly called a "new technique of Indo-Canadian style."

There was a modest amount of grant money from the National Research Council of Canada (NRCC) funneled through the university for his research work, as Raj took pride in telling me. I observed that when it was time for the annual grant application, Raj would make sure that everyone within the department knew that he was applying for it. He seemed to be even more particular about spreading this news among the city's Indian community. His way of spreading this news was also as unique as he himself was. He would make sure to attend some community function, and then in such gatherings, he would continuously complain about how difficult it had become to receive any grant from Canada's federal sources, even for recognized scientists. Perhaps that was how he tried to impress others. Many people had seen this year after year, and felt sorry for his pathetic attempt at feeling important. Someone once told me that it was a well-known fact, both within the mathematics department and the Indian community—*especially* the Indian community—that his wife's salary covered his funding needs for his mathematical theories.

I had not met Raj's wife; I didn't even know what she did for a living. I met him quite a few times afterwards, but Raj never mentioned her in any of our conversations. Over the time that I was at the university, there were many parties and get-togethers in the graduates' lounge; I had noticed that many faculty members brought their spouses, but I never saw Raj's wife attending any of these events. I also never inquired about her.

Raj told me once that his basement must contain at least a ton of paper. That was because his research entailed work on the number *pi,* denoted by the Greek letter π. It was one of the most ancient numbers known to humanity, and apparently also the most famous ratio in mathematics which deserved a lot of work, as Raj told me in one of our conversations. I made the mistake once of asking him what *pi* contained, and he went on talking about it tirelessly.

"3.141592653589793238...this is known as the decimal expansion of *pi*..." Raj went on and on. I had to rudely interrupt him in his recitation of the digits of *pi,* as I almost reached the point of feeling dizzy, and started visualizing the digits marching into infinity in a predestined yet unfathomable code.

"No one, I mean *no one* will ever find out the exact system of these digits of *pi,*" Raj said. He was relentless.

How do I stop this pi-nerd? I thought. I had to quickly think of some way. "So, what you are telling me is that among all mathematicians, there is a strong universal feeling that it will never be possible, in principle, for an inhabitant of our finite universe to discover the system in the digits of *pi.* Is that it?" I said as I faked interest.

"Huh?" Raj said. He seemed confused, not understanding what I said.

"Okay, let me ask you again in simple terms, so that you will understand my question." It was my turn to hold the upper hand. "I meant to say that no one in this world will ever find out about the *pi.* Is that it?" I reiterated. He nodded with a victorious smile.

I was smiling victoriously too, for a non-mathematician like myself could also baffle him sometimes with whatever tools I could find.

"What exactly do you research in *pi,* Dr. Panday?" I asked. I became quite brave one day and pretended to be genuinely interested in his research.

"Oh, you can call me Raj," he said. I was successful in sounding honest.

"The *pi* is not the only unexplored number, you see, but also an interesting one. I am curious to find out if the digits contain any hidden rule, you see. Something like the mind of God, you see..." Raj said this with a firm belief.

"What is the big deal anyway? *Pi* is just a ratio between the circumference and the diameter of a circle." I retrieved my own little knowledge about *pi* from my high school days, and tried to undermine it. That was a mistake, I soon realized. He thought I was demeaning "his" *pi*.

"You don't understand *pi*—nobody does!" he said, getting angry. "The complexity of the sequence it spits out in digits is really unbelievable, don't you see?" He jumped at me instantly.

"What you are calling a complexity of sequence is really a sequence of digits that looks like gibberish," I said, insistent in my attack.

"If you print in ordinary typewritten format a billion decimals of *pi*, they would stretch from here to the middle of Atlantic Ocean, can't you see?" Raj retorted, as if he was rescuing *pi* from my attack.

"But what is the point in stretching the decimals of *pi* to the Atlantic Ocean? I feel it is all a useless endeavor." I didn't know why, but I was insistent in my attack on *pi*.

"Maybe in the eyes of God, *pi* looks perfect," Raj said. He was hurt by my calling the research on *pi* a useless endeavor. He defended his *pi* with a very serious voice and quietly walked away.

Since that conversation, Raj made it a point to provide me periodically with new information about *pi*. And out of guilt or whatever, and I still can't figure out why, but I made an honest attempt to listen to him quietly without posing any questions or attacking his *pi*.

He informed me once that since the age of supercomputers, every so often a new scientist comes forward and generates yet another big number of digits of *pi*. He also said that each renowned mathematician beats the previous one in setting a new world record for *pi*, invariably labeling the previous renowned mathematician's efforts trivial. The irony of this situation was that no one found anything new or special about *pi*.

"Why do they do that, Raj?" I asked him.

"Do what?"

"Why do they try to prove the previous scientist's theory trivial, as you told me? These mathematicians spend immoderate amounts of time in researching just to declare each other's work trivial, is that it?" I asked him.

"Well, unfortunately, that is true," he admitted reluctantly.

"Why?"

"There is actually a very good reason for this, you see. Because once you dig out the solution to a problem, the problem itself becomes trivial." He smiled sheepishly.

"But that doesn't mean that the problem *was* trivial in the first place." I was confused.

"Maybe, or maybe not, but once the solution is there, who cares whether the problem was initially trivial or not?"

I didn't quite agree with this logic, but I didn't pose any more questions and let the conversation end.

What did I know about mathematics anyway, or mathematicians, for that matter? However, after getting to know Raj and having a few brief conversations with him, I had developed a certain impression that many mathematicians value the *struggle* to understand and solve the problem *rather than the problem itself.* But then, why do they work hard to prove each other's theories trivial? I always carried a genuine respect for mathematicians, but at the same time, felt sorry that the brilliance of many such mathematicians was getting wasted in a struggle for a futile cause!

After a while, I stopped posing questions to Raj about mathematics, himself, or *pi.* I was facing enough problems in my own life, such as being alone and adapting to a new lifestyle in a new country. The graduate study work had picked up considerably, which left me no time to think of Raj's confusion or problems.

The fall semester was in full swing, and so was Mother Nature. It was a beautiful, warm autumn day. All the maple trees on the university campus grounds had put on a magnificent show of colors that even an expert painter would not be able to catch it on a canvas. My room in the graduate residence was at one corner of the university campus with one tiny window, and I could get only a glimpse of this beautiful scenery. I decided to step outside and walk through this heavenly rainbow of colors, and if possible, soak myself in its beauty. I started walking leisurely, looking at the splendid colors of the trees, mesmerized by this dramatic presentation of nature. My mind and eyes were having a dialogue between them, with my eyes receiving this beauty, and my mind perceiving it and converting it into pure delight. I, like a mere observer, calmly enjoyed the peaceful time.

Suddenly I heard a holler directed at me. I was startled!

"Hello, Neila."

It was Raj. Out of nowhere, he appeared in front of me and greeted me with a big smile.

"Oh hi," I answered, still feeling startled.

"What are you doing here?" he asked.

"Oh nothing, just..."

"Just loitering on the campus I see..."

"Loitering?" I answered. I was irritated to say the least. Why was he interested in my *loitering* anyway? And what business was it his if I was loitering?

"Well..." I started to say, but was rudely interrupted.

"I live very close from here, a walking distance of merely seven minutes and twenty-two seconds," he said, looking at me with anticipation.

Seven minutes and twenty two seconds—is this how a mathematician describes a very close distance in a casual way? I wondered—but I kept quiet.

"My wife would be home right now if you want to come with me," he invited.

No, I don't want to, I felt like saying, but still kept quiet. However, the idea of meeting his wife intrigued me, so I nodded agreeably. I didn't even know her name. Unlike the spouses of other graduate students or faculty members, Raj's wife never visited him. Raj also never mentioned her or brought her for any events held on the campus. As soon as I nodded, we started walking towards his house.

Raj was glancing periodically at his wristwatch to make sure we reached his house in time as calculated by him, seven minutes and twenty-two seconds. The thought of missing the precision of his calculation made me a bit nervous. Inadvertently, I also started looking at my own wristwatch, and was overtaken by the precision of time. Completely forgotten was the splendor and beauty of nature around me that I was so much enjoying only a few minutes before. As the seventh minute was over, I started feeling overly stressed with these doubts. *What if it takes longer than his calculated time? Would I be responsible for the delay?*

Just then, Raj said, "There it is—my house!"

I looked at my wristwatch. It was only a few seconds after the seventh minute. I felt relieved, for I was spared the trauma of being guilty of causing any inaccuracy. We had arrived at his house in seven minutes and twenty-two seconds, after all.

We had come to a modest-looking, small bungalow with a gray roof and cream-colored aluminum siding. There was a small driveway leading to the house. A small green car was parked in the driveway.

"Oh good, she is home," he remarked as he glanced at the car. He rang the doorbell. "I need not use my key, now that she is home," he said. He didn't have to explain, but he did, anyway. His wife answered the door and tried to open it, but it wouldn't open completely. He pushed it with his shoulder and the door opened just wide enough for one person to pass through it.

"Come, come." Raj got in first and invited me in while pushing with his left foot what seemed like a huge cardboard box. I managed to get in. We were now standing in what Raj referred to as the *vestibule*. It consisted of a small, dark hallway with boxes of papers stacked all over the place. A couple of boxes had blocked the door from opening it completely.

"Mukta, meet the new graduate student; she is out of India." He never got rid of the expression *out of India*, which sounded like *out of the box* to me.

"Oh, you are from India," his wife said. She knew the correct expression. "Are you in the same department?" she asked.

Just as I was about to say something, Raj volunteered information on my behalf. "No, no, oh no, she is not in mathematics, she is
in some branch of biological science, I don't know which one." I felt
a bit of sarcasm in his tone but I ignored it. I always found him to be
demeaning of all subjects that were outside the realm of mathematics. Perhaps he was really ignorant of everything that was not related
to mathematics or the number theory, especially *pi*.

"Hi Mukta, nice meeting you," I said, and extended my hand for
a handshake.

Mukta had a pleasant face with big brown eyes. Her smile looked
genuine. She was much shorter than Raj and unlike him, a little on
the chubby side.

"What branch of biology are you in, umm..." she asked
me cordially.

"Neila—my name is Neila," I added, as Raj had not told her
my name, "I am studying towards my Master's degree in Clinical
Biochemistry," I answered.

"Oh, that's wonderful. There is a lot of research going on these
days in Clinical Biochemistry, isn't there?"

"Yes." I was still being cautious and answered in monosyllables.

"Oh yes, now I remember, Raj did tell me once about a new
graduate student from India, but he never told me in which faculty
you were studying. Neila, what are you working on?" she asked me,
sounding genuine.

"Plasma membranes of the red blood cells," I answered, realizing
that Raj had never asked me what *I* was working on. We only ever
talked about *pi*.

"The ghost cells?" she asked.

I nodded with a bit of a surprise. "How do you know about the
ghost cells?" I asked. I felt a bit better that at least Raj's wife was aware
of subjects other than mathematics. The ice had been broken.

"One of the senior doctors in my group is supervising a similar
project where they need these ghost cells for their work, and sometimes, we provide them with the red blood cells from our hospital. It
is a very interesting concept, isn't it?"

Our conversation had gone in a direction I liked.

"Yes, yes indeed. Are you also a researcher or a doctor?" Raj had never mentioned anything about his wife.

"I am a doctor," she said softly, and smiled again.

"Oh, wow! I honestly didn't know you are a doctor. Raj never told me so." I was impressed with her credentials.

"Mukta is *just* a GP, a general physician, that's all. Nothing great. And she doesn't have her own private practice; she is a salaried physician at the hospital," Raj said, trivializing her credentials.

"That's true, I am just a general physician and I don't have my own practice," she said. She seemed happy to concur with him. "I am with the department of Family Medicine at the university's teaching hospital. I have been there for, let's see, for..."

"For thirty years, three months and six days." Her mathematician husband provided precise information about her employment history, in his usual way.

"There you go. Now you know how long I have been working there." She smiled again, ignoring Raj's "butting in," which I found completely unacceptable!

"Would you care for something to drink, Neila?" she asked politely.

"Yes, sure."

"Hot or cold?" she asked.

"First provide her proper information, Mukta. What would the hot drink be and what would the cold drink be?" Raj snapped at his wife.

"Well, hot is usually coffee or tea, dear, and cold, some kind of juice or a soda," Mukta said placidly.

"What do you want now, Neila, hot or cold?" Raj looked at me and asked, sounding a bit irritated.

"Anything is fine," I said.

"No, no, be precise, hot or cold, now that you know what it is," Raj said impatiently.

"Something hot would be alright," I said.

"Hot what, coffee or tea?" He sounded irritated.

"Coffee would be fine, Mukta. Thanks," I said.

"How do you take your coffee? Tell her that, too. I take mine with three lumps of sugar, two spoonfuls of low-fat milk, and a pinch of cinnamon powder. Be precise like me," Raj said. I looked at Mukta. Her face was still calm with a smile on it.

"I take mine with one lump of sugar and a little bit of cream, and if you don't have cream, whole milk would be okay, too," I tried to say as precisely as Raj wanted me to.

"Mukta, bring one coffee for her just like she has asked and bring mine in my usual mug," Raj ordered his wife. *Ordered!* There was no request in his words or tone of voice.

"How about you, Mukta? Won't you have coffee with us?" I was feeling a little uneasy witnessing his behavior with his wife.

"No, she won't. She has to cook our dinner. We eat precisely at 5:45 pm, you see, otherwise that disturbs my schedule completely," Raj said. How rude of him to answer on her behalf! How rude of him to say anything to his wife in that tone!

"Oh, another thing, Mukta—fry some *pakoras*[2] for us!"

"No, no, no need for anything special like that," I said, feeling hesitant.

"It is alright. You have come to our house for the first time today, right? Pakoras go very well with coffee, you see. Mukta, prepare a plate full of pakoras to eat with our coffee, okay?" Raj ordered his wife again, and then turned to me and said, "Let's go and sit in my study room now. She will bring the pakoras there." Looking thrilled with his own idea of pakoras, he asked me to follow him to his study room. I was still standing there, hesitant and completely bewildered at everything what I had just seen—and even more so to see Mukta's face with an expression of total indifference.

"Come, come! Come to my study, she will go in the kitchen now to prepare pakoras." He sounded excited to lead me to his study room. I reluctantly followed him, looking at Mukta going straight into the kitchen with no qualms, wondering to myself how she could take his rude and arrogant behavior so casually.

"This is my sanctuary, you see. I do all my research work, my thinking, and everything in this sanctuary." He seemed to love the name *sanctuary* for his study room. "My research is very important; I try to keep everything in this sanctuary so that nothing gets lost, you

---

2 Pakoras are deep fried fritters of onions in batter.

see." Raj started showing me with great enthusiasm his degree and diploma certificates that were hanging on the wall, and a few other things that were all related to the field of mathematics. However, what little interest I would have had was lost by now as I was genuinely perturbed with his rude attitude towards his wife. I pretended to exhibit mild interest in whatever he was showing me. Nicely placed on the table was a small beer mug made of glass, with some writing on it. He pointed at that and went on for a long time about some conference where he had presented a paper and how he was awarded that mug after a round of applause.

"People still talk about my paper, you see," he said while handing me the mug to read. His name and the date were on it; the date was some twenty years old. Obviously, nothing much had taken place in the last twenty years—no more research had been done nor had any paper been presented by this man.

Just then, Mukta walked in the study room with a tray holding two mugs of coffee and two plates full of *pakoras*. She laid the tray on his table and was about to leave when I requested that she join us for a few minutes. She looked at Raj, as if needing Raj's permission, and then agreed to stay only for a few minutes.

"As soon as I get home from the hospital, I start cooking dinner and keep it ready," she said by way of excuse for staying only a few minutes with us.

"Yes, yes, she has to," Raj said.

"Why does she have to?" I asked with an emphasis on *have to*.

"Because Raj gets very tired from his research work, so when he gets home, he has to have his dinner ready," she said, defending him while grabbing a nearby stool.

"Don't you get tired after your full day's work at the hospital as a *doctor?*" I emphasized the word *doctor*, but saw nonchalance on her face, and kept quiet.

"Now that you are in Canada, do you miss eating Indian food?" Raj ignored her completely and asked me. I looked at him. He had his mouth full of pakoras.

"Yes and no," I said while taking the plate of *pakoras* that Mukta handed me.

"It is either yes or a no, it can't be both," Raj said while munching on the pakoras.

"I know, I know, I should be precise, right? Well, it's *yes,* because I do miss it. But it's also *no,* because I like trying all kinds of varieties of food. Food varieties are readily available here in Canada. Aren't they?" I asked, purposely looking at Mukta to pull her in our conversation. Sitting on a small stool, she looked like his obedient servant.

"Yes. This is an amazing country, especially this city. There is absolutely nothing that you don't get here," Mukta joined in the conversation and agreed with me.

"Two negatives make it positive," Raj said. He wouldn't quit talking with his mouth full.

"That's exactly what I meant, Raj, you get everything here," Mukta calmly explained.

"You didn't answer my question." Raj said to me, completely ignoring her while referring to his earlier question of whether I miss Indian food.

"That's okay dear; she doesn't have to answer your every question." Mukta tried to calm him. She then turned to me and said, "Neila, eat the pakoras while they are still hot, that way, you will enjoy them better."

"Please, you have some too, with us," I asked Mukta again, and held my own plate in front of her.

"Don't bother offering her anything. She must have eaten a lot at the hospital," Raj said. I couldn't believe his audacity or rudeness. But she ignored his remark and picked up a couple of pakoras from my plate, placing them on a paper napkin. She then started eating them. The pakoras were absolutely delicious. I was genuinely enjoying eating them.

"You must be a wonderful cook, Mukta," I said as I commended her pakoras.

"Well, I try to be, I guess," she said as she smiled.

"I am so impressed with you, Mukta, a full-time physician at the hospital, and such a good cook, too." I was genuinely complimenting her when suddenly she interrupted me.

"Did you see Raj's honor beer mug?" she asked, changing the topic completely. I just nodded. Was she uncomfortable in receiving a compliment? Or was it a simple case of his insatiable need for attention that she knew about all too well? If so, I was also beginning to see that by now.

"He had presented a paper on the concept of randomness in a conference," she said, her face expressing some kind of praise for him.

"Oh really? I didn't know that," I said.

"I didn't think you would understand the subject, which is why I didn't tell you," Raj said in his usual condescending manner.

"Ask him, then," Mukta said.

"What is random?" I asked. I didn't quite care about this topic nor did I understand it, but out of politeness, mainly to Mukta, I asked him about the subject.

"Oh, that is a big philosophical question, you see." Raj looked happy now that the attention was directed at *him*.

"What is the concept of randomness?" I asked again.

"It is a very difficult question, but you know Einstein's famous remark," he said.

"Which one? Many of his remarks have been famous." I was totally disinterested in him by now, and quite irritated, too.

"Remark that God does not throw dice!"

"What does that mean?" I was lost in his explanation.

"Simple. It means that Einstein did not believe that there was an element of randomness in the construction of the world. Can't you see such a simple thing?" Raj was gleaming while explaining Einstein's remark.

"But, then, I was not asking you whether the entire universe is a random process or not. All I wanted to know, from you Raj, was how the concept of randomness was related to *your* paper. Can't *you* see that?" I was slowly beginning to lose my patience. It was impossible to have a normal conversation with this arrogant man. My body language must have also been exhibiting my state of mind by then.

"Oh, but that is still a very important question, you see."

"So, do you have an answer to this question?' I stuck to my point.

It became obvious that Raj got restless with my question and my insistence on getting an answer. He got up from his chair and walked towards another one and sat in it. Then he stood up again and paced on the floor, then sat at his table, got up again, finally settling down on a beanbag chair, completely sinking in it. I wondered whether he was demonstrating the concept of randomness with this activity.

He then picked up a rubber band that was lying nearby, made a harp across the thumb and forefinger of his left hand, and started playing it with the forefinger of his right hand, generating some kind of a tune at a regular interval. Now *this* was a system that made some sense to me! It was a system that was completely devoid of randomness!

Mukta and I were looking at him and then at each other consecutively, staying quiet. We were waiting with anticipation that Raj might say something, anything, perhaps a further explanation about the concept of randomness or whatever he claimed that he had presented in his paper. We stayed quiet for a few more minutes watching him get more and more restless and flustered. Finally, just as Mukta was about to say something to ease the tension, Raj blurted out, "Mathematics is broken into too many specialties these days, can't you see that? Twenty years ago, it was a different story, you see. I was considered to be a great mathematician then. But now I am too specialized and too advanced in my specialty. To answer your question in simple terms today, you have to go back many, many years to find an ordinary general mathematician, you see. Only then you may be able to satisfy such silly inquiries, you see." He looked totally upset. His voice had gone up to a higher pitch and volume, raised more than necessary.

His lack of ability to answer my question led him to call my question a silly inquiry. That was his defense, but in doing so, he failed to realize that he had trivialized my intelligence, just as he had trivialized everything else in his surroundings, including his wife and her profession. It was out of sheer politeness that I had asked him a question about his paper, and at the prompting of his wife, at that. I certainly didn't need this insult. I was almost livid with his arrogance. However, he seemed totally oblivious to my state of mind and started explaining further. "By asking about the concept of randomness, you are automatically posing a question about the system, you see. And to inquire about a system in *pi* is like asking 'Is there life after death?'"

"What? What are you talking about? Who was asking anything about your *pi*? Or even life after death? I think, Raj, you don't have any answer, and that's the truth." I clearly expressed my anger in my attack.

"How can you say that, Neila? I do have an answer to your question about the concept of randomness. My answer to that is something like this: when you die, you will find out." Raj started laughing at his own joke. Was it really a joke? If so, what a miserable attempt at humor. He had safely landed on his favorite topic, the *pi*. He had obviously no clue whatsoever about any other phenomena in the realm of mathematics. Did he really have any knowledge at all in that field other than *pi*? Was he really haunted by the digits of *pi*? Why? Especially when he knew that the answer to the digits of *pi* might never be found.

I was restless, completely losing my desire to stay there even a minute longer. To my surprise, Mukta also seemed quite restless. Her usual calm face with the casual expressions that I was accustomed to for the last few hours was now gone, and a new expression of extreme tension was spread on it.

"The salt seems to be too much in these pakoras, don't you think?" Raj asked me, completely unaware of what the two women in the room were going through because of his arrogant, child-like behavior.

"Pardon me?" The topic had changed so suddenly, from the concept of randomness to that of the pakoras that I got a little startled.

"I said, the salt in the pakoras is too much, right?" Raj asked me again. I just shrugged.

"Yes, yes, taste again, and you will also find it salty," he insisted.

"No, it is not salty at all. It is absolutely perfect," I said unduly loudly, as if in total defiance to him, and as if to condemn him completely.

"Oh no, really Raj? Do you find them salty?" Mukta suddenly got up from the little stool that she was sitting on, sounding defensive.

"Yes, they are too salty," Raj said and looked at Mukta.

"No way Raj, they are not salty at all. Mukta, you tasted them too, right?" I looked at Mukta expecting her to agree with me and prove the point that Raj was wrong. But she agreed with Raj, not with me.

"Yes, I think so too. You are right Raj; these pakoras are quite salty," she said in a soft voice as she turned her head down. Strangely, I saw the tension on her face quickly disappearing as she agreed with him.

"See Neila, I told you they are salty," Raj said jubilantly, looking at me.

"I'm sorry, I'd better be careful next time," Mukta said. I saw her face slowly coming back to its normal, calm expression.

"Yes, you'd better be careful, not just next time, but all the time. You know I shouldn't be eating too much salt." Raj turned his gaze at her while munching on the last pakoras from his plate.

"The pakoras were not salty at all. And if they were, why did you devour each and every one of them? Look at your plate, it is empty," I retorted, but as I said it, I instantly realized that it was none of my business that his wife agreed with him completely.

I was angry at myself for trying to irritate him or defend her. Why did I get so perturbed with this whole episode? I could clearly see that I was reacting to the unjust way one member of this household was treating the other one. Still, there was no place for me to unnecessarily interfere in all this. I started getting very uneasy.

"I'd better go in the kitchen and start cooking now. Bye Neila," Mukta said. She must have sensed my uneasiness. With a smile at me, she picked up the two empty plates and walked away in the direction of the kitchen.

"Watch the salt in your cooking!" I heard Raj holler at her. She nodded at his warning. I also quickly got up from my chair, and after thanking him for inviting me to his place, I left, promising myself never to visit him ever again.

I started walking back to my residence. The sun had just gone down, and all those varieties of colors in that beautiful scenery of the campus grounds had assumed different shades of orange and red. They were absolutely magnificent! Yet I was in no mood to enjoy it. I was thinking about Raj and his wife—*especially* his wife—and what had transpired that afternoon. His arrogance and rudeness towards her were as annoying to me as was her subservience and excessive submission to him. This was causing me mild mental distress. I could understand a little dominance here and there, sometimes, by the husband over his wife, but what was this? Was this for real? The wife was a highly-educated woman, a medical doctor, a provider of the family, which only highlighted the contrast to the husband. Though well-educated, he was an unsuccessful researcher with no income, and was totally dependent on her income for support. How then could he insult her continuously?

And furthermore, how could this happen here in Canada, where everyone was treated equally and there were no social pressures? Could these people not shed their orthodox, traditional baggage after they landed on Canadian soil? Could all Indian immigrants be like this, with the husbands controlling and commanding their wives like masters of the universe, with the wives obeying them unconditionally?

I almost shuddered at this thought, and I started walking even faster, as if to run away from these thoughts. It was depressing to even think of that whole afternoon for a long time, which I came to call, later on, the "pakora afternoon."

I was absorbed in my own thoughts, and I didn't realize when I reached my residence. It was only five o' clock, but was already looking dark outside. Then I realized that the clocks had gone back by an hour just a week earlier, a system that was totally new to me. I went into my room and walked straight to the desk. There was a stack of papers and a few books staring at me. I sat at the table, turned the lamp on, and started working towards a term paper that was due for submission in just a few days.

About a month later, I saw Mukta walking in the corridor in front of my laboratory.

"Hi Mukta," I said, surprised to see her there. I ran up to her to greet her.

"Oh, hi Neila, how are you, stranger?"

She was right in calling me a stranger, for I never contacted her after the pakora afternoon. We exchanged some pleasantries, and then

I asked her the reason for visiting our department. Apparently, one of her doctor colleagues at the hospital was supervising some project in biosciences at the undergraduate level and he had requested Mukta's help in coaching a few of the students in that project. She had gladly agreed to help him and had come to the department to meet those students who were involved with the project.

"Will you be visiting here often?" I asked her, hoping she would.

"Not very often, once or twice a month, at the most, but that would be enough for the time being, I suppose. I am also quite busy at the hospital these days," she said with her usual inviting smile.

"Well, if you need any help from me in this project, I will be glad to help you," I said genuinely.

"Oh sure, thank you." There was sincere gratitude in her tone.

During that semester, Mukta came to the department a few times, and in every visit, she made it a point to meet with me. Once I gave her a tour of my laboratory, explaining some of the modern equipment we had recently procured for our research.

"It is so wonderful to be a student, isn't it? I really miss my days as a student."

"Yes, yes indeed! It is wonderful. We live below the poverty level, mind you, but yes, there is a lot of fun in being a full-time student," I said, trying to joke a little.

"You never called me or visited me after we were introduced. You know where I live."

"Well, you are right, I didn't." I was thinking of some excuse for not visiting her when she interrupted me.

"And you know it takes only seven minutes and twenty-two seconds to reach my house from the campus," she said with a teasing tone and a twinkle in her eye. We both had a good laugh.

"Listen, I am going to be on call at the hospital for the entirety of next week, but then I am off for a couple of days after that. Why don't you come and visit me at home? Come for lunch," she invited. There was so much affection in her tone.

"Who would deny to eat your meals knowing the way you cook, Mukta? But before I accept your invitation, let me see my class schedule."

"Please don't disappoint me, okay?" she said. She smiled again and left.

I liked meeting her on the campus, and I always looked forward it. This was a woman of class who could discuss many topics with grace and ease. I enjoyed her company every time we met. But I didn't want to visit her at her house, as I was totally reluctant to meet her husband, Raj, again. Ever since the pakora afternoon, I avoided meeting him altogether. His overt condescension towards his wife (and perhaps all women) was so repugnant to me that I had decided never to contact him. I could successfully do so in the university, but how could I avoid him in his own house? I declined Mukta's invitation every time she called me to visit her, with some reason or other.

The semester was over and so was my meeting Mukta, as she stopped coming to the campus for her work, and my going to her house was out-of-the question. And then it happened: there was a huge year-end event planned for all the graduate students and faculty members of the biology department; everyone who was involved in some capacity in the department activities was invited. It struck me that Mukta would be on the invitees' list as well. Immediately, I telephoned her to inform her about the event. I was happy to learn that she had been invited already—but she was thinking of declining.

"I really miss meeting with you though, Neila," she said.

"Then why don't you come to this event? We'll meet there," I said, and added, "I also would like to see you."

"Who's coming, any idea?" she inquired, hesitating a little—but I understood what she meant.

"Well, it is limited to the staff and students of biological sciences only, and from no other faculty," I informed her.

"Are you sure?"

"Yes, absolutely," I assured her.

There was a small pause; then she agreed to come. I thought I heard her breathe a brief sigh of relief.

The Graduates' Lounge was crowded with professors and graduate students. This was going to be our last get-together before the final examinations. Free food and coupons for drinks were two huge attractions for most of the students. Everyone was eating, drinking and enjoying the party. I myself had a plateful of food in one hand and a glass of wine in another. I was munching on the food and chatting with a fellow student when I saw Mukta walking in. She was wearing a sky blue colored pant suit with a navy blue jacket, had on light pink lipstick, and had tied her hair in a bow. She looked very elegant and professional.

A few of the students and professors knew her too, since she had come to the department regularly in the earlier semester.

"I am glad you could make it to our get-together today, Dr. Panday," said one of the professors who knew her well. She seemed to like his greeting. He led her to the bar and handed her a glass of wine.

"Hi Mukta," I said, approaching her as she was sipping the wine and conversing with the professor. After a few minutes, we both went to a table that was holding all kinds of food items. We helped ourselves with our plates full of food and started talking softly. "This is a very good party," she said as she looked around. She seemed quite pleased.

"Yes, it is," I said. "The parties in the Graduate Lounge usually are. I am very happy you could make it to this one."

"Do you know I have never been to a party at the university?" she said.

"Really?" I said. Then I realized that I shouldn't have expressed my surprise.

"Raj doesn't like me coming to the university. He himself never attended any party. In all these years, I have never attended any function, any party at all." She looked at me and smiled, but this time the smile seemed a little sad.

"Hmm…" I said. I didn't ask her directly, although I could very well guess the reasons why.

"It makes him very uncomfortable, he told me once. When he was a sessional instructor in the department of mathematics…"

"Sessional? Was he a sessional instructor?" Raj had never told me this.

"Yes, in the beginning, he was a sessional instructor here. He was supposed to get the Assistant Professorship in a couple of years—at least that's what he told me, but for whatever reason, it didn't work out that way. Poor Raj! He couldn't find anything outside the university as well, so he had no choice but to join the faculty as a researcher. Ever since then, he's been here. He is not even attached to the faculty; they have just given him a small room—more like a desk, a chair and a telephone, where he can sit and do his work. He comes here regularly and carries out the research in the way that he pleases."

"But then, why does he come here?"

"Well, because he has to feel that he is a somebody, that's why," Mukta said.

"But does he not carry out his research from home?" I asked innocently.

"Yes, but only a handful of people know that. To all others, he tells that he is attached with the mathematics department of the university. He *feels* that he is a somebody only by being with the university and not by working at home. It is quite simple to understand his thinking, isn't it?" she said.

"And why does he want to be *somebody*?" I dared to ask.

"Doesn't everybody?" she asked. She smiled at her own quip of logic, and then looked off into space. She waited for a few minutes, as though the combination of wine and exhaustion had taken away all her words, leaving her totally blank. Then with a serious face, she said, "You ask me *why*? Because that is the only way he feels *secure* about himself." Mukta emphasized the word *secure*, and looked around to see if anyone could hear our conversation.

"And what about funding for his research?" I dared to ask her in a low voice, as if asking her a secret.

"Me." Mukta had lowered her voice even more. "*I* provide the funding for his research. *I* am his funding source. Do you know that he never applies to the NRCC for any funds? He simply cannot. With no attachment with the faculty, he does not qualify for even applying for any grant." Mukta said all this in her usual casual tone.

"Oh my, really? But he tells everyone that." I looked at her and saw her shaking her head. "Oh my God, you mean to say, all that talk and fuss he makes about getting funding every year is just a ...."

"It is just a façade! A façade to cover his, his, his ...."

"His *sorry ass*! Pardon my expression, Mukta, but I have no respect left for him any more after I saw..."

"I know." I had really dared this time, but Mukta interrupted me with just a nod. She quietly took another sip of her wine. I was totally puzzled.

"Can we go and sit? I am feeling a little too tired to stand and talk," Mukta said, and pointed to a corner table. There was nobody sitting at that one. We both walked in that direction, greeting a few people on our way. I laid my plate and glass of wine on the table and sat down. She pulled her chair closer, sat down, and started sipping her wine slowly, looking around the lounge. I sipped my wine quietly too, wondering whether Mukta wanted to share with me some more information about Raj.

"I wanted to talk to you someday, anyway. Today might be the best day. Who knows? I may never get another chance with you alone." She started talking. She was really in the mood now. Perhaps this was my chance as well, although it was none of my business, to ask her about his rotten attitude and rudeness that I had witnessed during the pakora afternoon. And why was she allowing all that with so much understanding?

"You are right, actually, Neila: all that façade is to save his, what did you say? His *sorry ass*, right?" She looked at me intensely. "I knew that afternoon that you were really very upset with him and his attitude towards me. I could clearly read it on your face. The pakoras were not at all salty, I knew it, but I had no choice but to agree with him. I could see that you were almost exasperated when you were defend-ing me, but I purposely didn't agree with you, and let you down."

"Well, pakoras being salty or not is not the question here. That's too damn trivial, but it is his... " Mukta gestured me to silence.

"Wait, let me tell you more. When you asked him a question about his paper, at my insistence, you looked a little irked with his silly and pointless explanation. His flustered attitude made it worse. Do you think I didn't notice anything? Seeing your face and your open dis agreement with him, including your defending me against his false accusation about the pakoras, I knew immediately that you had spark and guts. But you also had no knowledge about him, or about us two. I wanted to tell you someday, but there never was a right time or a right place, until now, I guess to tell you that…"

"Tell me what?" I interrupted her with impatience.

"That Raj is like a sick child, a truly sick child." She said it with almost no emotion, and started sipping her wine slowly.

"A sick child?" I stopped sipping my wine and just held the glass in my hands, looking at her with a questioning expression.

"Yes, he has this psychological condition where he gets into moods of extreme insecurity. And when he gets into those moods, he starts throwing tantrums, and then the whole situation gets out of control in no time."

"Oh my God! Really?" I couldn't believe what she said.

"Yes, and I can't figure out where his psychological condition stemmed from. I do know that he had a very messy childhood and a very unstable time during his youth. The psychologist diagnosed that a few bad traits were ingrained in him when he was growing up. In addition, some of those traits could be of genetic nature, too, I don't know, but the sickness has continued to this day."

"What happened during his childhood to call it messy, if I may ask?" My concern was genuine.

"Well, although the only son, he was born as a very and weak sick child, in a family with practically no money. The parents couldn't afford the doctors' services or expensive medication. So he couldn't get any medical attention. To make matters worse, his father passed away when he was still quite young. His mother, a young widow, was left with no money or support at all, and just a sick young son, who couldn't help her."

"Oh, how sad…"

"Yes, sad indeed. Just imagine, Neila, a long path of life ahead of her, or worse still, imagine a high, dry mountain of life ahead of her to climb with not even a fragile walking stick at hand to use for support.

To add to the treacherous climb, she had this young sick son. How can the climb be any easier? That was his mother's situation."

"Hmm." I could not say anything.

"With this sick son, my Raj, what could his young widowed mother do? She started doing some menial jobs to provide them with the basic necessities of life. Poor woman, I feel so sad when I think of her. But she was determined. She worked very hard to provide Raj with the best possible things of the world, and that was education. She knew that her son may be sick physically, but he was intelligent. So she made sure he got into a good school."

"That sounds good."

"Yes, but then she had her own shortcomings. She was very loving but very strict. She was a good mother, working very hard to provide for food, shelter and good schooling, but she was also too much of a disciplinarian. She expected too much out of him in his school days, and would beat him regularly and hurt him very badly if he didn't get the marks she expected. On one hand she pampered him, on the other, she never could give him a feeling of trust and stability. When he would do well in the school, there was no end to her pampering him, but then, there would be no limit to her beating him when he failed to do so. As a doctor, I strongly feel that in that process, Raj lost his sense of security completely, a sense that a young boy develops while growing up. The consequence of all this was that he loved his mother dearly but secretly despised her, too. It's a horrible story, really!" Mukta shuddered and waited for a few minutes.

I shuddered too to listen to all this about Raj's childhood. A sheltered and well-raised person like me had never experienced or even seen any such thing in my life.

"He was doing his final year of a bachelor's degree in mathematics when his mother passed away. He was totally devastated with the loss, but also felt completely free—a weird combination of two extreme emotions. He was also financially broke and needed money to complete his degree. He talked to a few people in one of the nearby temples for some financial help when someone guided him to my father. He approached my father asking for some kind of a teaching job that would help him financially. My father, thinking that he was a bright young man who wanted to study further, gave him a helping hand. That was about the same time when I was trying to get into medical school and was preparing for the entrance exam. So, my father hired Raj to teach me Math and Physics. That's how we met."

"Oh how nice? A teacher and a pupil."

"Yes, it was. I did very well in the entrance exam and got into the medical college. I was happy, really."

"Yes, I can see that."

"Raj had also become my close friend by then. Just imagine, going through the medical training in a prestigious institution, and having a great friend like Raj."

"Yes, I can imagine. You must have felt like you were on cloud nine."

"I did actually. My father was a genuine promoter of good qualities in a human being. He didn't care for anything else but those qualities. He gladly encouraged me to have Raj as my beau! By the time I finished my medical degree, Raj finished his master's and doctorate degrees in mathematics. We decided to get married. My parents were very happy to get such a polite and well-educated husband for their daughter. We got married and decided to come to Canada. It was much too easy for doctors to come here in those days. We just had to write and pass the qualifying exams and residency was almost guaranteed. That's what happened in my case. We both were very happy to say the least, and I was happy for Raj. I felt that God cared, finally." Mukta stopped for a while, staring into space. It was as though she was trying to relive those happy days!

"He used to tell me all those loving stories about his mother then. How she cared for him and what a wonderful cook she was and on and on. For quite some time, I didn't know what was really underneath that love for his mother. I remember teasing him a few times and getting annoyed! 'Are we ever going to be alone or will your mother be always there?' I would ask him when I would be totally frustrated with his mother stories. Can you imagine? But then, honestly I couldn't figure out what happened. His behavior started changing, and his stories about his mother changed too."

"What do you mean?"

"Slowly his suppressed feelings of negativity and anger that he felt towards his mother started surfacing."

"Towards his *mother*?" I asked with surprise.

"Yes, towards his own dead mother. A man who had nothing but praise for her, nothing but wonderful stories about her that I was hearing all this time, exhibited a strange mixture of love and hate—actually, more hate than love. Eventually, this strange duality started dominating his emotions and everything went astray. He became suspicious of everything, literally everything, thinking nothing positive about anything, especially women. At the same time he also became a wishful thinker, thinking relentlessly that nothing positive was ever going to come his way. In his terrible mental fight, he ended up losing everything, his own accomplishments, his prospect of becoming a faculty member, his confidence and what's more, his self-respect too."

Mukta sounded very sad. And I felt sad hearing all this about Raj. What could have triggered this strange duality in him? Mukta and I were quiet for some time, both immersed in our own thoughts.

"But why does he treat *you* the way he does?" I broke the silence.

"Why? That's because," Mukta knew what was I going to ask.

"Because he looks at everything—especially all women, including me—in the same light as his mother, a completely negative one. I used to try to convince him that not everything is negative, not all women are bad, but it was like pouring water over a covered pot. Nothing went inside, nothing at all. Anything that was negative in his judgment, and everything was so, made him very anxious, and his anxiety got worse and worse, making him extremely insecure about himself. I tried to convince him that not everything in life is negative, but he wouldn't listen to me. When my attempts of talking to him failed, I tried to talk to him about medical treatment, but he took that almost as a personal insult."

"But then the diagnosis of a psychologist you mentioned earlier…"

"This psychologist is a good friend of mine, and his diagnosis is based solely on my description of Raj in our conversation as two doctors. Raj has never been to one, no matter how much I try to convince him."

"But then, you are his loving wife and a good doctor too."

"Yes, even I, who loves him dearly and who is a good doctor, could not convince him to seek medical treatment. It is all in his mind, his own mind, and that's the way it is going to be. He will never change, never." Mukta closed her eyes and shook her head, which clearly indicated that there was no hope at all for her situation.

Neither of us talked for a few minutes. She opened her eyes and continued. "And, as if to worsen that problem, he has chosen a field, that of research in mathematics, wherein the whole game centers on creating something out of nothing. It is almost like working in the *world of dreams*. I very much doubt if he really understands what he is working with! Sometimes I genuinely wonder if he just wants to get lost in some fictitious, 'make believe' world he calls *research on pi*. My poor Raj." She was quiet again for a few minutes.

"Now can you imagine why he is so haunted by the digits of *pi*?" she asked. She was the one to break the silence.

"Why?"

"Solving the digits of *pi* is almost as fictitious as what goes on in his mind. Just think, in order to be interested in any problem, there has to be a possibility of solving it, right?" she asked me.

"Right." I said.

"If you are an athlete, you ask yourself if you can run ten miles. Then there is a definite goal set in front of you to start working on. Or if you are a musician, you ask yourself if you can play 'The Blue Danube' the way Bach intended, or play a raga on the sitar the way Ravi Shankar does. This is how you set a precise goal and then start working at it diligently. In short, you make focused efforts, right?"

"Well, yes." I nodded.

"But the digits of *pi*? Does that offer him any goal, really? Why has he taken upon himself a task of solving such a problem when he is fully aware that it could never be solved?"

"May be, Raj likes to do something that is utterly impossible?" I tried to guess.

"That's exactly it. He has taken upon himself an impossible task merely to camouflage his bungled-up emotions, to hide his sick mind from everyone." Mukta became suddenly quiet again, giving a few gentle shakes to her wineglass.

I couldn't utter a single word, for I was stunned to hear about Raj's hidden sickness. Was he a case of a congenital personality disorder? Or was this an intense reaction to extreme frustration due to his failures in life? And why was he denying proper medical treatment and an opportunity to better his life, and Mukta's life too? I was equally overwhelmed to see Mukta's loving and nurturing attitude towards him.

Two very highly-educated people who had otherwise everything in life had nothing at all, in spite of living in the new world! Was it their destiny? If so, why would destiny play such a cruel game and curdle their joy? I started feeling very sad for both of them.

At the same time, I started feeling a bit enlightened and hopeful as well. Mukta's extreme understanding with her husband was almost spiritual. This was a splendid style of behavior that was suitable only to the perfect members of the human race, and I was newly acquainted with it through Mukta after hearing this story. I was completely awe-struck with her, and just kept looking at her in this new light.

As I was greatly regarding her honor and dignity, I could see that a terrific wave of pain had sprung up in her big brown eyes. It had become suddenly evident to me that the pain was there inside her all the time, like something alive but *controlled* by love and balance. She never cried or shed any tears while telling me her life story, but her self-control was worse than crying. The awesome struggle that she had endured was overwhelming. What was even sadder was that, in spite of the awesome struggle, everything was going to remain the same, with no hope for a change!

A strange somberness hung in the air around our table. We had become totally oblivious to the joyous party that was going on just a few feet away from us. We were completely silent for a few minutes, sitting and just staring at each other. I didn't know why, but I felt an almost unbearable tenderness in my heart for her in those quiet moments.

"Does Raj love you?" I cleared my throat and asked her in as soft a voice as I could.

She took in a long breath, exhaled it as if to blow away the somber mood that was lurking around us and said, "I think so! No, no, I *know* so." She looked at me with a calm face and gave me her usual sweet smile.

"He will never change, never," Mukta had said earlier about Raj, with a great remorse and total hopelessness in her heart. Looking at her calm face and sweet smile, I felt the same thing about her, with a great solace and hope in my heart. *Thank God, she will never change, either,* I thought.

Epilogue

Mukta has downsized her working hours in the hospital to only two hours per day. That is because she has a baby, named Raj, to care for at home. Dr. Raj Pande is officially "retired" from the research position that he claimed to have held at the university and now stays home whole day. He has given up figuring out the complexity of *pi*, and is secretly happy that no one at the university has figured it out, either. He is, therefore, no longer haunted by it.

Beyond the Rigid Fence

Ramesh Joshi must be in his early thirties. He originates from India. He is of medium height, has very little fat on his body, and has dark brown eyes and hair that suit his coffee-colored complexion. He keeps a thin, sword-shaped moustache, which compliments his boyish face. Ramesh is a mild-mannered man with a pleasant smile, giving the impression he would never hurt anyone.

I first met Ramesh at the badminton club, which was on the university campus in Ontario. Badminton was not a very popular sport at the time when I immigrated to Canada. It was mostly played for fun by families and friends in their backyards during summer months. I had a tremendous liking for it, and could boast a little expertise, too. I played this game for many years regularly when I was in India.

After joining and settling down at the university, I inquired about badminton in the phys-ed building, but was disappointed to know that no one played this game.

One day, I dropped in to the students' association office to find out if there were any activities run by students from other countries, like myself, and if there were, if I could join. There was no badminton played by anyone there, but I saw on the notice board a request for volunteers. I took an application form and filled it out, with a brief comment that I would start and run a badminton club there, if the association could give some money to run it. I was hopeful since there were a few students from other Commonwealth countries who were familiar with it. My application received a positive response and a small amount of money was granted from the association. I was elated to see the result of my effort and immediately started putting together all the necessary equipment. I prepared signup sheets with a brief description of the sport and pinned them on all the notice boards of the university campus. With a mild response from a few students, a badminton club was finally established, and a day and a time were assigned in the main gym.

After running the club for a few days and playing with all the registered students, I soon realized that most of the players were beginners. I was quite disappointed and was seriously thinking of giving up the whole idea when I received a call from the students' association, inquiring if our club was open for people outside the university as well.

"Yes, for a small fee," I said, quickly adding, "It would be a win-win situation, as the association would receive some money and the non-university-going people would get a chance to play this sport." The prospect of playing with people with better badminton skills motivated me to encourage the association to accept outsiders. The club liked my suggestion and allowed a few outsiders to join the badminton club. Just as I had hoped, there were some good players joining the club, and Ramesh Joshi was one of them.

Ramesh had immigrated to Canada a few years before I did. He had passed the stage of being impressed and overwhelmed by the grandeur and freshness of the New World, while I was still in awe of it. He was working as a loans officer in a local bank and lived in a small apartment near the university. He drove to the phys-ed building, and many times offered me rides to my residence after the games were over. I always declined, since my residence was nearby. He seemed to be polite and always helped me put away all the stuff and lock up after the game was over.

Once, Ramesh brought his friend Daryl to the club and introduced us to him. Daryl was working as a bank teller at the same bank as Ramesh, and was curious about this game, we were told. Daryl was lanky and tall, and was quite young-looking with a head full of curly hair. Daryl must have liked this new sport, because he started coming regularly with Ramesh. They always came together and left together. Since he was a novice at this game, Ramesh always partnered with him in the doubles game. I liked Ramesh's attitude.

One day, as I started setting up the nets while preparing for the game, I heard a gentle "Hi," from behind.

"Oh, hi," I said, slightly startled. Daryl was standing next to me. He was alone.

"Where is Ramesh?" I asked him.

"He is not coming today." Daryl grabbed the other end of the net.

"Oh? Is he feeling okay?"

"Yep, Ramesh is fine. He's busy this evening."

"Busy on badminton evening?" I was surprised as Ramesh had never missed the game night, but Daryl ignored my question. He seemed uncomfortable to say anything more and continued setting up the nets. All other members showed up and started playing. I noticed that Daryl had picked up the sport quite well.

That night, as I was about to go to bed, I remembered Ramesh not being at the club that evening and wondered about his absence at the game. I promptly dismissed the thought and fell asleep.

Ramesh did not show up at the badminton club for three consecutive weeks; Daryl came alone all that time. This was highly unusual. Everyone noticed it and also felt Ramesh's absence on the court. Many people, including me, asked Daryl about it, but no one got any answer from him, except just a shrug. Finally, when Ramesh showed up after three weeks, everyone was happy and welcomed him with enthusiasm. Strangely, Daryl was absent and Ramesh came alone.

At the end of the evening, Ramesh helped me clean up and lock up the place.

"How come you didn't show up for the game the last few times?" I asked him.

"Oh, I know, it was a long absence," he said softly. "I just couldn't." He kept on rolling the nets with his hands.

"And now that you were here today, Daryl didn't come."

"That's right." Ramesh finished rolling the nets and put them in the closet.

He obviously didn't want to tell me anything, so I didn't press the matter. We finished putting away everything, turned off the lights, locked up the place, and waved goodbye to each other with our rackets. I walked for a few steps in the corridor, and bent down at the water fountain for a quick sip. When I stood upright, I saw Ramesh standing next to me. I moved away from the fountain and wiped my mouth with my towel.

"I was just waiting for you," he said.

"Waiting for me? Why?"

"I think I should give you a ride to your residence," he said.

"No, no, not necessary. It's not that late." I looked at my wristwatch.

"It's not that late but it is very dark outside. Look." He pointed to one of the windows.

"It's dark, but really, I can walk to my place, it's not that far," I politely declined.

"Neila, listen to me. I think it is a bit too dark to walk alone. Let me drive you to your place." He sounded sincere.

The university campus was very safe and secure. Walking to my residence late at night, either from the library or the research lab, was my regular habit. But Ramesh looked so concerned about my safety that I couldn't refuse his offer.

We went to the parking lot. He opened the car door for me, and after I got inside, he closed it. *What a gentleman!* I thought. He requested me to buckle up the seatbelt and then started the car. It was a good car with a leather interior in an olive green color. On the dashboard was a magnet in the shape of Lord Ganesh, and next to it was a small photograph of a little girl.

"What a lovely little girl," I exclaimed, hoping he would tell me who she was.

"Yes, she is very pretty. She is my cute little daughter Asha," he said, keeping his eyes straight ahead.

"Your daughter? How wonderful! I didn't know you had a daughter."

"Well, now you do, right?" He glanced at me and stayed quiet. He obviously didn't want to talk about his family. We drove silently for about three or four minutes and then reached my residence. He stopped the car in front of my residence building, got out of the car and walked around to open my door, and then escorted me all the way to the front door.

"Thanks for the ride," I said.

"Any time," he said pleasantly, and then drove away.

I went upstairs to my apartment and took a long hot shower, thankful every minute for the ample water supply and the incredible plumbing system of this country. After making a fresh pot of herbal tea, I sat at my desk with books wide open. Mid-term exams were not too far away, so it was time to burn some midnight oil. I poured some tea in a cup and opened *Lehninger*—we in our study group referred to our books by their authors' names. Thoughts about Ramesh, his daughter, or anything else disappeared in seconds once I got deep into the course material.

In the following week, when I stepped outside my residence building to head for the game, I saw Ramesh standing outside his parked car waiting for me. As soon as he saw me, he opened the passenger door and gestured me to get inside. He had a smile on his face, as though assuring me that everything was okay. A little surprised, I got inside the car.

"You need not give me a ride on the way there, it is not dark *now*," I said, laughing.

"I know it is not dark right now, and you don't need a ride, but I wanted to." He drove us to the gym. He gave me a ride back to my residence too, explaining that it was dark.

This routine continued for a few weeks. His gesture was sweet, but it started bothering me. I didn't like this overly protective gesture, nor was I fully comfortable with this excessively friendly gesture. I was too independent to be so much cared for. *Is there a purpose to all this? If so, what would that be?* My mind started getting busy, but I couldn't figure out what it was. Sometimes Daryl would also be with him, in which case, we three would drive together to the gym. Daryl's presence or absence didn't make any difference at all. Ramesh would still pick me up and drop me off at my residence after the game.

All these times, I would invariably look at his daughter's photograph on the dashboard of his car and wonder about her or his wife, but there never was any mention about them in his conversation. Where were they? And where was his wife? Was she alive or dead? Or could he be divorced? But I never asked him anything, and sure enough, he never volunteered any information on his own, either. Eventually I just stopped thinking about all these details about him.

"We are having a 'Customer Appreciation Party' at my bank on Friday evening," Ramesh told me one day. "Would you like to come to the party?"

"Are you inviting me?" I asked him with a smile.

"Yes, yes of course. I am inviting you. That's my way of inviting." He smiled sheepishly.

"But I am not a customer of your bank. I am not a customer of any bank, for that matter," I said. "No bank would show any interest in a student like me with her 'fat' pay cheque. Get it?" I joked about my paltry earnings at the university.

"It really doesn't matter. Look at it this way, you could be our future customer."

He got back at me with his joke.

"I am not sure I have time." I hesitated.

"Then pretend it is our game night. How is that?"

"Well, okay, but how do I get there?"

"I will pick you up and drop you off after the party."

"Umm, okay then, I will come. Oh, one more problem: I don't own any good clothes to wear for a bank get-together."

"It is completely informal, Neila. What you wear for your daily routine is just fine, you will see. Come, I would like that very much." He finally convinced me to go with him.

He was absolutely right about the informality of the party. Everybody was in casual attire except a few of the bank officers. Ramesh himself was dressed up in a full three-piece suit and so was Daryl. There was a lot of food, mainly finger food, and a few kinds of non-alcoholic beverages. A clown show was organized for children under ten in one corner of the bank. All the children had gathered around the clown and were enjoying the show. A few of them were getting their faces painted. It was a very pleasant atmosphere. When I saw all the children, I immediately thought of Ramesh's daughter and his wife. Where were they that day—at least the daughter? Something didn't seem right, but I let it go without saying anything to Ramesh.

Winter had started to set in and the outside temperatures were reaching below zero. Ramesh and I were on our way to the gym in his car. As we approached the double doors of the gym, we saw the superintendent of the building sending everyone away. The heating system of the building was malfunctioning and there was no heat in the building. The maintenance crew had been called in for the emergency.

"Oh my, what do we do now?" I asked, mostly rhetorically.

"Well, can't play in there, obviously. But now that we both have this free time, we can do something together," Ramesh said.

"Such as what?" I wasn't sure what he had in mind.

"We can go to the cafeteria and have coffee and something to eat," Ramesh suggested.

"Sounds like a plan," I said. I had readily agreed as I was not in a rush to go back to my residence. We drove to the campus cafeteria, got coffee and something to eat with it, and walked to the cashier. Ramesh, the gentleman that he was, paid for my food as well, and we sat at a nearby table.

"Thank God the heating is on in this building," Ramesh said as we were settling down.

"Yes, but instead of playing and exercising, we are eating."

"Let us just say that a different part of the body will start the exercise now," he quipped.

We started munching on the food and engaged in some small talk. I thought this would be a good time to ask him about his wife and daughter. Just as I was thinking about this, Ramesh interrupted my thoughts.

"Asha just loves French fries." Ramesh said.

Oh my! Could he read my mind?

"You know, whenever I take her out for a treat, she wants me to buy French fries for her. Then when she finds a long one like this one in the bucket, she holds it between her upper lip and nose and pretends it is her moustache, just like her daddy's." He was holding a long French fry in his two fingers and was looking intently at it.

"Really?" I was looking at him in amazement.

"Yup." He looked at me, smiled, and bit into the fry.

"Do you take her out a lot?"

"Umm, sometimes, only when her mother permits me to do so."

"What do you mean?"

"Asha lives with her mother. Urmila, that's my wife's name, she doesn't live with me anymore. Fortunately, their apartment is not too far from where I live, so I get to visit my daughter as often as I wish." Ramesh was still munching on his fry.

So, his wife is alive, not dead, as I had thought once, and lives very close from him, I thought. My mind was in overdrive.

"Are you divorced?"

"No, oh no, no. I wish I were though."

This was confusing to me.

"I really want a divorce, but Urmila is reluctant to give me one. She insists that I stop living separately and move in with them. But it doesn't really make any sense at all, really any sense at all to me." He shook his head and continued eating.

"What makes no sense at all?" I finally dared to ask him about his personal life.

"All this! Both of us living separately but without a divorce, having separate lives but with a legal attachment on paper. I have been advising her, almost imploring her to get a divorce from me but she just plainly refuses."

"Why a divorce? Do you two not get along with each other?"

"It is a long and complicated story, Neila. I hope there is a happy ending to it. Someday, some day for sure, I hope." He sighed.

"Do you want to tell me?" I dared to ask again.

"I am not sure I want to. My story could embarrass you or could even make you feel really ill at ease, I don't know."

"I am a good listener if you wish to share your story with me," I said.

"Oh, I'm sure you are, but let me tell you something about me." He hesitated a bit, and then said, "In plain and simple words, I am not, what people from India would say, *normal*."

"What do you mean by *normal*?" I felt a bit irritated.

"Normal as in normal! You know, someone who is not abnormal."

I sat there, my eyebrows raised in expectation.

"I'm sorry I can't explain. But I just know that I'm not normal according to people in India, especially my folks."

"Listen, no human being is normal, or to put it another way, all human beings are normal." I said.

"That's refreshing to hear from someone from India. But do you actually believe in that, or you are just saying it? More importantly, do you practice what you just said, Neila?" he challenged me.

"Yes, absolutely," I said firmly, as if accepting his challenge. "By the way, why are you looking down upon people in India like that?"

"I'm sorry, I didn't mean to insult all the people in India." His hands were clasped, close to his chest, displaying a *Namaste* gesture. "It was more like I was talking about my folks."

"Apology accepted," I said with a smile, but his face looked a bit serious.

"If you think you are really broad-minded, then all right, I don't mind sharing my life story with you. But please remember, I have warned you."

What could be so drastic, so abnormal, as he put it, that he needed to *warn* me? I was a well-educated person with a broad and liberal mind. I was also too well brought up to think that there could be an abnormal human being on this earth.

"It all started when I was a boy, a teenager," he said as he started his story.

Oh God, this is going to be a long story was the thought that crossed my mind the moment I heard his opening line, but I had opened my big mouth and assured him of my beliefs and my good listening capability, so I had no excuse. I just smiled and started listening to his story.

"I came from a typical middle-class Indian family where education carried the utmost importance. My parents were not rich, but they could afford good education for me. Besides, I was their only son. I was a good student all through my school years. I must be in middle school when I entered adolescence. Going through adolescence must be one of life's tough learning processes. Like any other normal, healthy boy, it was time for hormonal changes for me, too. I knew all my friends were experiencing this; we used to discuss these things among us quite freely. There was no sex education given in the school system in India at that time, but it didn't matter. By the time we were barely fourteen, we boys knew everything. From what source, I really can't pinpoint, but we did. The adults in my family, especially my father, never discussed this with me, but he should have. Discussing these things was like violating a sense of personal privacy for him. It was not polite of me, or of any younger folks, to ask the elders direct questions about it." Ramesh waited for a minute and then continued again.

"In the type of family that I come from, it was expected that a man and a woman would meet as virgins on their wedding night, with little or no knowledge of what was expected of them, and then work it out naturally as they progressed in their married life. It was never the responsibility of the elders in the family to dispense any such information to the newlyweds ahead of time." Ramesh stopped talking and took a few sips of coffee. His throat sounded a little dry to me. And so was mine getting a little dry just by listening to his story. I started getting a little uneasy, too. I didn't expect him to talk so openly about his private life to me. But I sat quietly sipping coffee, and courteously lending him my ear.

"Listening to my friends talking about all these things was fun for me, but whenever they talked about girls or teased them, and they did that plenty, I never participated in their antics. I didn't know why, but I used to shy away from the girls. And this attitude of mine bothered me a lot. As I grew older and more knowledgeable about my body, I felt that I was definitely different from the rest of the guys in my group. But different in what way? I was terribly confused. Was I normal? I kept questioning myself. The more I thought about all this, the more doubtful I became about myself. Eventually I became totally confused, to the point of developing a fear."

"Fear of what?" I asked.

"Quite honestly, I didn't know what my fear was. It is only much later that I figured out that my fear was about someone finding out about me, that I could be different from the rest of my friends—that was something terribly wrong, something *abnormal*. Once I convinced myself that I was abnormal, I started isolating myself completely from my friends. I avoided all my friends and spent most of my time alone. I became aloof. And to camouflage that, I hid myself in my books, started studying hard, I mean really hard. That was my private refuge where solitude was kept, like secret wisdom, as an answer to my problem."

"A wise answer," I said.

"Yes, and that worked like a charm. My parents were so happy about my immersing myself in studies all the time; they showed complete approval of my behavior. As a matter of fact, they encouraged it."

"That flies very well with our middle-class Indian families, doesn't it?" I remembered parents of many of my friends in India putting an undue emphasis on their children's studies. The more a child studied, the more he or she was appreciated by all.

"Oh yes, it does. After all, I was a very studious son, showing respect to their efforts of educating me well. You know, I became a role model for many boys and their parents."

"I can imagine that," I said.

"My studying so hard paid off. I passed my high school exams with flying colors and got into a prestigious college on a full scholarship."

"Wow!"

"My parents couldn't contain their happiness. As I was going through the college years, I was getting a little calmer. However, my confusion and fear of someone finding out about my self-confirmed abnormality would still pop up in my mind frequently. "

"Hum, strange..."

"Strange, yes. It is really funny when I think of all that today. As I got calmer, my confusion and doubt started wearing out considerably. I was settling down mentally, but then, that calm state of mind made me neglect my studies. There was no need for me to hide behind the books any more. I didn't do well in college, just enough to get my bachelor's degree in Commerce. Can you believe it?"

"Yes." I did not know how else I could respond.

"That's why, as soon as I finished the undergraduate degree, I applied for a job in the bank. My father was surprised that I didn't opt for studying further, but they agreed happily with my decision. I was their ideal son, right? I started working in the bank and, believe it or not, I actually felt better. I developed confidence, started mixing with people, and became a bit social. This was good news to me, for I thought my abnormality was finally over and I had become a normal person, like the rest of the men in my circle. With this newly developed confidence, I started looking for better prospects elsewhere, preferably outside India. That is when I came to know about Canada's requirement for people in the area of commerce and banking. With my commerce degree and experience in banking, I applied. And as luck would have it, I got employment with a Canadian bank immediately. I jumped at the opportunity and here I am, in the free world."

"So, that's how you came to Canada."

"Yes, but you know what? That's also when the whole equilibrium of my life collapsed." Ramesh started looking intently at the food on his plate.

"What, in Canada? In this free world, as you put it?" I was surprised.

"No, no. Not *in* Canada, not in this free world, oh no! The whole problem started in India when I decided to come here."

"Why, what happened?" I really couldn't guess what he was alluding to.

"Everything happened. Anything and everything that *shouldn't* have happened, happened." He looked up. "When I declared that I was going to Canada as an immigrant, my parents were shocked. Being an 'immigrant' to another country was a shocking word to them. It had this strange and ugly label of permanence that also meant failure in your own country. And they didn't like it. According to them, people went to other countries only for higher education, after which they returned home. They could never imagine that their only son, an ideal one at that, would ever go to a far off land like Canada, and abandon them. They thought they would never see me again. My mother started crying as though I was dying of some terminal disease. Poor woman! She had no idea that immigration to Canada didn't mean that I was abandoning her or I would never see her again. Nobody, not even my father, could convince her otherwise, but I stuck to my decision."

"Good for you, but it must be very hard."

"Oh yes, it was very hard. But get this. When my mother saw that I was not budging from my decision of going to Canada, she took a new approach."

"What was it?"

"She demanded that I get married before I leave for Canada."

"Marriage is a sweet thing... why would you call it a demand?"

"It was a demand because I was not ready for it. I wanted to explore myself first before I could think of marriage and all that."

"Oh, I see. Did you tell this to your mother?"

"No. Of course not. Tell my mother about me trying to 'find' myself? She wouldn't even understand what I would be talking about. Besides, Neila, do you remember what I said about my fear and confusion during my adolescence?"

"Yes," I said.

"And about my abnormality?"

"Yes, yes, I do."

"Well, I really don't know how to tell you this, you being a girl that is, and an Indian one, but my fear was that I wouldn't be able to give happiness to a woman. You know what I mean." Ramesh quickly tuned his face down, with no chance of raising it for long. He obviously didn't want eye contact with me, an Indian woman. I didn't know what to do or say either, as I was also feeling very uneasy and embarrassed after hearing this. I started looking elsewhere, avoiding eye contact with him completely, at the same thinking about this gentle and seemingly kind man who was sitting in front of me and telling me his personal story; he was openly admitting that he was incapable of making love to a female, and calling it his *abnormality*. What could I to say, or how could I respond to him? I said absolutely nothing and just sat quietly, waiting for him to raise his head and break the silence.

"How was I to convey my fear to my mother? Or to my father, for that matter? I finally gave up and agreed to marry a girl of their choice. I agreed to go through the arranged marriage process in a typical Indian fashion. You know how it is, right?"

I nodded.

"My parents were ecstatic, especially my mother, when they got my approval for my marriage in the traditional way. Immediately they got into that typical long and complicated process of selecting a suitable girl for me. Funny as it may sound, I wasn't involved with it at all; it was *my* marriage, but I was left out completely. So sad, I tell you."

"Sad indeed, yes, and not just for boys, but for girls too. I would say it is worse for girls, but what can you do, really? This has been the Indian tradition for generations." I was sympathetic. "So, did they select a girl for you?"

"Yes, yes they did. They selected a good looking, young, healthy girl from a good family, who would make a great life partner for me, as they put it. *They* selected my life partner." Ramesh vigorously shook his head.

"Hmm"

"When they informed me about finalizing a girl for me, I decided to make one last attempt of cancelling this whole thing."

"What?"

"Yes, I told them that I wanted to meet this girl alone, absolutely alone, and not surrounded by ten different people from both our families. The idea was that I wanted to talk to her directly about my problem, tell her frankly that she will never be happy with me as a husband and thus talk her *out* of marrying me."

"Oh?" I was surprised to hear that.

"Yes. She was young and educated, and from a good family, so I thought after listening to me, she would understand and decline marrying me."

"Then?"

"Then what? Nothing, nothing at all. The girl's family sent a message to my parents that she was too shy to meet me alone, and that's it." He turned his face down again. "That was the end of my participation in my marriage. I gave up completely. I knew I was doomed for life." He held his head with his hands.

"Is that the same girl, Urmila, your wife?" I felt a little awkward to ask him, but I did, to which he nodded.

I didn't quite agree with him, that his life was doomed for good. Wasn't hers doomed too? Wasn't she getting into a marriage that may not prove to be a happy one? Why would he call this *his* tragedy? Urmila was not his choice for a wife, but nor was Ramesh hers. I knew very well that most of the Indian girls and boys married people of their parents' choices. Most of these marriages lasted their lifetimes, and most of these people led happy married lives, so what was the big deal here?

"Ramesh, you very well know the Indian traditions, and you just told me that your parents selected a good girl for you. Then what's the problem here?" I said this out loud.

"That was the most ridiculous way to meet my life partner, Neila, especially when I could not tell her some of my genuine problems." Ramesh raised his voice considerably, so I became dead silent.

"I got married, and almost immediately after my wedding, I came here to resume work at the bank. My parents were very happy that I had a wife of their choice. They told me so again and again. I could guess that they were especially happy because the possibility of me marrying a girl from some unknown culture or caste of this foreign land had been erased completely. The epitome of their happiness was that I was tied down nicely to a girl of their choice, a girl of Indian culture. Why the hell did I not stop them, or her, or all of them? *Damn* me! *Damn* her! *Damn* all of them!" Ramesh was scowling intensely and his hands were in tight fists. This was the first time I had heard him swear like that.

"Well, let it go now. You have a lovely little girl, think about her now," I said, trying to console him. However, I wasn't still quite clear on exactly what was biting him more—his own perceived problem about himself, or being forced by his parents to marry a girl of their choice.

"Do you remember a few weeks ago, when I couldn't come for my badminton games for three weeks in a row?" he asked me after he quieted down.

I nodded.

"Urmila had appointments with a psychotherapist."

"Did you say a psychotherapist?" I almost dropped my coffee cup.

"Yes, she needed to see a psychotherapist for her problems. So I had to drive her there. And while she was having her session with the doctor, I looked after my little girl. She did two sessions every week with the doctor for three weeks in a row." He said this in a relatively calmer voice, but that put me into a complete daze. So it was *she!* Ramesh's wife needed a psychotherapist! A girl born and raised in a middle-class family in India, like myself, *needed* to see a psychotherapist! I couldn't believe it. There was such a big taboo attached to it that anyone who saw a psychotherapist or a psychiatrist was labeled as 'insane' by all the folks. Young men and women talked to their parents, siblings, and friends or someone loving and caring to solve their personal problems—they never visited psychotherapists and psychiatrists. Even such doctors were labeled as 'Doctors of Insanity' and were not considered on par with the regular ones.

I just shook my head in awe. Now it was my turn to be dead silent.

One of servers in the cafeteria approached us and politely said that the place was about to be closed for the evening. We hurriedly got up from the table, apologized for having stayed so long, put on our winter jackets, and walked out the door. We went to the car and Ramesh drove me to my place. Neither of us talked during the drive. Perhaps he was wondering what made him share his personal story with me, and I was still in my own surprised state about his wife needing a psychotherapist.

We reached my place. I thanked him for the treat in the cafeteria and the ride. I was about to get out of the car when he said in a very gentle voice, "Listen, I really don't know how to thank you for your kindness. You were so patient in listening to my stupid life story. I honestly don't know what to say."

"Not to worry about it, Ramesh, but now that you have shared your personal life with me, can you please introduce me to your wife some day? I would like to meet her." My tone was genuinely compassionate.

"I am not sure of that," he said. His voice suddenly became very dry.

"Oh, please! Since she is seeing a psychotherapist now, perhaps meeting an Indian female like myself could be of some value too, who knows?"

"Well, maybe, some day. Let me think. Let me talk to her first, and only if she agrees, then I will introduce you to her."

"Fair enough." I was not in a rush.

"Goodnight," he said. He drove away and I went upstairs to my apartment.

I walked up to my room, and lay on my bed after a quick shower, ready to fall asleep. I was in no mood to study that evening. Instead, I was thinking about Ramesh and what he said about himself. And I was also thinking about his wife and her needing the services of a psychotherapist. Up until then, I always thought that only the rich and privileged folks in Canada needed services of such doctors, since only they could afford them; just as only the rich folks in India could afford to have servants and handymen. It was ignorant of me, until then, to carry an impression that while anxiety in India was structural, in Canada it was existential. What a misconception on my part! In Canada, even plain, ordinary folks could afford, and therefore needed, the privileges of the rich and affluent!

My thoughts slowly switched over to Ramesh; a thousand and one questions raced through my head. Did Ramesh create problems for his wife? But then, he seemed like a sensible and balanced guy, so why would he trouble her? Did they have marital problems right from the beginning, since the girl he married was not of his choice? But then, having marital problems is as old as the marriage institution itself, so what was the big deal? And if it was really the case, why did they have a baby between them? Was it really fair to the child? Perhaps their problem developed after the birth of their child. But then, why was he letting his sick wife live by herself and take care of his daughter?

Too many unanswered questions were crowding my mind, and I started getting annoyed with myself. Why in the hell was I thinking about them so much, or showing so much interest in their story? Especially when I didn't have an answer to any of these questions? One thought that made me mildly happy, however, was that there could be an outside chance of me helping them in some way. The chance was based on a common thread between us—the common thread of coming from the same culture and same pool of traditions of India. I truly believed, through my own experiences, that hailing from the same culture helped people feel comfortable with each other; when they ate the same kind of food, cherished the same beliefs, spoke the same language, and had the same processes of being raised and nurtured, this made them connect instantly with each other. And there was magnificence in this connection, for, people soon realized that they were not alone, and that there were no boundaries, and more importantly, no fears.

A simple thing like playing badminton together, although completely outside the realm of culture, but popular amongst Indian folks, had exhibited this point to me. It had made Ramesh and I connect with each other to the point where he developed enough trust to share his personal distress with me. Perhaps the same could work with Urmila, too. Just by being Indian females, with a common thread of culture, we could connect and develop some kinship with each other. With this thought, I felt confident that I might be able to help Urmila one day. Surprisingly, I started feeling a little connection with her already, when I hadn't even met her.

Not long after, when I was up to my neck in my studies one afternoon, I received a buzz at my door. A little startled, I hurriedly got up and pressed the button. It was Ramesh wanting to see me—urgently, it seemed. I went downstairs. He was standing in the hallway, looking quite upset. He removed his sunhat and started wiping sweat from his brow.

"Well?" I had a big question mark spread on my face.

"It's about Urmila," he said

"What about her? Is she okay?"

"Yes, yes. She is okay. I visited her this morning. When I told her about you, and that you were also from India, and fond of wearing a sari and all that, she got quite excited. When I mentioned to her that you wanted to meet her, she literally jumped with happiness and now she can't wait to meet you."

"Oh, that's wonderful!" I gave a big sigh of relief. There was nothing wrong with her, healthwise. I asked him when we could meet.

"Right now!" he said.

"What? Why the urgency?"

"No, there is no urgency, but seeing her happy face after such a long time thrilled me, so I thought I should come to your place right away and take you to my house right now. Do you have time right now?" he asked me politely.

"Well, I am in the middle of studies right now, so…" I wasn't sure what to say.

"Oh please, Neila." He didn't let me finish my excuse. "Please come right now. For my sake! Besides, you were also quite keen in meeting her someday, so why not right now?" he insisted earnestly.

"Okay. You wait here in the hallway. I will go upstairs to my room, wrap up my books and meet you here in few minutes." With a little hesitation, I agreed and went upstairs to my room—but then, instead of spending time in clearing up my study stuff, I pulled my suitcase from underneath the bed, took out a sari, and quickly wore it, with an idea that this attire could be a good tool to connect with Urmila and make her feel comfortable with me.

Ramesh was surprised to see me in a sari, but he got the idea behind my gesture and appreciated it. We drove to Urmila's place and he introduced us. Wearing a bright yellow silk sari, some fine gold jewelry, and a bright red dot on her forehead[3], she looked like she was expecting my visit. She had long, beautiful brown hair that reached almost to her knees. She had a gentle face and she looked very pretty, like a daffodil in full bloom. However, her face looked tense and she seemed a little nervous. Asha, the little girl, was dressed up in a pink

---

3 *Old Hindu tradition requires all married women wear dots, preferably red, on their foreheads.*

jogging suit with white frills on the sleeves. That was her favourite outfit for going to the park with her father, I was told. *So, Ramesh is going to leave us two women alone for a while,* I realized. After our initial introduction, Ramesh and Asha (who looked very eager to go to the park with her daddy) stepped out.

Urmila gestured me to sit down. I glanced around. Her gesture meant literally down on the carpeted floor. There were no sofa sets, chairs, or dining table. The apartment was clean and tidy, and was decorated in the old, traditional Indian style. The floors in living room and the dining room were carpeted from wall to wall with small Persian carpets laid on top of it, with a few decorative throw pillows stacked neatly in the corners of both rooms. You could sit on these pillows and lean against the walls comfortably. There were picture frames of Indian deities on all the walls, with plaques of Sanskrit scriptures written in calligraphy in the center of each wall. There was a provision made to burn incense sticks in each corner of the two rooms. I was sure they were burnt just before I entered, as I could smell a mild jasmine fragrance in the air. There was a huge *Mandir*[4] made out of sandalwood, set up in the center of the dining area, right underneath a small chandelier that came with the apartment as a decorative light fixture. Innumerable small statues of Indian deities made out of brass were laid out within the Mandir. She must have just finished worshipping the deities, for I could see, on either side of the Mandir, two small silver lamps with candles still burning in them. For a minute, I thought I had entered my grandmother's house back in India! Grandma never kept any chairs or tables in her house, had a huge Mandir with innumerable little statues of Hindu deities neatly laid out in it, and always had a few small oil lamps burning in front of it. Even the smell of incense burning in Urmila's house reminded me of my grandmother's house. The old fashioned, traditional decor of the apartment told me a lot about Urmila. I pretended to exhibit interest in all those deities she had in her Mandir and complimented her for keeping up with the old traditions, although everything I saw there

---

4 *Mandir is a temple. Many Hindu families keep small models of **Mandir** in their homes to place small statues of Hindu deities.*

was against my own natural grain. But that did the trick. The tension on her face had disappeared and she didn't seem nervous like before. She showed me her family pictures that were hung in the hallway to the bedroom, enthusiastically explaining about every member in the family photographs. Two large picture frames, one of herself in her wedding attire and another of Ramesh and his family, were hung on either side of her bedroom door. Urmila looked very pretty in her wedding outfit in the picture. Ramesh's parents were right in selecting this girl for Ramesh; she was very pretty.

"He told me that you wanted to meet me sometime," Urmila said very politely in *Marathi*[5].

"He, who?" I didn't quite understand whom she meant.

"He, Asha's father."

"Oh, yes, yes." Silly me! How could I forget the proper way of referring to a husband? My grandmother never took my grandfather's name either, a custom followed rigorously by most of the old fashioned Marathi women. 'Good girls don't take their husbands' names or address them by their first names' Grandma had told me once.

"Asha's father told me about you and that you wanted to meet me sometime," she said again.

"Yes, yes, I wanted to meet you, now that I know your husband so well." I didn't take Ramesh's name either.

"He told me that you two have been playing badminton at the university club for many weeks now, and that you are a very friendly person," she said with a smile.

"Thank you. Do you play?"

"No, I played when I was a little girl, just for fun, that's all. It is very difficult to play in a sari."

"Then wear a jogging suit. I don't wear a sari when I play."

"You wear pants like men do?" she asked me with surprise.

"Yes, I do." I didn't want to tell her that I seldom wore a sari since I arrived in Canada, and jeans and tee shirt or a jogging suit were my regular, every-day clothes.

"I can't do that, no way," she said emphatically.

---

5 **Marathi** *is one of the major regional languages of India, and spoken in the state of Maharashtra.*

"Asha is a very cute girl," I said, changing the topic from my clothes to her daughter.

"Thank you. She takes after his family. She looks just like his mother."

"Really?"

"Yes, if you see his family's picture carefully, you will see that Asha is completely like his family—same eyes, same forehead, same everything. Even her nature is just like her father's." She seemed to be proud of the fact that Asha resembled her husband's family. I wouldn't have been so generous to give all the credit to my husband's family if I had a pretty daughter.

"She is also quite attached to him," she continued. "Not a single day passes without her wanting to be with her father. But what can I do? It is all up to him." She sighed and then kept quiet. I was glad that she had touched the subject that I was thinking of bringing out.

"What is all 'up to him,' Urmila? Will you please tell me?" I asked her directly, because to me, she appeared to be a woman of old traditions with a simple mind.

"I don't mind telling you. Whom do I have to talk to in this country, anyway? Honestly, it is really all up to him for three of us— that is Asha, him, and I, to stay together like a nice family," she said as she sighed again.

"Really? Do you believe that it's *all* up to him?" I asked her again.

"Yes. It is *all* up to him and him alone."

"Ramesh is a very good man. He comes across as a very loving man."

"Yes, he is very loving, but he doesn't love *me*." She held her lower lip tightly with her upper lip as if to stifle herself from crying, and became abruptly quiet.

I didn't know what to say. Should I ask her why she thought so? Should I dare to enter the tricky and private area of a husband-wife relationship, or just shut up?

She slowly relaxed her lips, letting her mouth open a bit, sighed, and as though talking to herself, said, "Everything seemed so normal, so good when I was getting married to him, but then I didn't know what happened. Things just went downhill so fast. I still don't get it."

I sensed an opening and decided to ask her, after all. "What makes you feel that Ramesh does not love you, Urmila?"

"He does not love me, that's why he lets me live alone here. He does not love me, that's why he lives separately. He loves our daughter, but then why does he let her be without a father?" She sounded desperate.

"What are you saying?"

"He provides everything for us but doesn't want to live with us. He visits us almost every day, plays with Asha almost every day, but continues to live in his own apartment. He doesn't want to be with us, and that is because he does not love *me*." She said this again, making me speechless. "And you know what? Now he is asking me for a divorce. He is actually asking me for a *divorce*, can you believe that?" Then she looked at the ceiling as if trying to find an answer straight from God Himself. "He is asking divorce from a woman who reveres her great traditions, honors and respects her husband and never eats before praying for him every single day since the day of her marriage to him."

I knew of many women in India who prayed for their husbands' wellbeing every single day. They fasted for long hours, took penance, and followed many rigorous rituals with a strong belief that this would bring prosperity to their husbands. But these women were of my grandmother's, occasionally my mother's, generation. Most of the women of my generation and age had openly questioned the credibility and validity of these rituals and eventually had stopped following them.

"Not a single day has passed since our marriage that the two silver lamps you saw in the Mandir were not lit." She said this as though she could read my mind. "I have given him a beautiful daughter. I am sure I will give him a son too one day, but he, only he..."

"Only he, what?"

"Only he can do all this. He has to give up that hideous thing and get back to me as a normal husband." She sounded a little hyper with excitement.

"What hideous thing?" I was totally confused.

"That! That hideous thing he does with Daryl." She closed her eyes, raised her shoulders and shook her head, emitting a big *uuuuuu* sound with her mouth shaped in a pout. With Daryl's name taken, I right away knew what she was referring to.

"Are you telling me that Ramesh, your husband, is *gay*?" I was as direct as one could be. She nodded and broke out in a loud cry. I was dumbfounded.

Ramesh was gay! Ramesh was gay? Was he really? Is that what he was trying to tell me the other day in the cafeteria? Is that what he meant when he said he felt being abnormal during his adolescence? How stupid and ignorant of me that I could not guess what he was trying to tell me! Had I guessed it then, I would have reassured Ramesh that gay people were as normal as anybody else was. I personally didn't know any other gay people, but I could very well imagine that their sexual preferences were not special, or abnormal; they were just different!

I was flabbergasted to find this out from Urmila, though. I looked at her. She had collapsed on the floor with her head down and her long brown hair spread haphazardly on the carpet, hiding her face. She was crying loudly like a child. With her loud cry, she looked like a little girl crying for her favorite doll that had been snatched away from her with force. She had become completely oblivious to me. I didn't know what to say or what to do. I just kept on staring at her. There she was lying on the floor, an old fashioned young woman with love and deep faith in her orthodox traditions and customs, but now forced to live in a new and free world with its total freedom, including a sexual one—therefore, she was caught in a conflict between the conformities and boundaries of the old system and the beliefs and notions of the new system! What was worse was that she had no one from *her* own world to talk to or understand her or explain to her such unfathomable realities of the New World! And someone who could have done that was himself the source of her problem, her gay husband. *A gay husband*! Just then, a bizarre question arose in my heart, about any woman born and raised in this New World with its sexual freedom: *Wouldn't she feel betrayed if she found out that her husband was gay?* No answer came to me. I felt laborious and unbearably heavy.

I quietly walked into the kitchen. Even in that awkward moment, I noticed Urmila's kitchen was the typical Canadian kitchen that I was used to, with a stove, fridge, cabinets, counter tops and a tap with its sink. I grabbed a glass from the cabinet, filled it up with water, and came out in the living room.

"Come now, Urmila, please get up. Have some water."

She raised her head and looked at me, took the glass from my hands, and in one gulp drank almost half. Then she wiped her face with the drape of her sari, looked at me, and made the sounds of a person who was trying to wrestle an enormous sorrow to the ground. I was feeling painfully sad to look at her condition.

"Are you feeling a bit better now?" I asked. She nodded slowly.

"I am so sorry. I am really so sorry! You are my guest, you came to my house for the very first time, and here I am, making you feel awkward." She could barely talk, but she was coming back to her senses.

"Don't worry about it, Urmila. Consider me as your friend and not your guest, okay?" I was talking to her as though she was a child who was hurt and I was an elderly person trying to console her. She nodded quietly. It took a few more minutes before she could collect herself. She sat on one of the pillows and started talking.

"Do you know how I found out about him?" I shook my head. "I will tell you the whole story. When my marriage was fixed with him, everybody was happy. I was the happiest person on earth. I was going to get married to a bright man who, after my marriage, was going to take me to a beautiful land where women had white skin, blue eyes, and golden hair, and I was going to live among them. It was just like I used to read in storybooks when I was a child."

Oh, my good Lord, Urmila *still was* a child.

"My girlfriends were teasing me and warning me that I'd better take care of myself, remain slim and always try to look beautiful, and that I should also take the best care of him all the time, otherwise he might fall in love with one of those women with white skin, blue eyes, and golden hair. Even today, these thoughts give me such sweet goose pimples. I decided that I would pray to God every day and serve my husband diligently every single day as long as I lived." I saw Urmila's face light up. My thought was confirmed. Urmila was *still* a child living in her dream world.

"Soon after we got married, we boarded the plane to come to Canada. I had never sat in a plane until then. As the plane was flying, so were my thoughts, those beautiful thoughts: *I am going on my honeymoon now, a honeymoon in a beautiful land, far, far away from the in-laws and all the hassles of typical mundane married lives of girls in India.* My whole journey was so thrilling." Urmila had entered her dream. Her eyes seemed bigger and rounder to me and I could clearly see those dreams in them.

Just then, she suddenly shook her head vigorously and exclaimed loudly, with contempt, that startled me, "Ha! Some honeymoon!"

"Why, what happened?"

"All those wonderful dreams I had, and all those romantic thoughts I held in my heart that I'd cherished all along our journey were crushed—I mean *totally* crushed to pieces. Every one of them, totally crumpled, as if someone had violently trampled on them." She started sobbing. I handed her the glass of water again. She took a couple of sips, wiped her face with the drape of her sari, and handed me the glass. Then she got up, grabbed one pillow, walked to a corner of the room with it, and sat on it. She then lifted her hair, made a cluster of it on the top of her head and tied it into a big bun, all this while sobbing, and with every sob, her chest going up and down like a bellows.

"You want to tell me now why you said your dreams were crushed?" I asked her gently after her sobbing tapered down.

"Yes, I want to tell you what happened, I want to share with you all that, I really do. I am all alone, Neila *Tai*[6], really alone!" Her addressing me as *Tai* hit my soft spot. I walked up to her and started stroking her back gently. That seemed to work because she calmed down and seemed more in control of herself. She started speaking.

"Every night I would dress up in a beautiful silk sari, let my long hair loose, wear some perfume and go to the bedroom with my heart

---

6 In **Marathi**, an older sister is addressed to, as Tai.

filled with love for him. But he wouldn't even notice me. He was so very disinterested that he wouldn't even look at me. He was my prince charming, my everything, and I was his princess, his everything, right? But nothing like that would ever happen in our case. Not on the first night, or the second, or night after night for weeks together. Nothing. Can you believe it?"

She looked at me for sympathy. I wasn't married, and didn't know anything about married life, nor about the first night, second night, or whatever. I never ever had conversations with any of my married friends about their intimate times with their husbands either. However, being a young and healthy woman myself, and having read a few romantic novels or seeing some 'dirty' pictures with my friends behind the backs of my parents, I had a pretty good idea of what must happen on those nights. I could easily guess that something was not right in Urmila's case. I nodded to support her.

"He didn't touch me for a long time. And willingly? Never, not even once. After waiting for a few weeks, I tried to overcome my own hesitation and shyness, and dared to make some advances. Just imagine, I made advances, like an uncultured woman, but he remained unexcited, totally disinterested. I was completely frustrated by then. I was angry too. I started making a big fuss about it, but then he would just ask me irritably, 'Why do you insist on lovemaking? Go to sleep now.' 'Well, what do you expect, we are newly married, remember?' I would reply in anger and be even more frustrated. 'I don't like to indulge in this activity like you do.' he would say. Totally exasperated, I would start stomping my feet, pulling my own hair and throwing things around. At times, I would summon my courage and ask him directly, 'I am your wife, we are newly married, and why don't you show any romantic interest in me?' But then he would dismiss my question and just remain quiet or pick up a book and start reading."

Urmila took a long, deep breath and sighed slowly. "You know, I used to get letters[7] from India, from my girlfriends, family members,

---

7 In the early 1970's, 'writing letters' was the most common means of communication for people living in different cities or countries. Communication via telephones was expensive, and 'Internet', 'electronic mailing', 'skype', etc. were yet to be invented for the use of common folks.

and *Aai* and *Baba*[8]. Each letter would be filled with curiosity about me and my life here. I would reply to each letter joyfully. What a liar I was! Nobody, I meant nobody, not even my mother, could have guessed that I was in so much pain."

"You could have told your mother, at least."

"No. Oh no, no! I figured that these were *my* troubles, even though they were too big for my endurance. I was raised with love and care, and during my growing up, I saw my parents preserve and develop the good in me by their own dignity. I thought I should do the same and tell them nothing. I wanted to preserve their ignorance about my life by my own reserve." She said this very calmly. I couldn't help thinking how thoughtful and well-bred Urmila was.

"Days went by, even months, and my horrible life without any romantic love was going on. It was as dry as it could be. My pain was like a headache, something that no one can see or feel, and so never gets any sympathy, but I felt it every step of the way. In spite of my pain and agony, I kept on praying for my husband and his wellbeing and prosperity."

"That is very sweet of you, Urmila," I said.

"Well, sweet or whatever, that was my wifely duty, right? Many months later, after I made a big fuss and threw too many tantrums at him, he did *manage* to make love to me, finally. Love? Right, a pathetic effort on his part, and total pretense of satisfaction on mine! Whatever it was, it was better than nothing. I had acquired a new key now, and I used it every so often with him. However miserable it was, we did come together a few times over a period. And what do you know, Mother Nature did the trick!" A faint smile appeared on Urmila's face.

"What happened?"

"My tedious and dull life of long days and dry nights finally ended. My natural craving to love and be loved found its miracle of true satisfaction in me being pregnant."

"With beautiful Asha!" I exclaimed.

---

8 In **Marathi**, mother is addressed as **Aai** and father as **Baba**.

"That's right! In spite of all its obstacles, I was soon to give birth to another human being! Whatever little and lousy 'love life' I had, it had done its job!" Urmila's smile widened and her eyes shone.

"And how did Ramesh feel?"

"Oh, he was surprised at first, but happy, yes, very happy, I would say. I could see that in his eyes clearly. He told me that whether girl or boy, I get to name the baby. I got a beautiful girl, so I named her Asha! It means 'hope', right?"

"Yes, Asha means hope, indeed!"

"And you know very well, what I was hoping for, right?"

"Right."

"With a child between us, I knew things would get normal now. Everyone in India was very happy too with this news. When Asha became two years old, I wanted to visit India. I was craving to meet my parents with my baby, so I asked him if I could go for a visit to India. He was happy to let us go. Since all airlines gave discounted fares on their transatlantic flights if taken for four months, we wanted to use it, and so, Asha and I went to India for four months. During the visit, I never told anybody, not even my mother, about my miserable married life. And why would I? I looked good, and Asha was there, a proof enough to support my lie, right? I thoroughly enjoyed my stay with my family and friends. I tell you Neila Tai, ignorance must be the bedrock of bliss, and therefore, the linchpin for the survival of human species, as I was taught. I returned to Canada all happy, and with confidence that things would be all normal now."

By now, I could understand what she meant by "normal" in her conversation.

She continued. "When he came to the airport to pick me up, he looked quite happy and quite healthy too. I was happy to see him and so was little Asha, who jumped in his arms as soon as she saw him at the airport. We came home. I went inside the bedroom to change my travel clothes and lie down for a while. As I opened the closet door, I noticed something different there. His side of the closet was completely empty. I was shocked. I hastily called him in the room and asked him why his side of the closet was empty.

"Oh, that, that's because I have moved out," he told me calmly.

"What? Moved out? Did you say *moved out?*" I questioned him frantically.

He just nodded. His calm nod gave me a terrible jolt. I shouted out loudly, something I had never done before in my life. He walked towards me and told me to sit down on the bed. I refused. I had never disobeyed him like that in my entire married life. I was standing at a distance from him, staring, wondering what other shocking things were coming my way."

Urmila took in a long breath, closed her eyes, flared her nostrils and exhaled hard as though she was releasing pressure from inside her head.

"Neila *Tai,* when I didn't listen to him, he called me again, very gently, 'Sit down, Urmila please.' When he saw me still standing, he said, 'Okay, come and sit on the bed near me. I have to tell you something very important.' But I was not budging at all, as if in total defiance. Finally, he walked closer to me and said, 'Please listen carefully. There is something very important I need to tell you, Urmila. I should have told you a long time ago, but let's just say I didn't have the guts to tell you earlier. First hear my story and then decide if I was a coward. My story goes back to my adolescent days. It was during that time that I started to have this suspicion of something being different in me.' I started listening to his story reluctantly."

"Urmila, does this story have anything to do with his feeling abnormal during his adolescence?" I interrupted Urmila and boldly asked her.

"How do you know that?" She raised her eyebrows in surprise.

"Well, Ramesh told me once, very briefly. That was the day I requested him to introduce me to you."

"Oh, so you know how he felt and all that?"

"Yes."

She was a little bit surprised to hear me say "yes," but she collected herself quickly and said, "In that case, I don't have to tell you that part of his story. He then said that when he held me in his arms for the first time, he felt no thrill or anything at all in the touch. But he dismissed it, thinking it could be just stress or something. However, he felt no excitement or electricity towards me at any time, ever. Not only that, but my insistence on making love caused him great anxiety. That's when he realized that he wasn't interested in a female partner.

"'I am sorry Urmila,' he said. 'I am so sorry that an innocent young woman like you had to be a victim of my situation. That was *my* folly, *my* mistake. I was a complete coward for not exposing my true self earlier, I've cursed myself for hurting you, and actually for hurting me too, in the process. I very much wanted to make love, yes, but not to you, my dear wife, not to you or any other woman. My heart was full of passion for making love, but only to a *man*! Unfortunately I found out who I really was *after* I married you.' Then he put his hand on my shoulder, looked straight into my eyes, and said 'Urmila, I am gay! That's what they call people like me here in Canada, *gay*! There is nothing wrong in being gay. Nothing at all. When I was growing up in India, I thought I was abnormal, some kind of a pervert. There was a terribly wounded boy within me who thought constantly that something was drastically wrong, something malfunctioning, in my body. In this confused state of mind, I hated myself and cursed myself for too long, but now I know better. It has nothing to do with perversity or abnormality. I am not abnormal and I am not a pervert. I am *gay* and I have no problem with my being gay! I don't hate myself anymore, not today! Today I know I am healthy and normal, as normal as any male can be; my sexual preference is different from others, that's all.' Neila Tai, I was dumbfounded to hear what he was telling me."

Urmila stopped talking for a few seconds and flared her nostrils to breathe deeply. Her heart must have been palpitating, for she had both her hands held firmly on her chest. She looked at me with anticipation. Although I had an enormous faith in my own capacity of handling any situation, including awkward ones, I couldn't say anything at all. I just stared at her.

"After he finished telling me all this, which I didn't quite understand, I said, 'I don't understand this gay stuff or anything. Just tell me why you moved out!' I took his hand off my shoulder and moved away from him. I didn't even want him standing close to me. He asked me if I remembered Daryl from his bank. I did remember him, as he had been to our home a couple of times for Indian dinner.

"'Daryl is my partner,' he said.

"'Partner? Partner in what?' I asked him with a blank face.

"'You silly girl, partner of my life. Daryl and I are like husband and wife now,' he said. I was totally confused.

"'Like husband and wife? But, but, then you both are men, how can that be?' I got excited and almost shouted. He again came closer to me and said, 'Well, that's the way it is, Urmila. We both are men, but we live like husband and wife, and that's why we are called a 'gay' couple. Did I not just explain it to you? Men like us don't like to go to bed with women. So do you understand now?' He was patiently explaining me all this, but I was just too confused and too dumbfounded to understand what he was talking about. My gaze at him was completely frozen. He kept asking me if I was okay. He held my shoulders and started shaking then gently. I don't remember anything that happened for a few moments; I went totally blank, as if I'd fallen in a bottomless pit. Slowly I came out of the black hole and noticed that he was still holding my shoulders and shaking me. I looked at him. *Is that how a 'gay' person looks like?* I wondered. *But then, he was born and brought up in a traditional family like mine, so how could he be like that?*"

Urmila stopped and closed her eyes. I silently watched her for a few seconds. "Neila tai, that's how I came to know what 'gay' meant, that's when I came to know that my husband was gay." She said with a blank face. "That's also when I understood, after he explained so explicitly, why my husband didn't want to touch me after we got married. And that was why he had moved out, to be with Daryl, his life partner, a *man*! I was no longer his life partner even though he married *me*, a woman to whom he had solemnly declared, in front of our parents and the whole community, his total commitment and love for life. No, that didn't matter to him anymore." Urmila was shaking her head vigorously as if she was saying an emphatic *no* to someone.

"After what he told me, I remember my whole body shaking hard and my mouth being crooked, uttering a long 'uuuuuu' with total disgust to what he had just told me. The whole thing was so very ugly and repulsive to me. He looked upset with my response to what he told me, but he didn't get angry. He just took his hands off my shoulders and said, 'Well, that's the way I am and that's the way it is going to be from now on. And that's whom I live with now—Daryl, my partner.'

"I felt a tremendous tremor in my both legs and all my energy was completely drained out. I fumbled towards the bed and managed to sit on it. Feeling absolutely helpless, I started crying really hard. He walked over and sat beside me on the bed. He held my hands and tried to pull me close to his chest. There was so much kindness in his gesture, but I felt a terrible repulsion towards him. He had been holding a *man* to his chest with love and now he was holding me! I pushed him away hard. He almost fell off the bed." Urmila held her head with both hands as though to stop it from shaking.

"He didn't seem to mind me pushing him like that; instead, he asked me, 'Why don't you understand? Why are you being so childish?'

"'You call *me* childish! What about you? And what about our child? The real one? Asha, *your* daughter?' I started shouting and yelling at the top of my lungs at him with total anger and frustration. 'Asha will be fine, and so will you be,' he said. He calmly ignored my shouting and left me alone in the room, with a promise that he would take care of Asha and me, and that we would never face any financial problems.' Neila tai, I never thought I would be coming to face such a bizarre and tragic end of my married life the day when I returned from India." She started crying silently.

I sat close to her, quietly looking at her, and thinking about the events she had just narrated, asking myself why these two decent and civilized people were going through such agony by no fault of their own. Why were they victimized like this—Urmila by the orthodox and traditional upbringing, and Ramesh by the extreme pressures of his family? Or was the closed-mindedness about homosexuality in Indian society the real culprit?

I felt a tremendous compassion towards both of them; I truly believed that when two people loved each other, it really didn't matter what their genders were; what really mattered was love itself, love that brought to them that supreme and the most intimate of all experiences. I thanked heaven that this seemingly simple definition of love between two people was prevalent in Canadian society, a mark of a truly liberal society, in my judgment.

During my formative years in India, I was led to believe that there were two essential attributes of the Divine, the masculine one and the feminine one; and that they both were present in every human being. The one that overpowered the other took control of the human being. As such, I was taught, one could not claim to know God in entirety unless both these attributes were recognized and accepted. Simply put, it meant that accepting the presence of God was also recognizing and accepting homosexuality, that was present in every race and creed of mankind. Was it not the goal of every civilization to explore the origin of divinity and humanity? And if so, why were there many like Ramesh in the world getting smothered, and therefore many like Urmila who suffered?

Whatever peripheral knowledge I had about homosexuality was only after coming to Canada. It was freely discussed in the media as well as on the university campuses, with no taboos or reservations. Why not do a systematic scientific study of the sexual impulses of people of various cultures that would shed fresh light upon it? And what better place to conduct such study than Canada, with her people of all cultures and all races? A thought crossed my mind in that fleeting moment.

The doorbell rang. We both were startled for a second to hear it ring. Urmila hurriedly wiped her face, straightened out her sari, and tried to look normal. Then she got up and opened the door. Ramesh walked in with Asha fast asleep in his arms. Urmila went inside, brought out two blankets and spread one on the carpet. Ramesh gently laid Asha down, and Urmila spread the other blanket over her, making sure she was properly covered. They both looked at the sleeping child for a moment and then moved away from her. I could clearly see tender love and care in both their actions towards that child.

Ramesh looked at Urmila and then at me, and in just one glance, he could guess what had happened in his absence. "So you know the complete story of my life now, eh?" He made an attempt at smiling but his smile seemed more sad than joyful.

"Well, you had already told me your story in the cafeteria, remember?" I said.

"But I never told you that I was gay, did I?" He sounded accusatory.

"No," I said.

"Now that you know I am gay, how do you look at me?"

"Should I look at you differently?" I was pretending to be calm.

"I don't know. Why don't you tell me?" He sounded a bit sarcastic.

"Well, as far as I am concerned, you are still the same old Ramesh, my badminton buddy and the same caring person who drives me home when it's dark outside," I answered. He looked relieved.

"But Ramesh," I continued, what I think about you is not really the concern here. The real concern is about you and Urmila. She thinks you don't love her." I made a bold statement.

"What?" he almost shouted. I could see the child startle even in her deep slumber.

"And that's why you are asking her for a divorce." I was unduly bold to tell him that, in spite of his shouting. He looked over at Urmila intently.

"Oh my good God, is that why you are upset about the divorce, Urmila? You think I want a divorce because I don't love you?" He shook his head vigorously as if in complete disbelief.

"Yes, that's why you want a divorce from me," Urmila said firmly. "You hate me, and that's why you live separately."

"That is one hundred percent wrong. Totally, totally wrong! Listen Urmila, listen to me." He moved closer to her and put his hand on her shoulder. "I am not asking you for a divorce because I don't love you, or as you put it, I hate you. I love our baby very much, you know that very well. And I love you too, not as a husband perhaps, but certainly as a good friend. You know that too, right? Do I anytime complain about having to provide for both of you? Do I? Don't I always ask you if you need anything else, besides money? Don't I? Don't I try to be with you and Asha as much as I can?" His voice was soft, friendly, and she was nodding to all his questions.

"I want a divorce from you for *your* sake, Urmila. I want a divorce from you so that *you* can be free!" He emphasized *you* and waited for her response. She tried to say something, but kept quiet. While this was going on, I tried my best to keep a poker face.

"Urmila, I know you are confused. But hear me out first. Just think of how our love life has been since we got married."

"What love life?" she said defiantly, in a low but firm voice.

This was definitely a husband-wife conversation about their private affairs and I had no business being there. Without making the slightest noise, I started moving towards the door, but Ramesh saw me and gestured for me to stay put. I shook my head and continued walking, but he walked towards me and said, "Neila, please stay here." Turning towards Urmila, he said, "You are absolutely right. What love life? There was almost none, right? Did I ever fulfill any of your romantic notions you carried all those years? No. Did I ever give you total satisfaction in our lovemaking? I am sure, no!" He continued to speak softly.

I was feeling extremely uneasy to hear all this, so I made an attempt to leave the room again without disturbing them, but he again gestured me to stay back. I saw no choice but to stand there and reluctantly become an audience to their private talk.

"Urmila, you have spent enough time feeling sorry for yourself and feeling angry and frustrated. I know it because so did I, especially after we had our Asha. I thought we could have a family life like many other young families. But I was wrong. I had realized that I *was* gay, and was to remain so all my life, and I was quite happy and relaxed about it. Listen to me, this is Canada, and she gives her people an opportunity to have a free choice, even in their sexual preferences! I want to take that advantage in this new country; I refuse to be suppressed anymore, like I was in India all those years. I suggest you don't waste your time either. Don't waste your life in a sorry state. The liberal society here does not thwart anyone—be a part of it, Urmila! A divorce will set you free, free from me! You will be free to get married again, free to have a truly fulfilling married life with someone; free to have someone who would make passionate love to you, the way you always dreamt. You have been dreaming about the pleasures of this most intimate of all experiences all these years, I can imagine that. Now, don't settle for miserable experience like you had with me. I have already chosen to have that supreme pleasure with someone, and I want you to taste it too. I don't want to live in denial and ride on the wrong bus all my life, nor do I wish that you should. My dear Urmila, this free world has given us one more chance to restart in life, so let us honor it. Get a divorce from a gay husband and find someone who would make you truly happy. I promise you I will always remain your friend and a father to our daughter till I breathe my last. You believe me, don't you?" Ramesh's voice had gotten even softer than before. What a wonderful gentleman he was! What a splendid human being! My eyes were filled with tears.

Urmila looked like she was listening intently to all his suggestions, and then asked him, "But then, what will they think of us when they find out about our divorce?"

"They who?" he asked her.

"They, our folks in India, your family, my family, all those people," she said.

"Oh, so you mean our folks in India! They may not like it, but they have no choice. They will have to accept it," he assured her.

"And what will they think of *you* when they find out how you are," she questioned again, a little hesitantly.

"You mean gay?" he asked. She just nodded. She seemed to have an inhibition when saying the word *gay*.

"Well, the same thing I suppose. They may not like it, but they have no choice but to accept me the way I am. Quite frankly, I really don't care what they would think of me," he assured her again.

"You don't care, but I do. I care about what they think of you. They will talk ill of you behind your back, and that's what would bother me the most. They will ridicule you, they will laugh at you with contempt, and that's what would bother me, even more than the divorce itself. They will ridicule you endlessly when they'll find out that you are..."

"Gay?" he very obviously had no qualms about his homosexuality. She nodded. "You mean to say that you are objecting to the divorce because that would make me look ridiculous in front of our families. Is that it?" he sounded genuinely surprised.

"Yes."

"And how will *not* getting a divorce help this situation?"

"With a divorce, it will all be out in the *open,* because that would be the reason for our divorce. Whereas, with no divorce, no one will ever find out that you are..."

"Gay..."

"And then there will never be anyone ridiculing or despising you. You are my husband. I pray for you, so I really don't want anyone, not even my parents looking down upon you with disgust. That's why I don't want a divorce. I request you, please don't ask for a divorce, please don't."

"So you think people look down upon gay folks with disgust?"

"Yes, in India, they do, whether you accept it or not." She straightened her shoulders and started talking again. She sounded in full control of her emotions.

"Even I personally don't believe in this kind of relationship, the one between two men. The real husband-wife relationship is only between a man and a woman. Perhaps nature intended that way, or perhaps my traditional thinking taught me so, I don't know. I am only requesting you not to ask for a divorce and to come home and live with me. I am not even telling you to stop your relationship with Daryl or whomever you choose, I will never object to it, I promise you that. I will never demand anything of you, I promise you with all my heart, but please, do not ask for a divorce. Divorce will make our private life wide open to everyone, especially our families. Let us maintain our secret, and keep our private life private; that way, no one will ever be able to point a finger at *you.* You called my life miserable, you may be right, but don't forget that it is *my* misery and *my* pain. I am willing to bear it all my life, for the sake of your honor and mine, and for the sake of honor of our families back in India." She spoke earnestly. She was standing straight and looked confident. There was a layer of tremendous self-confidence spread over her face that gave her a compelling quality that defied analysis. Ramesh's face revealed nothing but a big surprise.

"We have our little girl, Asha, the wonderful fruit of our married life, the exalted achievement of our marriage. Let us live together and raise Asha together, but please don't break our marriage. Please, oh please, I beg of you ..." The layer of self-confidence wiped out completely. She broke down and started crying silently and softly, like a well-bred lady.

Ramesh just stood there, completely frozen, silent, in awe of his wife. He looked defenseless.

And I was standing there, myself all frozen, looking at them in uneasy silence.

Suddenly I remembered that Urmila was seeing a psychotherapist. Could a psychotherapist of *Canada* even comprehend her, let alone help her? A *Canadian* psychotherapist of this *New World* would perhaps diagnose her as having fear of the consequences—however, could he or she be able to undo her fears, especially when they were rooted firmly upon the traditions and beliefs of the Old World?

Age-old traditions and customs have a powerful hold on most of us. They display and glorify infinite patience and infinite devotion from us. However, their artificial demands also produce from us responses of unimaginable kinds and magnitude to various situations. This was one of those unimaginable responses that Urmila gave to her predicament.

No Canadian psychotherapist could have helped Urmila unless he or she became a part of her traditions and surroundings first; this was the conclusion I came to in those few frozen moments.

Epilogue

A few years back, I received a wedding invitation from Ramesh. When I couldn't make it to the wedding, I received a note from him a few days later, where he wrote a brief description of his wedding. A few of his friends and colleagues gathered together, Ramesh and Daryl swore vows to spend their lives together, signed the necessary paperwork, and then cut the cake! After getting officially married, the newly married couple moved into a beautiful condominium overlooking Lake Ontario. This was a wedding gift they bought for each other, he added.

I was elated to see that Canada has the distinction of recognizing and sanctioning the gay and lesbian marriages in modern times.

At the same time, I have since wondered about where would Urmila and Asha fit in this picture.

A Slippery Path

Baljeet Kaur must be in her mid to late thirties. She is a tall woman, only a couple of inches short of six feet. She has light skin, much lighter than most of the people from India. She has long brown hair, which she always ties in a bun right at the top of her head with hairpins, which makes her look even taller. Her deep brown eyes with long lashes compliment her round face. Baljeet Kaur is a strikingly beautiful woman by any definition.

In the many years that I have known her and seen her at work or at her house, I have never seen her in disarray. Her great taste and style seem to be everywhere, in the way she dresses, in the way she arranges the objects in her house, or in the way she plants her garden. One can see her taste even in the chemistry laboratory, a place that doesn't offer much latitude for any aesthetics. She works as a laboratory technician in the chemistry laboratory. What I like the best about her is that in spite of her beauty and sophisticated bearing, she is not at all stuck-up and there is always a feeling of inviting comfort about her!

Baljeet, or Billie as everyone addresses her, is a superb technician in the university's chemistry laboratory. She has been in charge of preparing mixtures that are called the "unknowns" by the students and the staff. These are the chemical compounds which the students working towards their bachelor's degree in science are supposed to analyze, discovering which elements they are composed of. Very meticulous and innovative in her approach in making these chemical compound samples, Billie has been every instructor's and every professor's favorite technician.

For a long time, I didn't know that she was originally from India. Nothing about her, including her physical attributes, spoke of Indian heritage. Her name, Billie, a Canadian name as she has labeled it, didn't disclose her identity as an Indian, either. Therefore, I was quite surprised when I came to know that she was originally from India. It was only after knowing her heritage that I started noticing her "Indian-ness," especially in the way she talked. Anytime I told her something that intrigued her or surprised her, she would say out loud, "Really?" A purely rhetorical question, with a long sound of the *lly* part of the word, in the same way that people from India always seemed to ask when they felt surprise or pure intrigue.

When I joined the Graduate school of the university, I received a Teaching Assistantship in the chemistry department as an aid to my scholarship. The scholarship money was so paltry that I needed this part-time job to support me as a full-time student. Fortunately, there was no competition for this job from the experts of the outside world. This job was given only to the graduate students of the faculty with a purpose to provide a small additional income. Nothing was challenging about this job at all. It entailed a task where a demonstrator was required to conduct a laboratory for about three hours, teaching and showing the students a few of the basics of the subject. I accepted this job and resumed my duties immediately as a chemistry laboratory demonstrator.

It was my first day at this new job. I was heading towards the chemistry laboratory with a laboratory manual and a pad of papers with brief lecture notes scribbled on them. That day's course work was required to cover a topic of the nonmetallic elements and their compounds. While I was walking, I was unknowingly reciting within myself the names of all the nonmetallic elements (hydrogen, nitrogen, oxygen, boron, carbon, and so on) that I was supposed to talk about on that day. I was also a little too ambitious for my own good because I had secretly decided to cover, along with the chemical and physical properties of the nonmetallic elements, their uses in society. That was my own idea, and not the requirement of the course. Why did I come up with this idea? I honestly couldn't tell. On the one hand, I was eager about my new idea, and on the other, I was almost sure that my first class was going to be a total disaster with this unnecessary material. I was thinking and rethinking this new idea, finally deciding to include it anyway and take my chances. I must admit I was feeling a little apprehensive at the prospect of facing twenty freshman students. All the butterflies of the world were slowly gathering in my stomach.

In that peculiar state of mind, I went into the laboratory. It was a huge laboratory with big, wide windows on both walls. The benches were navy-blue colored and clean, which I didn't expect at all from my previous experiences in other laboratories. All the equipment that I required for my demonstration was very neatly laid out on a table at one end of the laboratory. There was enough room around this table for students to gather for the demonstration and watch me conduct some experiments. I walked around the benches and saw that every bench had the same equipment neatly laid out and ready for conducting the same experiments. I was pleased to see all this preparation. My first impression of the laboratory was good, giving me some relief from my tension. There was still some time for the students to enter the laboratory. I put my lecture notes and the lab manual on the table and went into a room adjacent to the lab. It was a small room with twelve small tables holding twelve very clean and shiny chemical balances. A chair with a wooden pad attached to its right hand armrest was kept in front of each table.

"Is everything okay?" said someone, asking this polite question from behind me.

I turned around and saw a beautiful, tall woman wearing a clean white lab coat. She had a polite smile on her face to match her polite attitude. She was standing in the doorway of the chemical balance room with one hand in her lab pocket.

"Oh yes, yes, everything looks just perfect..." I replied hastily and started walking towards the lab, not knowing who the woman was, and if I was disturbing her.

"I am Billie. I work here as the chief technician. I just finished laying out everything that you will need for your lab demonstration," she said, politely introducing herself.

"Nice to meet you, Billie. I am Neila Singh. I am..." Knowing that this remarkably beautiful woman was a lab technician, I felt a little at ease. I tried to introduce myself too, but she interrupted me, again very politely.

"I know who you are. You are a graduate student in the department of Biochemistry, correct? And this is your first class to teach here, isn't it? I got all the information from the department head last week. That helped me keep everything absolutely ready for your class today." She provided me the information. I nodded in agreement and started walking towards the lab.

"Good luck and have a great class," she said.

"Thanks." I nodded, appreciating her gesture, and went into the lab.

The students had started coming in one by one, and within a few minutes, the class was full. They all gathered around the table where I was standing. I introduced myself first and then started talking.

"Chemistry is that branch of science which deals with the nature of matter and energy. As you all know, one of the most important aspects of chemistry is the experiment, during which you observe and collect information to study a certain phenomenon." I noticed that the students were listening intently. I was gaining confidence and the butterflies were leaving my stomach one by one as I was talking.

"In the next twelve classes, starting today, we are going to conduct experiments to study the chemical and physical properties of the nonmetallic elements and their compounds, and more importantly, in my judgment, discuss their uses in society. We will start with hydrogen today."

I finished my introduction and the brief lecture covering the topic of that day, including the idea I had thought about earlier. I looked at the students. They seemed pleased, which boosted my confidence even more than before. Then I conducted one experiment, demonstrating the entire procedure with some explanation. Following the experiment, I told them to disperse and approach their own respective places at the laboratory benches and start conducting the experiments as written in the manual. I was very pleased with my own performance and felt completely at ease.

As the students dispersed and started conducting their experiments, I decided to walk around observing and providing help as they needed. Just as I finished helping most of them, Billie approached me and said in her polite way, "Very good, very good indeed! I liked your way of introducing the subject, if I may say so."

"Thank you. Were you there?" I was pleased. Although I had not noticed her, Billie had apparently stood in the doorway of the chemical balance room looking at my demonstration and listening to my talk.

"Yes, I was watching you the whole time. Your way of explanation is very friendly. You make chemistry an interesting subject." She smiled and complimented me.

"Well, it *is* an interesting subject, don't you think? I have always enjoyed chemistry for its universality." I emphasized the *its* part of my statement.

"True, very true. But that way, *all* sciences are universal, isn't it?" She emphasized the *all* part of her statement. I nodded with total agreement and we both laughed at each other's profound statements. I suppose I was hooked by her charm, too.

She proved to be a great help for my demonstrator-ship throughout the semester, and even after the completion of my assistantship, we met frequently for one reason or another, and eventually became good friends.

"You may call me Baljeet if you wish," she told me once.

"All right, Billie—I mean Baljeet. Is that your real name?" I asked.

"Real or whatever. It is the name I got from my parents, and it is okay if you call me by that name."

"Alright. I'll call you Baljeet. By the way, what made you change your name to Billie?" I asked her, trying to sound as casual as possible.

"Oh, I just wanted to. It has nothing to do with 'Canadianization' or whatever." She dismissed my question. She obviously didn't want to get into any explanation or argument about her old name. She knew my views on the subject and also knew that I had not changed my Indian name to a Canadian name. Since that day, however, Billie became Baljeet to me.

"Let me tell you a little story to illustrate my point..." was how Baljeet always started her argument and made her point. I believed for a long time that we held almost diametrically opposed points of view on every subject, and that my values and viewpoints would always evolve more as a result of protest and rebuttal. Needless to say, we argued a lot on all issues.

Over a period of time, I found out that Baljeet had interests in a wide variety of fields, especially the literary, cultural and culinary fields, all of which she was quite involved in. She would go to the library or a book store specifically to attend reading sessions, especially when they were done by the writers themselves. She was an active member of a local culinary club where they would get together once a month for a cooking demonstration of some exotic dish from a different country. Apparently, she had done a demonstration of some Indian recipe there and had received accolades for it. Therefore, all this had resulted in Baljeet having many social circles, and she was capable of maintaining all her contacts, which to me was an art in itself.

She had asked me once if I could join her some day for a cooking demonstration, but I had politely declined it. For some reason, cooking was not my cup of tea. I never enjoyed cooking and I never bought a cookbook, even out of curiosity. I did promise her, though, that someday I would definitely go with her to a reading session by the writer in the library.

It was from Baljeet that I found out that there was a university students' cultural society which would put on a show for the students and the faculty once every month. She was actively involved with it, helping them in everything, including fund-raising. Someone told me once that she was also a good dancer, and although I hadn't seen her dance, I could very easily imagine Baljeet being a good dancer. She had all the attributes needed for dance, including striking looks. The cultural activities attracted me equally as did the literary ones, and when Baljeet and I talked about it, I promised her that I would attend the monthly show at the earliest opportunity. The opportunity came soon enough and I became one of her admirers.

The students' organization was going to put on a show for the Christmas Festival. However, instead of carol singing, choir, or some mythological story from the Bible, the students had decided to present a total of four plays from four major religions of the world, one of the four being that of Christianity, at four different times during the weekend. The title was quite catchy too—it was the "One World Festival." Each play was about two hours long, with many actors and all the props. It was an ambitious project and needed some serious funding for the production. As expected, Baljeet was deeply involved in it, right from fundraising to writing, acting, producing and participating. The festival was going to be presented in the university theatre, which had a beautiful auditorium with a capacity to seat over a thousand people. As the selections were finalized and preparations and practices of the plays started for the festival, Baljeet became increasingly unavailable, and other than my class time, I never met with her. During the class times, I tried to pry into the details about the plays, but she never gave me any details, except one hint that one of the four plays was based on Hindu mythological stories and that she was participating in it.

"Sita[9] was not treated fairly by her husband Rama[10], was she?" she asked me one day, just as I was finishing the lab demonstration and was getting ready to leave. The question came suddenly out of nowhere.

"Well, depends upon what you deem fair," I answered cautiously, not knowing what she was talking about or what she intended.

"Neila, don't answer politically. You know what I am talking about and you know what I mean. In the epic Ramayana[11]. Sita was taken for granted by all, more so by her own husband," she said looking straight at me.

---

9 Sita is the wife of Rama, and the main female character of the Indian epic named Ramayana.
10 Rama is the Crown Prince and main male character of the same epic. He is one of the most worshipped deities by most of the Hindus.
11 There are two epics of India, Ramayana and Mahabharata.

"That's not what everyone thinks. Sita had a specific role and she fulfilled it beautifully. Therefore, Sita has become an embodiment of, of..." I was about to recite what I had learned about it since my childhood.

"Oh, come now, really! Sita's whole life was one *righteous suffering* after another, right from her birth to the very end. Then how can she be an embodiment of...of *what* were you going to say?"

"Embodiment of feminine grace and tolerance," I said, completing my statement calmly.

"Oh, what a pretense! Righteous suffering can ruin you faster than shame. Do people really believe that all women should follow Sita's example in life?" she asked me again.

"Yes, absolutely. She has been idealized as a perfect wife and a perfect daughter-in-law, according to the Hindu mythology," I said very calmly again, all the while observing her face. "And by the way, why are you throwing this volley of questions about Sita from the Ramayana epic?" I asked her while secretly making an educated guess that the Hindu play in the festival must be on the story of Ramayana. My guess was correct. She told me that they were presenting a play about the life story of Sita, the heroine of the Ramayana.

"She never rebelled against anybody, ever, especially against her husband, Rama, isn't that correct?" Baljeet asked me again.

"No, she didn't. She never rebelled against anybody, especially her husband Rama, but more importantly, Rama never stopped loving her, either."

"You know, all this makes no sense at all, none whatsoever to me, really." She sounded as though she was talking to herself now.

"What do you mean by a*ll this?*" I asked.

"All this, the whole story of Ramayana! A beautiful gal named Sita marries a Prince, the prince goes to the forest immediately after their marriage because he has to keep some promise to his father, she gladly follows him to the forest because she loves him dearly; there she gets kidnapped by a crook, and when her husband finally rescues her after killing the crook, instead of embracing her happily, he asks her to enter a fire to prove her chastity." She continued further. "And all this for what? For proving *her* chastity when *she was the victim*! And ironically, she willingly enters the fire at his command, knowing full well that she was pure at heart all along." Baljeet took a deep breath and shook her head vigorously as if to dismiss any such unfair thought.

"Very good Baljeet, that's *Ramayana in a nutshell*." I complimented her for describing the whole epic in literally two sentences, at the same time wondering what was bothering her.

"You must have read the story of Rama and Sita many times, right?" she asked me.

"Yes, I was told this story when I was a little girl. I also read the story when I was growing up, and I had almost digested it by the time I came to be in my twenties," I told her.

"Do you believe that such unfair and one-sided stories about women should be told to little girls?" she asked.

"Well, this is not just a story; it is about a great king who was like God to his people. He was an ideal son, an ideal brother, and an ideal king who considered his subjects to be his own children, and served them for their welfare." I tried to defend the story of Rama, as I knew it since my childhood.

"But what about his duty as a husband to his wife? What good is his idealistic behavior to everyone in his family if he is negligent to his wife? Umm, correction, if he is downright *unjust* to his wife?" She emphasized the word unjust with a face that matched her tone perfectly. I had never thought about Sita from this angle. Nor had anyone ever explained to me this story from such an angle. I made an attempt to defend the story of Ramayana. However, all my attempts were futile as Baljeet didn't believe me at all.

"So, are you going to change the story when you do the play?" I conveniently changed the subject and brought her back to the play.

"No, no, oh no, no! Who are *we* to change an epic, right? We are going to keep it exactly the way it is, of course! But since I am acting in it, I have been reading the script every single day, and every time I read it, honestly, this thing bothers me a lot." She really sounded quite perturbed with the story of Rama and Sita.

"Whose character are you playing in this play?" I asked her.

"You come to the play and find out for yourself," she said, giving me a smile. That was Baljeet, all right.

The play was a hit and everyone loved it. All the actors performed beautifully. An undergraduate student, who played the role of Rama, was a tall, handsome young man with a very pleasant face. He acted with a complete understanding of the role. What I found interesting about the play was that it was a 'Ramayana, *international style!*' The cast included students from almost all the nations of the world. That was the beauty of doing Ramayana in Canada. Almost all races had joyously participated in presenting this Hindu epic on stage. Rama himself was presented by a white Caucasian young man, and his three brothers, by students from three different races of the world. I had never seen it cast this way in my entire life, and I simply loved it.

I had also never seen before a more elegant and beautiful Sita than the one in this play. Baljeet played the role of Sita and was unbelievably wonderful. She had achieved an exceptional spiritual depth while depicting Sita's character. With her own strength of acting and grace, she had taken away the religious connotations, bringing to that character a more philosophical flavor. Although this character of Ramayana was initially intended to be the epitome of traditional Hindu women, the way Baljeet presented the character hardly met the conventional expectations of Sita. Baljeet's Sita was totally different from any "Sita" I had seen on any Indian stage or screen. It was unbelievable. The play received a standing ovation from the audience.

After the play was over, I immediately went behind the curtains to extend my heartfelt congratulations to all the actors, especially to Baljeet for her superb acting. The Sita that Baljeet presented not only delighted me—she intrigued me. And later on, the more I thought about Baljeet in that role, the more I felt I needed to know about her as a person. *Perhaps, someday...* I thought.

The festival ended with a gala finale, which was equally superb. It was a great success. All the plays were tastefully selected, and the students performed with honest effort. Everyone involved in the festival had worked very hard and deserved much appreciation.

Christmas holidays marked the first major break after school had started in the fall. The graduates' residence was almost empty, and most of the graduate students had gone away. Since it was a holiday season—a season to be jolly rather than to be working—most of the people from the cleaning and maintenance crew had also gone for holidays, with only a skeletal staff remaining on duty. I didn't go anywhere because I couldn't afford it financially. I was one of the very few people in the entire residence, and perhaps the only one on my floor. Exhausted from all the work and stresses of exams, assignments and part-time teaching, I decided to take it easy during the break and recuperate. I also needed to catch up with letter writing to my friends in India during the break.

My telephone rang early one morning. "Good morning Neila, how are you?" I could clearly hear Baljeet on the other end of the line.

"Good morning, what a pleasant surprise. How are you doing?"

"I am fine. Listen, we are going to the International Food Fair that's held in the Northern Mall during Christmas time. We will have our dinner in the food court there, would you like to join us? It's my treat!" she asked. She was sounding especially happy. I gladly accepted her invitation for dinner that evening, all the while wondering who she meant by *we!*

After taking a couple of trains and a connecting bus, I reached the Northern Mall. It was a huge shopping centre, with over two hundred shops of all kinds. I reached the specific spot where we had decided to meet, and saw Baljeet waiting for me. I also saw a gentleman standing with her. *So, this was the person who made it* we I realized.

"Meet Phil, Phil Wilson. And this is my friend from the university, Neila." She introduced me to her friend as we walked to the eating place. I glanced around. The crowds were enormous, and almost all the tables were occupied. With the International Food fair, the place looked like a miniaturized United Nations with people and food items literally from all over the world. There was no need for any reservation or anything. You were required to pick up a plate, fill it with the food items from any country you wished, pay at the cashier and grab any available table to sit at and enjoy the food.

"Why don't we go and pick up our food first, shall we?" She started walking towards the food stalls and Phil and I followed her, assessing each food stall with a keen eye to pick up something exotic looking and smelling. A few minutes later, each one of us picked up something that looked interesting, and with the trays in hand we all headed to a table at a relatively less crowded spot.

"Didn't you take anything to drink?" Baljeet asked me when she saw that I had only a plate full of food on my tray.

"I am okay with just a glass of water," I said.

"Neila, this is my treat, so don't worry about the money. Let us get a bottle of non-alcoholic wine for all of us, how is that? " Having said this, she almost ran to the wine shop in the same mall and came back with a bottle of non-alcoholic wine for us in five minutes. Phil quickly procured three plastic glasses and poured wine for us.

"I didn't think they allowed wine in the food court," I said.

"They do, only non-alcoholic ones, and only during these ten days," Phil said.

"Cheers!" Baljeet said. She gave the toast and we all started sipping the wine.

"What is the occasion for this treat, Baljeet?" I looked at her and Phil, wondering who he was and why he was here with us. I had never even heard anything about him earlier from Baljeet.

"Phil just finished his thesis for his bachelor's degree, so I wanted to give him a treat. And what better way for a treat than having it with a dear friend as well, right?" She looked at me, then smiled and held Phil's right hand in her hand. He smiled too. His smile was as pleasant as Baljeet's, and they both looked at each other with the same feeling in their eyes as was special among really close friends. I sort of got an idea who he might be!

Phil was not bad looking, and was tall too, with a pleasant per-sonality. With a bachelor's degree, I suspected that he may become a good provider, too. My head was busy at work. Why was *my* head busy at work, like a typical Indian mother? And who the hell cared for *my* assessment anyway? I mentally slapped my head and joined their small talk.

"B.Sc., that is wonderful, Congratulations Phil! What are your plans now?" I asked him politely.

"Right now, none! I have taken a six-month ticket to travel to the Far East. After I come back, it will be summer in Canada, and then I will decide what to do next." His voice was more like a baritone. *Hum, good voice, too!* I thought. Here I was, analyzing him again. I slapped myself again mentally.

"Phil may join the graduate school for his master's degree or do a job somewhere for a few years as a lab technician like me, and then pursue further studies," Baljeet said.

"That is a good plan. To be able to do what you like and what you want, that's very lucky, wouldn't you say?"

Phil nodded.

"He has time on his side—that's lucky too, I would say," Baljeet said.

"I am sorry, I didn't get that," I said, confused.

"Phil is about ten years younger than I am, so he has a lot of time on his side to do all these wonderful plans," Baljeet said.

"Billie darling, you are not *old*, for Pete's sake!" Phil said. He looked at me and said, "Look at her. Do you think she is old? If anything, *I* look older than she does." He held her hand in his hands and started playing with her fingers.

"You *both* are young, and young looking, too." I gave a diplomatic answer and we all laughed. Actually, that's how I genuinely felt about Baljeet, and now him, too. Looking at her, no one would have believed that she was closer to forty.

Incidentally, who was Phil, and what was his relationship to her? And why were they comparing their ages? I really couldn't stop thinking about it, but I was too polite to openly ask Baljeet. I decided not to think about anything and to just enjoy the evening. The food was good and the company even better. The festive season had spread its joyous feeling on everyone and everything, making the whole atmosphere blessed and cheerful. We had a great time together. We parted happily wishing each other a great start of the New Year!

It was the very first day of school after reopening in the new year. The students were slowly coming back from their holidays, still reminiscing about what they did during vacation. However, my own research work had started at full speed, and my time in the research laboratory had increased phenomenally. I had not gone to the chemistry laboratory as no course work had started yet.

Before the courses and my teaching job were to start, I felt I should visit the chemistry laboratory once, just to see if any preparations were needed prior to teaching. I went to the chemistry laboratory. All the undergraduate laboratories were located a little far from my research laboratory on the university campus. It was a bit late in the evening when I reached the chemistry laboratory. It was dark inside, except for a small streak of light coming from the chemical balance room. I followed the light and went to the room. Baljeet was sitting at one of the tables in front of a chemical balance, weighing a few chemicals and making notes after weighing each one. I was really surprised to see her there, as it was way past her quitting time.

"Hi Baljeet," I said.

"Oh, hi..." she said. She looked a little startled.

"I am sorry. I didn't mean to startle you," I said.

"It's okay—it's just that I didn't expect anyone to come to the lab right now." She turned around and looked at me.

"Well, I just thought I should come over to see..."

"To see me?" She laughed and got up from the table. She had finished weighing all the chemicals.

"Frankly speaking, no. I didn't expect to see you here at this hour of the day, but..."

"Oh, I was just kidding. Don't worry about it. I know this is after my working hours, but I wanted to get a head start on my work in this semester." She put away all the chemicals and started washing her hands. "How's your work going on Neila?" she inquired.

"Good, I hope, only the results will tell if it is satisfactory or not. It is so very frustrating at times, I tell you." I was about to begin my same old song of the endlessness of the research world when she interrupted me and said in a calm voice, "Phil left for Malaysia this morning."

I heard that, but just kept quiet.

"He is gone for six months now, can you believe it? Six months! It almost seems like an eternity." She sighed and wiped her hands with a paper towel.

Should I ask her more about Phil? I wondered. The question kept popping in my mind but I still kept quiet.

"I have just brewed a fresh pot of coffee in my office. Do you have time to have a cup of coffee with me?" she asked me. A fresh cup of coffee was tempting, especially after a long, hard day for me. I instantly agreed to her offer.

Her asking me for coffee meant that she desired my company at the moment. Was she okay? Was she feeling lonely that evening? Could this be the right time for me to ask her about Phil? I just quietly walked with her to her office.

Her office was on the same floor as the laboratory. It was a very small room with just a table, a chair, a small brass coat rack in the corner to hold her winter woolies, and a small coffee percolator that was kept on a stool. The office was clean and tastefully decorated with plants, posters, and a couple of unusual artifacts. A table lamp, a paper clip holder, and a pen rack, all uniquely designed and antique-looking, were placed in one corner of the table. Even the telephone was unique looking. The whole décor of the room revealed the taste of its owner.

The room was filled with the aroma of freshly-brewed coffee. She approached the coffee percolator and poured coffee into two mugs.

"Sugar and cream?" she asked me. I nodded. She added some white powder and then some cream-colored powder to the coffee and while handing me my cup, mischievously said, "Mind you, this coffee is a non-coffee."

"What do you mean?"

"It is a decaffeinated coffee with saccharine in place of sugar and a non-dairy creamer in place of real milk. Everything is make-believe!" She laughed mildly.

"Well, water is real," I said, joining in her humor.

"Not really—I took some distilled water from the lab."

"So even the water is not real!" We both started laughing and sipping the "non-coffee." The make-believe coffee was still quite believable after all!

"The whole world is one big make-believe entity, isn't it?" she said with a serious face, sounding almost too philosophical for my mood.

"Wow, that's heavy! Too heavy for a tired mind at the end of the day," I told her frankly. We were sipping coffee quietly for a few moments.

"How did you find Phil?" she asked me.

"Pardon me..." I was taken off guard. This subject was totally different from her earlier philosophical statement.

"I said, how did you find Phil? Did you find him interesting? Did you feel that he was a good man?" she asked me again.

"Yes, oh yes, he sounded like a good guy. Quite interesting to talk to. Mind you, I met him only once." I was ready this time.

"But we spent an entire evening together, right? Did he make a good impression?"

"Yes, he did. He came across as a charming man. And very polite too." I was being cautious.

"I met him four years ago, right here in the lab. He was a freshman then and I was the same, a lab technician," she said. "A good man, Phil is. A very good man, indeed! Quite young, too. Here I was thirty something and he was barely in his twenties. Strange, isn't it?"

I stayed quiet, unable to guess what she was getting at or what response she was expecting from me.

"You must be wondering why am I talking about Phil this way, right?" She looked at me with a questioning face and, seeing my receptiveness, was encouraged to continue.

"I have been working in this lab for almost five years now. I am completely self-supporting. I never accepted anything from anybody, ever. No money, nothing. I am totally self-made, you know." She took a few more sips of coffee and started talking again. "You know that I came from India, right?" she asked me. I just nodded.

"Do you know that I was about to get married in India almost ten years ago?"

"Oh, really?" This was news to me.

"Yup. About to get married into a rich family. A very rich family in Chandigarh, that's in the state of Punjab in North India."

"Oh, I see."

"Had I been married in that family, I would never have the need to work for money, ever. I would have rolled in money. Money and riches everywhere." She looked at me with a funny expression.

"Then what happened? Isn't that the dream of every young woman in India? Or anywhere, for that matter?" I was genuinely interested in knowing about her by now.

"Uh-huh! That's the dream of every young woman, all right—mine too; it was a heartfelt desire…like every young woman, as she is nicely led to believe right from her childhood, isn't it? Well, so was I, actually! I was born and brought up in a large family. The family included my parents, my four brothers, two sisters and me. We had both our grandparents living with us too. I was quite close to my grandmother; I called her 'Dadi Ma.' She used to tell me a lot of stories from the Ramayana."

"Oh, so you *did* know the story of Sita very well then?" I asked her.

"Yes, very well indeed! I would say I knew it too well. Dadi Ma was one of those women who worshipped Rama and Sita and all the others from the Ramayana. She totally believed in them, and so did my whole family—except me, of course! I think I was born a rebel. All the customs and traditions that were followed by my family, and the entire society that we lived in, for that matter, were not at all acceptable to me. No way! I just couldn't tolerate them. They must be at least a thousand years old, no exaggeration, I tell you. My Dadi Ma always told me, 'A woman is always dependent on a man: before marriage she is dependent on her father, after marriage she is dependent on her husband, and in the event of her husband's death, she is dependent on her son!' Oh God, what a colossal way of wasting women's talents! And what a brutal way to regard her! I used to get so angry at this insane idea that I would start arguing with Dadi Ma. At times I would argue so fiercely that my parents would meddle in our argument and come to the rescue of Dadi Ma, but this was how literally *all* the women that I knew of thought, even my mother and sisters."

Baljeet was sounding excited and had started breathing faster, so she waited for a few moments for her breathing to come back to normal. She seemed quite riled up and looked genuinely disturbed by the old belief she had described.

"Can you believe that all our upbringing was centered on this belief? And God only knows how many million other families raised their daughters with this belief." Baljeet shuddered for a moment and continued. "There was hardly any room for expressing a doubt or question in all this. As a matter of fact, it was considered downright rude and arrogant to doubt or question this belief."

"And you did it."

"And I did it—you're damn right I did it. And not just this belief: I questioned everything. I used to have so many arguments with my parents and grandparents on these issues, like you wouldn't believe. They called these arguments *fights*. The fact was that utmost obedience was required of us girls, in all respects. Simple arguments or questions were labeled as *fights* by the elders in the family." Baljeet took a long breath and took a few more sips of her coffee. "And then it started happening..."

"What started happening?"

"The *marriage game*." She said the word *marriage* as though it was a curse straight from hell. "You know, most or all of the marriages in my family and in my community were essentially arranged ones. The young women had no say in it whatsoever. I was born a beautiful girl, right? Well, in my case, my beauty became a curse."

"A curse? How so?" I was surprised to hear her say this. It was my long-held belief and innocent conviction that anyone gifted with physical beauty was a blessed soul.

"It raised too many expectations from me, not *from me as a person*, but because of my physical beauty. I was supposed to be what all beautiful girls were expected to be: the wife of a rich city man...the trophy and proud possession of the rich and the famous! Dadi Ma used to tell me over and over again, 'Puttre, you are a beautiful girl; you should be able to hook a rich boy from a rich family.' Great, so a beautiful young woman like me was more like a *bait* to catch a big fish from the pond! When my parents and Dadi Ma spread the word about my coming of marriageable age to the matchmakers, an endless supply of names of 'suitable' boys from the rich class started flowing into my family. I knew that it was just for my physical beauty. And get this, Neila: these matchmakers would tell my folks that all these guys were ready to marry me *in spite of* my humble background. Do you know what this means? It meant that these men were kind enough to accept that my parents were ordinary, with no social status. Can you believe that?" She emphasized the words *kind enough to accept* in a very sarcastic tone.

"Oh my God! What an insult! But how do you know that?"

"Oh, I know. I heard it straight from the horse's mouth. I actually *met* a couple of such idiots who had no reservations to say it to my face that they didn't *mind* my father's mediocre background if I married them. Can you believe their audacity?" She looked intently at me and shook her head.

"Unbelievable...really..." I was genuinely surprised to see some people insult a girl in such a manner.

"And get this: when I told this to my father and mother, do you know what they did? They just laughed it away and told me that they didn't mind it if I got one of those rich guys. According to them, the girls were not worthy of being equal to men. So if a rich man accepted a girl from a humble family like mine, she must consider that to be a great boon to herself and her entire family. This was an even bigger insult. A response like this from my parents was unbelievable. Honestly, that's when I realized I didn't know my own parents." Baljeet suddenly became silent. She finished drinking her coffee, placed her empty mug near the percolator, and started pulling out paper clips from the holder, one by one. After pulling out all the clips, she started putting them back in the holder one by one. The silence was like a pregnant pause.

"To tell you honestly, I didn't think even those boys had any say in this matter. It was purely a matter of chance, and to a large extent, a matter of economics. The matter of economics was controlled primarily by the older men of the family, with the older women dealing directly with the matchmakers, collecting all the necessary data about the girl, and then proceeding with the propositions to the older men in the family. In my case, the matchmakers always dealt with only my mother and Dadi Ma. They would bring in all the information about some rich dude to them, and my mother and Dadi Ma would present that to my father and grandfather. Then there would be elaborate discussions about the financial status of his family, but never ever about the boy himself. And that's exactly what happened with one guy to whom I was about to be married. One matchmaker brought this proposal to my family. My parents and grandparents thought this was absolutely perfect for me. This boy was not at all good looking, nor was he educated, but he was filthy rich. That was his only qualification, but that made him the best match for me in their judgment. When they told me about him, I was literally flabbergasted. I was about to protest, but they all sounded so very happy and excited that I thought I had no choice. So very reluctantly, I accepted this proposal. Everybody in the family was happy with this match, so who was *I* to argue against them, right? After all, I was expected to want what *they* all wanted, right?" Baljeet became silent. I just took a couple of long breaths and watched her silently for a few moments.

She had filled up the clip holder by now, and then, one by one, she was pulling the clips out again. She pulled out one clip, held it in her hand, looked up at me and said, "The moment I agreed to this proposal, they immediately sent an invitation to the boy's family to come for a discussion. A *discussion?* What for? What did it entail? That family came, and the discussion took place in my home for what seemed like eternity to me, a whole day. During all these discussions, everyone in my family was busy catering to the needs of that boy's family. My sisters were continuously carrying trays of food and snacks and beverages and some more goodies to the room. I came to know later on from my Dadi Ma that the discussions were actually negotiations about 'give and take' between the two families. 'Give and take? Why, Dadi Ma?' I asked her, but she just said, 'That's what the tradition dictates, Puttre.' I kept quiet. But later, I found out from someone in my family that the negotiations were completely one-sided. It was a much more 'give' from my parents to the boy's family, with almost nothing given by his parents. I got so angry, I marched straight into my Dadi Ma's room and started showering my questions on Dadi Ma.

'Dadi Ma, isn't *he* a rich dude? Isn't *his* family a rich family? Then why are *his* parents looting *my* parents?' I asked—but Dadi Ma ignored me completely, with just a flick of her hand, like this."

Baljeet waved her hand in the air and threw away the clip. Perhaps that is how her questions were dismissed by her Dadi Ma, with just a flick! Just then, I saw her make a fist and punch it hard on the table.

"I should have put my foot down right then and there. I should have objected to the shenanigans of that jerk and his family. I should have told my father that I didn't want to marry that bonehead or be a part of his family. But I was too damn obedient for my own good, damn me..." Baljeet was breathing very heavily by now.

"Cool down, Baljeet, cool down. Take a few long breaths and cool down a bit. You don't have to tell me everything right now. It is history, anyway." I meant every word but she insisted on completing her story.

"The preparations had already started for the big day, my wedding day, I called it my 'doomsday' or a day of defeat for all of us. Everyone was complimenting my parents for getting such a rich family as a *sambandhi*[12]. Everyone in my community was happy for me that I was going to be a daughter-in-law of such a rich family. In reality, no one knew that the rich family was squeezing my poor family to get even richer. And the irony of the whole thing was..."

"What was the irony?"

"The irony was that all this seemed to bother *only me*. Not Dadi Ma, not my parents, no one; everybody looked quite happy about the looting that was going on continuously by the groom's family. Now, isn't that strange? My father spent a few *lakhs*[13] of rupees that he did not have to buy all the things they had demanded of him. That family had prepared a list of things that they wanted from my father. Can you believe that? Man oh man! The more I think about all this, the more I ask myself, *Why the hell did I keep quiet that long or even stick around?*"

"*Stick around?* What do you mean?"

---

12 *The in-law-family member of a son or daughter is called a* **sambandhi**.
13 *One lakh is equal to 100,000.*

"Oh, just listen, the story gets even more exciting later on!" she said in a funny-sounding, mocking voice. "All the purchases were complete, just the way they wanted, exactly according to their demands. And then, do you know what happened? On the eve of the wedding day, one more list of demands was slapped on my father's face. A long *list*! A list of demands, with a condition that all the items in that new list be purchased and given to them right away or there would not be any wedding taking place the next day. Can you believe it? Those rotten, despicable people insulting my family like that? I overheard my father talking about the new list to my mother and Dadi Ma, behind the closed doors. He was almost on the verge of tears. A *father* on the verge of crying, can any daughter take it? Just imagine! My father had already taken a huge loan to do all the previous purchases, and now there was this new list of demands. He was totally helpless. I couldn't stay quiet after overhearing all this nonsense. I went to my father and told him that I wished to talk to my future husband. I don't know why I felt confident, but I even assured my father that once I spoke to my future husband, things could be alright. I guess I was too confident of my own beauty, or I believed in the basic decency of all humans. Ha! Boy was I wrong, or was I wrong?" There was another fist pounded at the table along with her *Ha!* That startled me.

"When I met him alone, he was ecstatic and tried to flirt with me, but when I tried to talk to him about the new list, he defended his family and came up with a million reasons and pretenses for not withdrawing their demand—the worst being his family's honor. That bastard had no balls, I tell you, Neila! That chicken shit of a man! So do you know what I did?" she continued. She was even more furious.

"I marched back to my house, and declared openly to all that the wedding was off! My parents were absolutely flabbergasted. 'I don't want to marry this eunuch,' I said, and then told my parents everything that had transpired between us. I even requested my father to return all the stuff to the vendors and return the loan money. They first tried to convince me—*convince me,* can you believe it? But I didn't budge even a bit from my decision. Eventually they gave up, I guess partly because they realized that it was impossible to carry out the wedding plan as demanded by the groom's side. The wedding was called off!"

"Oh my, the wedding was called off. Hmm..." I just repeated what she'd said.

"Exactly! My wedding was called off. Just imagine, a wedding being called off in a small community in India! And on the very eve of the wedding day! Because of the *bride!* Not to mention a bride from a very ordinary family that was a staunch follower of all the old customs and traditions! Just imagine."

What she said was absolutely true; I had never heard of any such incident before in India, a country of strict, orthodox customs and traditions.

"Neila, I have no words to express what happened after the wedding was off. My family was totally devastated. My parents had no credibility left in their society—and I had no credibility left in *my own family*. People started pointing fingers at me for my undue audacity. Even a few of my extended family members were laughing and ridiculing me for my stupidity. I was almost like an outcast." Baljeet waited for a few moments taking long breaths and then continued.

"Slowly, as some time went by, everyone started accepting my actions, except my mother. She was worried about my younger sisters being affected by all this. She was concerned that they wouldn't have any suitable matches because of their older sister's despicable behavior. You know what I mean? I personally had lost all my interest in this stupidity of arranged marriage, anyway. All those atrocities of dowry and demands and all that junk, almost suffocating the bride's family." In that vein, she started ridiculing the entire system of arranged marriages in India.

"Wait a minute Baljeet, just wait for a minute." I had to interject and object to what she was saying. "Listen Baljeet, *all* arranged marriages are not bad, and *all* families don't loot the bride's families, okay?" In her rage, she was generalizing every arranged marriage, although this tradition of arranged marriages had been successful for thousands of years in India, and perhaps elsewhere in the world. Therefore, I felt a strong need to defend it. This tradition not only brought two people together for a lifetime through matrimony, but also two families, and sometimes two villages. In the times of limited communication, this tradition of arranging marriages between people from different villages nurtured the progress of those villages. Naturally, there had to be some merit in it, and it couldn't have been all that bad. But Baljeet completely ignored my comment and went on.

"Oh, it is all rubbish, I tell you, Neila. There are thousands of Indian families who have to face gruesome situations in their daughters' marriages. There are millions of young women who start their married lives with a bitter taste. Does the bitterness ever disappear? No, and possibly, *never*. Does the bitterness affect their married lives? Yes, and quite possibly, it causes harm to their relationships for the rest of their lives. Then how can I think of this tradition being any good? And tell me one more thing, Neila: how many young women are gutsy enough to stand for their rights to happiness and honor? How many exhibit courage and refute such a horrible ordeal?"

She was right, actually. I personally didn't know anyone who had exhibited such courage. I did hear of a few such stories, when I was in India, where the honor of the bride's family was totally crushed by the groom's family during the wedding ceremony. However, the bride and her family members still went ahead with the wedding. They all left the fate of the bride in God's hands. These were very sad stories, no doubt, but unfortunately no one seemed to object to such customs, and everyone, including the brides themselves, accepted them and attributed it to their *poor karma!*

"As I told you earlier, I had no credibility left, and could not face anyone in the community or even my extended family," Baljeet continued, "and I became a prisoner in my own home, never venturing to step out of the house. But when I realized that I had lost the respect of even my own sisters and close friends, I decided to confront this horrific situation boldly. I tried to convince my parents that I should move out of town to another place as soon as possible. That would help them to save face in their society and in our own family. They didn't agree initially, but they finally gave in. Dadi Ma and my mother seemed more favorable towards my moving out of town than my father was. Well, I wasn't surprised, as I knew *their* reasons. And when I moved out, I did better than I'd expected. I moved not just out of our town, but out of the *country* as well. I was totally out of their hair, once for all!" Baljeet started looking a little bit happier.

"What do you mean, out of the country?"

"You see, I knew that my mother's youngest sister, who was living in New Delhi at that time, had a relative here in Canada. I left for New Delhi immediately, stayed with my aunt for a few days, got all the information about Canada from that relative of hers, and applied to the Canadian embassy in New Delhi for immigration. When the embassy granted me a provisional visa for nine months (to be converted to an immigration visa at a later date), I jumped at the opportunity. Without wasting any more time, I left for Canada right away."

"And what about your parents, and your Dadi Ma?"

"I informed them just as I was ready to take the flight."

"Oh my God, really?" I said, in awe of her courage and strength. Did any female in my family—or even among my friends—have the courage to call off her own wedding for the sake of self-respect and honor, and then fly off to a totally new and unknown country all alone? I didn't know anyone. Would *I* be able to do it? I honestly doubted it, as I didn't think I possessed the courage to be so aggressive and independent. That was a heroic deed as far as I was concerned. It displayed unique levels of strength. No words could convey my admiration for Baljeet or her heroic act.

My mouth was open with awe, my eyes were fixed on her in total admiration, and I was sitting still with an empty cup in my hand. She took the empty mug from my hands and said, "Let's go to the lab again. I don't have a tap or a sink in my room to wash these mugs. " She picked up both our mugs and started walking towards the chemistry laboratory. I followed her without uttering a single word. I was still in a daze. We went inside the laboratory. She approached the sink, opened the faucet and started washing the cups. Watching those mugs in her hands, suddenly it occurred to me that I had not thanked her for the cup of coffee. When I did, she said, "Actually I must thank you for listening patiently to all that garbage of my past." She smiled at me and started wiping the mugs.

"Garbage? You call that *garbage*? Here I am, totally in awe of your bravery, which I don't recall seeing in anyone that I know, and you call it garbage?"

"Well, thank you, Neila, it means a lot to me when you say that. When I met you, I knew I would one day share a story of my past with you, I don't know why." She pulled the top drawer of her table and kept the clean, dry mugs in the drawer.

"How did you support yourself though, after you landed here in Canada?" I asked her.

"Oh well, I managed somehow."

"No, really." I was a bit confused.

"Well, to tell you honestly, when I landed in Canada, I took some financial help from the Canadian government. I did some research while in New Delhi itself and when I visited the Canadian Embassy; I got all the answers to my satisfaction. That was an added attraction to me. You see, I not only could leave my country and settle in Canada: I could *study* further too, something that I always wanted but never got an opportunity to do because of my family's orthodox thinking. I had a chance to learn English since it was one of the two official languages, something that I always wished for. The people in the embassy also informed me that I could take some technical training as well with their help, if I wished. This was huge! Nothing could hold me back anymore. And when I finally arrived here, I went straight to the Canadian Immigration and Manpower. With their help, I first chose to learn English, and then studied for two more years in a technical school. I finished a diploma in chemistry laboratory technology and got this job. I have been at this job ever since. Neila, a strange sense of freedom came over me just by being here, wandering around this strange place, being economically independent and most importantly, knowing full well that I was free from having to answer to anyone from that old world."

"Wow! That's remarkable!" I was very much impressed with her daring move. I started shaking my head in total wonderment, asking, "How many young women of India can claim to be so daring and to have such self-respect? Wow! That's simply wonderful!" I meant every word of my compliment to her.

"Thank you, Neila, thank you." She looked genuinely happy to receive my compliments.

"And what about Phil? Who is he to you?" I had gained enough confidence by now to ask her openly and freely about Phil.

"Like I told you earlier, he was a freshman and I was a lab technician here. I met him at the same time and in the same way as I met twenty other freshmen in his class. But he was different. He was so charming, so understanding and so mature for his age, and I liked him a lot. Believe it or not, *I asked him* out one day." She looked at me with a naughty smile.

"Oh, I can believe *that* one hundred percent," I answered.

"After hearing my story, nothing would surprise you now, eh?" she said as she laughed. I just shook my head and joined her in laughing.

"Actually, I was averse to meeting any man for quite some time. But after I settled down in this job, the thought of scoping some guys started surfacing in my mind, you know what I mean?" Baljeet winked with her left eye naughtily and continued. "Especially when I saw these university-going women all around me dating regularly. Mind you, I was damn scared, and damn cautious, too. But with Phil, it was different. His maturity attracted me, I guess. Before I knew it, I was already falling in love with him."

"Oh?"

"Yes. Well, it is like this: say you stick one toe in the water. You feel comfortable, so you begin slowly sticking your entire foot in it. Soon you feel even more comfortable, and before you know it, you are already up to your neck in that pool of water. Later, you can never really pinpoint the moment *when* it happened, you just remember the first time you stuck your toe in it. Something like that happened here, too. The first date proved to be very comforting and assuring to me, so I started dating him regularly, and before I knew it, I had immersed myself in this relationship. I have a very good feeling about this relationship with him; I have never doubted it and have never got the feeling of wanting to get out of it, either. It has been a warm and tranquil feeling all along, well, so far anyway. To be in this loving relationship with Phil has been absolutely wonderful."

At this point, Baljeet had closed her eyes, as though she had immersed herself in that warmth already. I just kept quiet in order not to disturb her tranquil moments. After a few moments, she opened her eyes and said, "It has also been a revealing experience to me, which was even more important."

"A revealing experience?" I asked.

"Yes, a revealing experience because this experience has shown me my own *weaknesses and immaturity*."

"Weaknesses and immaturity?" I was a bit surprised to hear this.

"Yes, after I got burnt, I totally despised all men—until I met Phil and began a relationship with him. Even now, that feeling occasionally surfaces and makes me hate everything that concerns men, can you believe that?"

"I can believe that, yes."

"When I think of men, I invariably think of the injustice done to women by them. That's really very immature on my part to look at all of them with the same glasses. That has become my very big weakness, Neila."

"That's natural for you, Baljeet. But then, is that why you always question the injustice done to Sita by Rama, in the Ramayana?"

"Probably, yes! That's why, sometimes I can't see any virtue in Rama at all. I realized that I was bruising your love and respect for Rama, who is like God for you, but now you know my reasons why I kept questioning Rama's attitude and behavior, especially towards Sita."

"I don't know what to say, really."

"Neila, I sometimes strongly feel that the relationship between a husband and a wife is very complicated, be it between Rama and Sita or just plain earthlings like us. I feel that I need to stay away from married life altogether. I don't want any complications in my life, and no one can convince me otherwise."

"Oh, I see."

"Of course, over the years, I may be willing to look at this type of relationship without being judgmental, and with more of a mature perspective, but right now there's not a chance."

"And what may happen over the years?"

"Well, my experience in this relationship with Phil has been a very positive one and that has influenced me considerably, and perhaps in the right direction, I might add."

"That's good!"

"Right now, we are living together."

"Any plans of marrying him in future?" I didn't know why I made it my business to ask her this question.

"Perhaps yes, perhaps no! No such plans right now, anyway, I am too damn scared to walk on that slippery path of marriage, I tell you."

"Hmm…" I said, intently listening to her. Was she calling the path of married life as a whole a slippery one, questioning the whole institution of marriage itself? Or was she merely condemning a path that was bogged down by old customs and traditions—a path that would make such marriage a slippery path leading to total devastation?

"Phil and I feel very compatible with each other. Really, very compatible. More importantly, we have no expectations or demands from each other. *I* remain the same when I am with Phil, and I can say the same for him, too. And that's what is of utmost importance to me." She then looked at me intently and asked, "We may be polar opposites when you think of us as a couple, but…"

"What do you mean?"

"You see, he is a white Canadian, born and brought up in Canada, with a totally different set of values. In contrast, I am an Indian immigrant, born and brought up in India with a set of values that are totally *alien* to him. There is a wide age difference between us, too. He is at least ten years younger than I am. Yet there lies this tremendous chemistry between us which breeds a wonderful familiarity. This chemistry has in turn evolved into total congeniality and mutual respect. I feel confident that this is how it will remain in the future, too. The congeniality and mutual respect between us will guide this charming chemistry between us all the time!"

"That's wonderful, Baljeet, I am so happy for you."

She just looked at me and gave me her usual smile that extended from ear to ear. I looked at her and said, "Look at you. You are looking and sounding so very happy. And that's how you looked in his company that evening, when I met him for the first time."

"I did?"

I nodded again to confirm.

"I am happy, I really am! Perhaps he is my soul mate, I don't know. I don't even know what a soul mate is! All I know is that we are very happy with each other, as though we are in a state of *total bliss*. Isn't that the whole idea of two people being together in life as life partners, to be in a state of total bliss?"

"Oh absolutely. That's for sure. No question there."

"Then, where is that feeling of bliss in a typical Indian arranged marriage?" she asked again. In response, I just shrugged my shoulders.

"And why do people tangle up themselves with all these archaic traditions and customs which do nothing but destroy this bliss completely?" she sounded a little excited.

"Well, I am sure these traditions and customs are there for a reason, and I don't think *they* make the path of married life a slippery one, as you labeled it earlier. On the contrary, I think, they help it become less slippery to walk on, make it a little more *walk-able, so that the* path can lead them to the bliss that you just mentioned." I made an attempt to support the age-old traditions of arranged marriages in India.

"That's bull!" she said. She totally dismissed my contention.

"Oh, come now, not *all* arranged marriages in India are devoid of bliss," I strongly objected to her remark, protesting against her dismissal, although in reality I was well aware of many holes in my argument.

"Okay, I won't say that *all* arranged marriages in India are devoid of bliss. But surely you agree that *all* arranged marriages in India are complex, and seem very intricately woven, right?" She looked at me, expecting me to agree with her, which I did.

"All I am saying is that it is completely unnecessary," she continued. What she said was unfortunately true. "With all these intricacies and complexities, honestly, it is almost impossible for anyone to see any virtue in them. And in addition to that tangled mess, there lies a thick layer of expectations and demands at the very foundation of it; there are sky-high levels of expectations and demands of each and every person involved. Do you agree?"

"Yes, I do. It is really too bad, but yes, I do agree!" I said.

"You know very well how it goes: the groom and his family are out to get a pound of flesh from the bride and her family, leaving that family pretty much bankrupt; after the wedding is over their demands continue through the new bride, holding her welfare at stake; even the newly-married couple have their own demands and expectations from each other and from others. God, there is just no end to it. Expect, expect, and expect some more! What is all this?" She moved her gaze from me to the ceiling, as though it was written on it. "In contrast, there are no expectations whatsoever between Phil and me. We are not married today, but tomorrow, should we decide to get married, the same principles would apply then, too, with no expectations or demands."

"Yes, I know there is usually a long list of demands in traditional Indian marriages that goes on and on endlessly," I concurred with her completely.

"And in spite of fulfilling these series of demands and expectations, is there ever any happiness or satisfaction in these relations? No!" She looked at me expecting a concurrent response from me, and she got one. "The answer is a big fat no!" she continued. "And what's more, even after fulfilling these initial series of demands and expectations, the series of expectations continue, right?"

"Well, I guess so," I said. I agreed with her, albeit very reluctantly.

"Let me ask you then, Neila, what kind of traditions or customs are you really defending? That which supports *nothing* but endless demands and expectations from all the family members, wherein the idea of *total bliss* is completely buried?" Baljeet looked at me with a genuine questioning face, emphasizing her question in a rather high-pitched tone.

"Well, what can I say, really?" I was at a loss for words. She had proven her point with her own life's experience. After listening to that, and witnessing the unfortunate suffering that the system had caused within her, there was absolutely nothing I could say.

Being raised in the very same Indian traditions and customs as Baljeet, I could easily see the flaws and thorns in it. So far, I had not been a victim of it, for I had not gone towards that path yet. However, as a young and unmarried Indian woman, I was sure to walk on it someday. Heaven forbid that I would end up on a slippery path and be victimized.

I realized that something was badly needed to be done by women like us to avoid such possibilities, something concrete and profound that would awaken all women, young or old. We could spread a clearly-defined message among them that said, "Avoid the big circus of these traditional weddings and focus on the *real* thing: a union of two people that defines a *marriage* in true sense, and leave some room for the blossoming of love!"

Or perhaps, with an exposure to the new world and its freedom, we could spread a message that said, "Drop the tying-down for life with *expectations*, partake of the liberty and freedom of the new world, partake of those moments of deepest happiness which result from a union of two people, which were designed for *each and every one* on this God's earth, and not just for those in the newer world!'

Or perhaps, through the force of some fertile imagination, we could devise a method for combining both, the openness and freedom of the new world and traditions and customs of the old one. We could thus, make the slippery path of Indian arranged marriages not just a walkable one, but a long, pleasant journey, leading to the bliss!

However, sadly, I knew that nothing like that would ever happen. I knew it, Baljeet knew it, and hundreds of thousands of Indian women like us knew it too: the age old traditions and customs had silenced our free voice permanently, leaving us in an invisible cage.

Could there ever be a change in future? I really couldn't tell.

Epilogue

I met Baljeet almost two decades after I had completed my studies and left the university. She got married to Phil immediately after his return from the trip. They have two lovely, twin daughters; Surjeet and Teresa, names from the heritage of both parents.

In spite of being "polar opposite" as Baljeet had once said about herself and Phil, they are living happily ever since, like in any fairy tale!

Life Practitioner!

Chris Campbell was a graduate student in the same department as mine; I met her for the first time in my supervisor's office. Dr. Nichols—my supervisor—was talking about a research project with me when there was a light knock on the door. She asked the person to come in. A young woman, whom I had seen many times in the laboratory, walked in with a small stack of papers in her hand.

"Have you met Neila?" Dr. Nichols asked her as she was putting the stack on the table.

"I don't think so, but I have seen her here a few times," the woman answered.

"She is my new graduate student, Neila Singh. She is working towards her master's degree in biochemistry. Neila, this is Chris Campbell, also working towards her master's degree in biochemistry under my supervision."

Dr. Nichols introduced Chris to me. We shook hands while eyeing each other intently, as though we were two rivals competing for the same prize. Her long golden hair was loose, and was almost covering her entire back. In the laboratory, I had always seen her hair tied tightly with a rubber band at her neck, making it resemble a long golden tail of a horse; this had fascinated me. Another conspicuous thing I had noticed about her was her bubbly laugh that one could hear even at a distance.

Dr. Nichols finished whatever she was explaining me earlier and then said, "Chris is an excellent person to get help from in your research project. She did her undergraduate degree under me on a similar research topic."

I nodded and started picking up my stuff from Dr. Nichols' table when Chris quickly came forward and said, "Wait, let me help you. It looks like there is too much stuff for you to take in one trip." I liked her gesture and waited for her.

"What was it that you wanted to see me about, Chris?" Dr. Nichols asked her.

"Oh yes, I almost forgot my purpose in coming here." She laughed in her typical bubbly style for two seconds and said, "Dr. Nichols, the radioisotope I125 [14] is almost finished, and we need to order some more of it." She gave Dr. Nichols some papers to sign, and was explaining to her about few other laboratory items that needed to be ordered. While she was doing that and getting the papers signed, I waited and observed her. She was on the shorter side and had light hazel-colored eyes that you could clearly see through her rimless glasses. She had a slight nasal voice, and when she laughed, she took it to a much higher pitch. I liked Chris. Her whole bearing seemed so free and natural, a quality that genuinely appealed to me.

After they finished discussing everything, she turned towards me, picked up half of my stuff and started walking out the door. I picked up the rest of my stuff from the table and followed her.

"Neila Singh, you must be from India, right?"

"Yes, how did you guess that?"

"Oh, your looks and your name, too—that gave it away."

This was refreshing to me because most of the people I had met thus far had always inquired about my origin in spite of meeting me and knowing my name.

"My husband has a sister by the same name."

"Your husband has a sister by my name? What do you mean?" Now this was even a bigger surprise to me. Why would a Chris

---

14 I125 is a radioisotope that is used as a biological marker in medical research.

Campbell from Canada have a husband whose sister's name would be Neila, an authentic name from India?

"Oh, my husband is also from India. I am sorry. You obviously didn't know that. And you thought I made a well-educated guess, eh?" She looked at me with a mischief in her eyes and gave out a big bubbly laugh. I joined her in laughing. She had hooked me as her friend already!

We walked together through a long corridor to my office at the end of the corridor.

"You married an East Indian?" I asked.

"Yes, but I have kept my maiden name," she answered casually.

"Really?" Chris, or any woman, keeping her maiden name after her marriage was new to me. "Where is your husband?" I asked her.

"Have you seen a tall, Indian guy with similar glasses in these corridors? That's Kris, my husband."

"He is Chris too?" I was confused. How can her husband, who was from India, have the same name as hers? She laughed again and said, "Well, he is not *Chris* with a *c*—he is Kris with a *k*. His full name is Krishna Yadava, but he has been using only the first four letters from his Indian name, so it's been shortened to Kris. Everybody calls him by that name now."

Hmm! *Krishna* became *Kris!* That was my first time coming across a shortened version of an Indian name with a result that sounded one hundred percent Canadian. Perhaps that was one more way some Indians chose to assimilate with Canadian society. I felt amused.

We entered my office and kept all the stuff on the desk. "Thanks for helping me," I said, expressing my genuine appreciation for her help.

"Any time! Do you want to meet Kris?" she asked me.

"Oh, sure!"

On hearing my response, she immediately approached the telephone on my desk and dialed it.

"Oh, I didn't know you meant right now—some other time would be better, perhaps," I tried to say, but she had already arranged it in her telephone call to her husband.

"Let's go," she said as she put the receiver down and gestured to me.

"Where?"

"To the department of physics."

"Why?"

"Well, you said you want to meet Kris, right?"

"Yes"

"Well, that's where he works. He is a post-doc there."

"Oh really? I didn't know that," I mumbled. She was at the door already, waiting for me to join her. We started walking to the adjacent building.

The university campus was huge, and even if the department of physics was located in a building adjacent to ours, it proved to be a fairly long walk. Chris filled me up with a lot of information about the university, and about herself, too, during this walk.

"I did my undergraduate degree here."

"Yes, I heard Dr. Nichols mention that; when did you do that?"

"Oh, quite some time ago. It seems like a lifetime ago." She gave her bubbly laugh again. "Kris was doing his master's degree then, when I joined the school as a freshman."

"Was he your TA[15]?"

"How could you guess that?" She looked surprised.

"Believe me, it was just an educated guess, not like yours about me. Tell me first, is that correct?"

She nodded with a giggle and I joined her in laughing. A connection between a TA and a student was a close second to that of two high school sweethearts, culminating in matrimony. It was almost universal!

We entered the Physics Building, as it was usually referred to, and went up the stairs to the second floor. This was the first time I'd been there. The building had long corridors, with all the rooms and laboratories opening on one side of the corridor. The other side of the corridor was closed in with three-foot-tall parapet wall with glass panes extending all the way to the ceiling. There was a huge and beautiful

---

15 TA is a Teaching Assistant. Usually these assignments are given to graduate students in the university with a small stipend. A TA either teaches a lab or conducts a tutorial for the undergraduate classes.

botanical garden right next to this building, and with the glass panes of the corridors, one could look outside at that beautiful garden and enjoy the view.

"Beautiful, isn't it?" Chris asked me when she saw me look at the well-manicured garden through the glass.

"Yes. I wish we had a view like this one from our building." I was still looking at it when I heard Chris say, "Oh, hi honey."

I looked at Chris. She was hugging a tall Indian gentleman. That was obviously Kris, her husband.

"Meet my husband, Dr. Kris Yadava; Kris this is Neila Singh, the new graduate student in my department."

"Oh, your name is Neila too, same as my sister," he said with a smile. He shook my hand gently with a polite nod.

"I told her already that you have a sister with the same name."

"Oh, you did? " he said. I was observing Kris while they were talking about my name.

Kris Yadava, a post-doctoral fellow in the Department of Physics, was a tall and lanky guy with a headful of thick and curly long hair that he had tied in a short ponytail. He wore a pair of rimless glasses similar to those of his wife, through which I could see his dark brown eyes. His ears were pierced, and he wore a small gold stud in his left ear that was shining in the sunshine coming through the glass panes. He was wearing a pair of navy blue jeans that looked faded on the knee area, and a cream-colored cotton shirt that was tucked into the waistband of his jeans. He had used a piece of rope in place of a belt for his jeans, and it was tied in a knot at his waist. He was wearing a long white lab coat that bore his full name on the top left-hand corner. It read, *Dr. Krishna Yadava, Ph.D. Quantum Physics.* I was impressed. The man had a doctoral degree in a subject only the very intellectual dared to enter, and yet he looked so very unassuming and simple. I wondered in that brief moment about my own silly notion of making the possession of both a high I.Q. and humility mutually exclusive.

"When did you come here?" Kris asked me while I was dwelling on my own silly thoughts.

"I joined the graduate school just a couple of weeks ago."

"So you are quite new to Canada?" he asked.

"Oh no, not to Canada. I came to Canada from India a while ago; it's just that I joined the graduate school only recently."

"I see. So you are not on a student's visa then?" he asked me, and to answer that, I just shook my head.

"How do you support yourself, then?" he asked.

"Well, I am not on a student's visa, but I hold my immigration papers, right? So I have taken up some part-time work. That supports my meager stipend here, thank God." We both laughed at my answer.

"What were you doing until you joined the graduate school here?"

"I was working full time at the same place where I am working part-time right now. I needed to qualify myself for the graduate program at the university in the science faculty, so, while working full time, I was also studying for all those exams." I was answering him politely and truthfully, but at the same time, I was wondering why was he asking me so many questions about myself when we had just been introduced to each other.

I didn't know why all immigrants seemed to need to know all the details about other immigrants from their own country *as soon as* they met them. I had observed this trait, especially with immigrants from India. We just didn't seem to be able to resist the temptation of asking a whole host of questions to fellow immigrants from India as soon as we met them. Even a person with a Ph.D. in Quantum Physics could not avoid this temptation! I was amused.

"Are you going to take us to your lab and show us around or just carry out your interrogation further?" Chris interrupted, putting an end to Kris's volley of questions.

Thanks Chris, I murmured within myself; she didn't know that as an immigrant from India, I was quite familiar with this line of inquiry, and a presumption of this kind was always taken as a natural course on our part since we were always available for questioning from other fellow immigrants.

Kris just smiled and led us to his laboratory. It was huge and modern, equipped with the most sophisticated articles. Most of the people in the laboratory knew Chris very well, so she preferred talking to other people in the lab instead of touring with us in the laboratory.

"Why don't you come home sometime, Neila?" Kris asked me in Hindi. I was looking with curiosity at some article that looked like an incomprehensible apparatus. I was surprised to hear him speak in Hindi.

"Your home?" I just repeated what he said, not really understanding why he would invite me to his house so soon after meeting me.

"Yes. It is a bit of a long drive from the university, but we have a car and we can always pick you up whenever you decide to come over," he said, again in Hindi.

"Okay, sounds great. I'll let Chris know when I can make it," I answered in Hindi.

"Did you see the whole lab?" Chris came towards us and asked me. I nodded. After saying goodbye to Kris, Chris and I left his lab to go to ours.

"Do you know Kris has invited me to your home?" I asked Chris.

"Oh, really? Now tell me something, did he talk to you in *Hindi?*" I was surprised at her question and just nodded.

"That means he feels comfortable with you, and possibly sees a friend in you."

"Friend in me? I met him for the very first time today. I met even *you* for the very first time today, remember?" I said honestly.

"Yes, but I know my Kris very well. He never, I mean *never*, talks in Hindi to anyone unless he feels a little something about that person in his heart."

"But there are so many Indians here; I saw a couple of Indians right there in his lab."

"That's right. But believe me, he has never invited anyone to our house. I bet he never talks with them in Hindi either. Apparently, those guys in his lab tried to talk to him in Hindi a few times, but he answered back in English, he told me. That clearly indicates that he doesn't entertain any such ideas."

"Perhaps he saw a friend in me because his sister's name is the same as mine, right?" I asked her.

"Oh probably. Or not, I don't know. But my guess would be that he really wants you to visit our home." Chris responded to my doubt with an emphasis on every word matching the rhythm on each step of the staircase that we were using to go downstairs.

"Where is she, by the way?" I asked Chris.

"She, who?" Chris asked me.

"Neila, Kris's sister."

"Oh her. She's in India"

"Wouldn't she want to come here now that her brother is here?"

"No." Chris gave me a monosyllable answer and kept quiet. I could guess that she did not want to expand on this topic. We quietly walked to our building.

"Hey, thanks for showing me around and introducing me to your husband," I said as I entered my office.

"You are welcome! And don't forget, Kris has invited you to visit our home. So consider that as *my* personal invitation too, okay? Do visit our home sometime." She gave me a light hug and left.

I actually felt good when I received Kris's invitation to visit his home, but I also felt a bit amused, for I realized that although he was married to a white Canadian girl, or a *gori* as all Indians referred to them, he was still carrying a few streaks of Indian-ness in him, and a few of them were quite strong. Exhibiting curiosity about my status in Canada and extending hospitality to me as soon as we met were a few of those strong ones. My keen observation of Indian immigrants was that they were overly inquisitive about other Indian immigrants, but at the same time, they were very friendly and would be hospitable to them as soon as they met, as was reaffirmed by Kris. It was also a bit surprising that he hadn't invited his Indian lab buddies to his house. I let that thought go and decided to take him up on his offer sometime in the near future.

I asked Chris one Friday afternoon if I could visit them that evening.

"Sure, Friday evening sounds fine. Join us for dinner then," Chris said.

"Dinner would be too much trouble, Chris. I would like to come just for a cup of coffee or tea after dinner." I was hesitant to go for dinner since I had invited myself there.

"No, no, no trouble at all. Let me telephone Kris and let him know that you have finally decided to visit our home. He was asking me the other day about it." She immediately telephoned him and told him that I was interested in visiting them on that Friday. The plan was that Kris and Chris were to give me a ride, and we three were to drive to their place. So, after the lab work was completed on that Friday evening, Chris and I walked to Kris's lab, and we three drove together to their home.

When I entered their house, a modest looking, two storey house, the very first thing that struck me was the tasteful decoration of the living room that was done in authentic Indian style. The living room was L-shaped. It held a bright white wicker sofa set, set of a typical three-seater, two-seater, and a chair with a matching central table, laid out in one corner of the L. All the sofa set pieces had cushions with silk covers in beautiful bright colors. A tall floor lamp was set on one side of the three-seater which had an octagonal brass cover with small Ajanta and Ellora carvings. The second corner of the L-shaped room held a statue of Lord Ganesh that was made of black stone. The statue was mounted on a pedestal that was also made of black stone. A tall brass *Samayee*[16] was standing next to the statue which was not just for decoration; it looked used. There were many beautiful paintings hung on all the walls of the room. The theme of the paintings was obviously of rural India, and all the paintings had village scenes with village folks from India. The long leg of the L-shaped room had a beautiful Persian rug thrown on the floor with a couple of oversized cushions stacked neatly on it. A small folding table made of sandalwood was leaning against the wall.

Chris was proud to give me a guided tour of her house. A lot of care was given to decorate each bedroom with a specific theme. One bedroom had a theme of an African safari, with a lot of stuffed animals neatly arranged on a single bed. And the master bedroom was done in authentic Indian style, like a maharaja's room. There was a third bedroom which we didn't enter because the door was shut tight. After showing me the house, she led me to the kitchen.

---

16 *Samayee is an authentic Indian lamp that is lit with oil. The modern Samayee can be lit with candles as well.*

"Most of the cooking is done already, I just have to take it out from the fridge to warm it up," she told me.

"Do you want some help, honey?" Kris asked her. She just shook her head and then asked us to sit at the kitchen table to give her company while she warmed up the food[17]. Kris pulled a chair out for me at the kitchen table and asked if I wished to have a drink or something. I requested a glass of orange juice, so he poured some in two glasses and then sat on another chair across from me.

"You have a beautiful home here. Whose idea is it to decorate it in different themes?" I asked while taking a sip of the fresh orange juice.

"We both did it together," they both said simultaneously, and we three laughed heartily at that.

We were still laughing when a little boy came running and giggling into the kitchen from the back door. He was followed by an old gentleman who was obviously trying to catch the boy. The little boy, who looked to be about four or five years old, and the old man, who looked to be in his seventies, were obviously members of the family. I could easily guess who they might be.

"Hey guys, what's so funny?" Kris asked them, pulling a chair for the older gentleman to sit. As soon as the little boy saw me, a stranger in the house, he stopped giggling and ran to his mother.

"Hi sweetie, had a good play in the park?" Chris asked him. He didn't say anything. Instead he wrapped himself around her thighs from behind and stared at me.

"Neila, meet my father, Dr. Yadava." Kris introduced his father to me. I got up from my chair and said *Namaste*, a polite salutation in Hindi, as per the Indian customs.

Kris's father looked quite healthy and strong for his age. He had a thick white mustache to match his thick white eyebrows. He was of medium build with a dark brown skin color, and almost no hair on his head.

"And this is our son, Rishi. Say 'hi' to our guest." Kris got up from his chair and dragged the little boy away from his mother towards me.

---

17 *In the early 1970's, microwave oven, a common kitchen appliance used as the quickest method of warming up food, was not available.*

"Hi," Rishi said reluctantly, and then he disappeared from the kitchen. We all laughed again.

"What a cute little fellow," I said. Rishi was a cute little boy with his mother's color and his father's dark brown hair and eyes.

"You never mentioned your son to me. How old is he?" I asked Chris.

"Five years old," all three of them answered. I could easily sense a harmony in that family. "Soon he will be ready to start public school," Chris said.

"So Neila, what brings you here to Canada?" the father asked me after settling down comfortably in his chair. He had a deep voice. Before even I could answer him, Chris said, "*Tatah*[18], she is a graduate student in the same faculty as I am. She has the same supervisor as me."

"Dr. Nichols?" he asked. Chris nodded. I was mildly surprised and impressed to see that Chris's father-in-law had the knowledge of who Chris's supervisor was. He must have noticed the pleasant surprise on my face, because he said to me, "I know on what research project Chris is working and who her supervisor at the university is. I also know what topic my son is working on, although I don't understand it. I must know at least that much, don't you think?" I nodded. His face expressed genuine pride. Secretly, I wished that my parents were there too, proudly talking about me.

"Dr. Yadava, what kind of doctor are you, sir?" I asked him politely.

"I am not a medical doctor. I have a Ph.D." he answered and smiled.

"Tatah was a professor of Linguistics in one of the universities in India. He came here after his retirement," Kris said.

"Now you know what brought *me* to Canada, right?" Tatah said to me with a smile. Turning towards his son, he added, "It is almost five years since I came here, isn't it?"

"But it feels like just yesterday since you came here, Tatah," Chris said to him. I saw the old man's face light up a little. There was not a streak of complaint in his voice and I could easily guess that he must *like* it here in Canada. This was a bit of a pleasant surprise to me, because my own experience had shown me exactly the

---

18 Tatah is a common term used to address a father in some parts of India.

opposite; senior Indian immigrants were usually the unhappy and whining type after migrating to Canada, especially if they came *after* their retirement.

"Tatah, do you wish to eat right now with Rishi, or later with us?" Chris asked him. He gestured *right now* and added, "Why don't you all sit in the living room? I can manage Rishi's and my dinner." He immediately got up and started setting up their plates on the kitchen table. He surprised me even more with this action. He must have done it quite often, because Chris and Kris both picked up their juice glasses and asked me to come to their living room. I picked up my juice glass and followed them.

"You have a very friendly and helpful father-in-law, Chris." Although that was Kris's father, I felt more comfortable expressing my genuine feelings about the old man to Chris, and also because she could understand what *I meant.*

"Oh, I know. I know he is a very good man and a very 'easy to live with' type of father-in-law." Chris knew exactly what I had meant.

"Rishi is quite attached to him now, and so is he to Rishi. They play together a lot, go to the park most of the evenings together, and Tatah is quite particular about reading a bed-time story to Rishi every single evening."

"That's wonderful" I said.

"That makes us feel good, too. That way, it does not impose a burden upon us about how to entertain him. He could get so bored here otherwise, wouldn't he?" she said.

"Yes, what would he do for the whole day otherwise, right?" Kris said. Then he added, "He gets along very well with Chris, too. Not a day passes without him asking her about her work, her project, and all sorts of things."

"Yes. I sort of guessed that when he mentioned our supervisor's name," I said.

"He has been asking me to take him to our department for a visit. One of these days, you will see him there," Chris said to me.

"To tell you honestly, seldom you see the in-laws getting along so well with their daughters-in-law, especially in Indian families. I don't know if it's influence of some old traditional ideas or whatever, but the seniors in Indian families seem to have inhibitions in admiring or showing any compassion to the *wife* of their son," I said.

"Especially if the wife is a Caucasian woman of Canadian origin and therefore certainly not a girl of their choice, isn't that true?" Kris completed my sentence. It made me feel a little awkward, but what he said was true. That thought did cross my mind, too, but I didn't say it openly as politeness and simple decency demanded one not to mention one's race, color or even origin[19]. I just nodded to what he said.

"You should have been there to experience what happened when I declared my plans of marrying Chris to my parents," Kris said to me, while looking at Chris.

"Tell her, tell her everything," Chris said.

"I went to India immediately after finishing my graduate degree and told my parents that I was enrolled in the doctoral program in the same university. They were very happy for me, but at the same time, they were concerned about my marriage because this degree required me to be away from India and away from them for another five years. So they both started making a big fuss over me getting married, the 'arranged' way, of course. They wanted me to get married and *then* leave for further studies."

"And also because you were their only son," Chris interrupted.

"Yes, that too! My mother immediately went on a mission of finding a suitable girl for me. She said, 'I am finding you a nice girl. You will get married and then go wherever you want.' I flatly refused her idea. When she started nagging me every single day, showing me photographs of young women of marriageable age, that's when I decided to tell her and Tatah the truth." Kris looked at Chris momentarily and then said, "I told them that I had already met the girl of my dreams"

"And that was Chris, of course," I said.

"Of course! Oh my God, the moment they heard me say that, it was like all hell broke loose."

---

19 *The terms 'politically correct' or 'politically incorrect' were yet to be invented when I met this family. Simple decency and politeness sufficed in those days.*

"They asked you what my name was, right honey?" Chris said to Kris.

"Yes, and when I told them Chris's name, it was as if I had dropped a bomb on my family. My mother went completely berserk, and my father, a learned man, a college professor, hit his forehead with his right palm and said, 'Hey Ram, not only is she from Canada, a different culture, but she is also from a different race, *a white girl!*' I just didn't know what to say to them."

"Well, honestly speaking, they were right. I am white and I am from a different country, different culture, or *race* as he said," Chris said, interrupting Kris again.

"So what? I tried to convince them that although she had landed in a Canadian crib with white parents, she was a very loving girl with the same family values as ours. She would be a good wife to me, a very good daughter-in-law to them, and a fantastic member of our family. But my mother, and my father too, were too darn stubborn to even listen to me or my reasoning." Kris looked at Chris and held her hand tightly, giving her a sweet, gentle smile.

"Finally, I stopped convincing them and told them bluntly that I loved Chris very much and that's all that mattered to me. I told them, 'I am going to marry her.'" When he said this, I saw Chris hold Kris's hand too, reciprocating his earlier action.

"Oh, what happened then?" I asked him.

"Well, they both started throwing tantrums, hoping that I would be dissuaded from marrying a white girl by their angry outbursts. When I told them that I was absolutely determined to marry Chris, they suddenly became very quiet. Almost totally mute! A dark gloom spread over the entire house as if someone in the family had died and we were all observing mourning for the dead." Kris looked a little uneasy, but at the same time, he also looked like he wanted to tell the story. "I didn't budge from my determination. I *was* in love with Chris and I wanted to marry her. Finally they gave in, begrudgingly of course, and accepted my wish to marry her. It was more like a *surrender* to my determination, really." I looked at Chris. She had tears in her eyes and a smile on her face.

"We got married right here, in this town, with the JP," she cleared her throat and told me.

"What's a JP?" I asked her, thinking that that must be a position of some denomination in the church.

"That's a Justice of Peace," Chris said.

"Oh, so it was a civil wedding ceremony."

"Yes, oh yes. I didn't want to hurt his parents any more than I already had. A church wedding would have devastated them completely," Chris said.

"Why?" My question was genuine.

"Because they are *Hindu*. Neila, having their only son get married in a Christian surrounding with Christian rituals would have devastated them completely. So I insisted that we have a civil ceremony. Actually, I had dreamt ever since I was a little girl of my wedding ceremony, wearing a beautiful white, silk gown, holding a beautiful bouquet of pink roses and walking down the aisle to the tune of "Here Comes the Bride" but I refrained from being dreamy and unreal. A church wedding would have had a religious connotation to my wedding ceremony, and I didn't want any religious conflicts in my union with the love of my life." Chris said this and smiled again at Kris. What a wonderful and understanding person she was, and how mature, too, to show concern to other people's emotions! I was impressed.

I had not seen very many interracial marriages between white folks and Indian immigrants during my university years. They were not at all common in Canada at the time when I met Kris and Chris. However, whenever I did witness such a liaison, I always saw a kind of tension in both families, and more so in Indian families. It seemed to me that some Indian immigrants carried too many social taboos from their homeland to Canada, which remained fresh on their minds even after many years of staying in Canada; perhaps that prevented anything new from penetrating their minds or hearts. I had heard someone referring to it as "unavoidable baggage." What could be the reason for white Canadian families to resist accepting people of other cultures or races in their families? I couldn't tell why; perhaps they simply lacked exposure to new people.

"My mother was the first one to accept Chris in my family," said Kris. "She sent a beautiful *Mangal sutra*[20] for Chris and told her to wear it whenever she could, although according to Hindu tradition, it should be worn at all times. My father resisted accepting Chris for a lot longer time, but finally he accepted her, too."

"Oh, I am so very happy for you guys," I said.

"Yes, so are we. Look at my father now. He is very friendly with Chris and dotes on our son," Kris said.

"Where is your mother?" I asked, since I had not seen her.

"She died a couple of years ago," Kris answered.

"I am sorry to hear that. Did she die here in Canada?" I asked him, because I was told earlier by his father that he had been in Canada for the last five years.

"Yes, right here, in this house. It so happened that, after my father retired from his job at sixty years of age, he started getting bored at home. College work was his entire life. He had not done anything else or learnt anything else in his life. Out of excessive boredom, he started getting on my mother's 'nerves,' as she put it, whereas my mother was quite active still, getting involved with many women's organizations and associations. She was only in her mid-fifties, a relatively young age, I suppose. When mother saw that he was getting restless and bored at home and having a tough time adjusting to the excessive leisure, she wrote to me describing all these things in detail and inquired if there was anything I could do for them. I talked with Chris about all this, and that's when we decided that we should call them here so that they could be active again in something new, something challenging, in a new country."

"So you called them here?" I said in a questioning tone.

"Yes, I sponsored both of them. Under the 'Family Union' program that the Canadian Immigration Department operated, they were granted immigration in less than a year and they both came here immediately, leaving everything in their hometown."

---

20 *Mangal sutra* is a nuptial necklace, made by threading black beads in a gold strand. It is a tradition in many provinces in India that all Hindu women wear it after their marriage. The groom puts it around the bride's neck at the time of the wedding, and once worn, it is not to be taken out anytime, something like a wedding band.

"It must have been difficult in the beginning, eh?" I looked at Chris and asked her this, because Kris was their son, whereas she was a 'foreigner.'

"Yes, quite so. First of all, I was not used to having parents, because all I had was an aunt, my Aunt Martha who raised me after both my parents were killed in a car accident when I was a little girl. But I must say, it was wonderful. And I really meant it. I decided to like this new situation…"

"*Decided* to like it! What a profound statement!" I commented.

"Yes, and welcome them as *my* parents, an experience I deserved. Once I made this decision, it was relatively easy, and in a short while, I *really* started liking it," Chris said, sounding completely genuine and sincere.

Listening to her, I realized that, although she had stated it very casually, she had made a profound statement which was also an important yet practical philosophy of life! I was impressed with her mature attitude.

"They slowly started getting used to the Canadian style of living."

"That is, light, insignificant lunches and dinners around sunset times, right?" I asked Kris with a smile. The Canadian eating habits and timings were new to me in the beginning as well. He nodded.

"That's right—light, insignificant lunches and very early dinners. My father liked spending a lot of time in watching television shows and reading newspapers. 'The newspapers are huge with many sections here, not much news, but lots to read in it,' Tatah used to say all the time," Kris said.

"Yes, I had observed this too when I was newly-arrived in Canada."

"And he had lots of time to read every section in the newspaper. Going for long walks in the beautiful parks was another of his favorite pastime. He was impressed with their size and excellent maintenance. He also joined local senior's club and started going there regularly. My mother took charge of the kitchen. She was fascinated by the fact that she could make all kinds of foods with literally thousands of types of ingredients available in Canada, and sure enough, she would prepare a variety of dishes for us with her superb culinary skills. She was like a child in a candy store."

"His mother taught me a whole host of Indian dishes while she was here," Chris interrupted Kris.

"Yes, these two women got along just wonderfully with each other. Mother didn't know English and Chris didn't know her language, so initially I was their interpreter, but later on, they both could communicate with each other very well, though I didn't know how." Kris said.

"That's when we planned our baby," Chris said with a smile.

"And that's, Rishi, right?" I said.

"Yes ma'am! You should have seen *Amma*—that's what we called her—when I gave her the news. Oh my God, she was completely taken over by enthusiasm and zeal. She never let even one day in my nine months go by without preparing some new dish especially for me. Can you imagine that?" Chris sounded quite excited.

"Lucky for you," I said to her.

"The baby was a healthy nine-pounder, a regular heavyweight champ, just like his mother had become with Amma's cooking!" Kris teased Chris. She just slapped him lightly on his wrist with a big grin on her face.

"Amma was looking after Rishi—actually they both were looking after Rishi—when Chris went back to work after her maternity leave. I was still finishing my doctorate degree and the money wasn't enough," he said.

"It *still* isn't, honey! I am a full-time student and you are *just* a post-doc fellow, getting a paltry stipend, remember?" It was her turn to tease him, and his turn to discard what she said with a grin.

"That's when Amma got suddenly very sick. I was working as a lab technician at the time in the same lab," Chris started telling me with a serious face. "Kris telephoned me in the lab and was almost on the verge of tears. I immediately grabbed my purse and we both rushed home, but…but…" Chris stopped talking and looked like she was swallowing a lump in her throat.

"It was too late. Amma was gone already. It was a shock to all of us. The doctors could not figure out why she died so suddenly. It was horrible even to think of it." Kris shuddered and we all stayed quiet for a few seconds.

"That's when I met Neila, his sister, for the first time in my life. We sent her a ticket to come from India and visit us immediately, and to be with Tatah." Chris broke the silence.

"Did she?" I asked.

"Yes, she came right away. She is a wonderful woman, just like Amma was. She stayed with us for almost a month. She was a huge consolation to Tatah. Even Kris felt very good having her here at that time. A sister does make a difference in such times of grief, isn't it true?"

"Yes, yes," I said.

"Actually, she is younger than me, but she is quite balanced. She took care of all of us at that time," Kris said.

"I think that's why Kris felt a kind of closeness to you almost immediately after meeting you, Neila. You look a little like her, and coincidentally, you have the same name too, isn't that right, Kris?"

"Yes, most definitely." Kris was smiling at me while concurring with his wife.

"Where is she now?" I asked.

"She went back to India after she felt confident that we were alright. She is happily married and lives with her family in India," Kris said.

"I am so glad to see your father come out of his grief and reconcile..." I started saying, when I saw Tatah come out in the living room with his grandson. He turned to Chris and said, "We are all done, dinner and everything. The table is all cleaned out, and I laid out settings for your dinner, okay?" Then he pulled a chair in front of me and sat down. I was genuinely surprised to hear that.

"Tatah, was the dinner okay?" Chris asked him.

"Oh yes! Everything was just fine. Especially the curry, it tasted as if it was made by your Amma." His moustache quivered along with his lips when he laughed. Then he turned towards me and said, "Krishna's mother was a fantastic cook, you know, and she trained Chris wonderfully. She has left her legacy of some fine dishes with Chris now. You will soon taste and see what I mean." I admired him for complimenting his daughter-in-law. I was in equal awe to see him overcome his personal loss and adjust to the changed situation so soon.

"Mom, can I please go out with Tatah to the park again?" Rishi came and sat on his mother's lap and asked her.

"I don't think so Rishi. You played enough in the park earlier, right? Now it is Tatah's time to meet his friends, okay?" Chris said to her son while gently stroking his back.

"But Mommy..." Rishi said. He jumped off his mother's lap and started wallowing on the floor, throwing some tantrums, but Kris got up from his chair and approached Rishi.

"Rishi, get up. Get up right now and go to your room. Do some coloring or something, okay? It's time for Mommy, Daddy and their friend to eat dinner now," Kris told Rishi in a firm voice. Rishi got up and looked at his mother and then at Tatah for sympathy, but soon realized that no one was willing to rescue him from his daddy's order. So, while expressing his disappointment, he reluctantly went to his room.

I was again surprised to see that Tatah was not interfering in his son's disciplining of Rishi. Nor did he join Kris in scolding Rishi. He just kept quiet, like a wise man, staying out of it completely. It was unusual, and therefore refreshing, to see an Indian grandfather doing so, and not causing any tension within the family with unnecessary interference.

"Do you have lots of friends that you meet in the park, Tatah?" I tried to divert attention from the little boy.

"No, no, just four friends. We meet at one fixed place in the park, and after a brief chat, we play bridge or some other card game for a couple of hours, except on Thursdays. On Thursdays, we four go to the Veteran's Center for two hours to do some volunteer work," Tatah said.

"Oh really? What do you do at the Veteran's Center?" I asked him.

"Anything that the supervisors tell us to do, like serving tea and cookies to the veterans, or playing cards with them, or sometimes just talking to them. A few of them are in wheelchairs, so we take them around on the grounds for some recreation," Tatah said.

"That's wonderful. Do you like it? " I asked him.

"Well, yes, being with them makes me *feel* young." Tatah laughed and I saw his moustache quiver again while he laughed.

"Tatah, you *are* young, and thank God, you are healthy too," Kris said to his father.

"That is because my *daughter* here makes sure I eat healthy food," he said with a look of genuine appreciation for Chris.

"Talking about food, let's eat now," Chris said. She asked Kris and me to come into the kitchen and sit at the table. The table looked immaculate with three settings for dinner, with dinner plates, napkins, cutlery and glassware all properly arranged. Chris took the food from the oven and laid the containers one by one on the table on hot mats. The aroma of the delicious food spread instantly everywhere, activating my salivary glands. She served us and we all started eating.

"This tastes absolutely exquisite. It is all authentic Indian," I said, complimenting Chris.

"Thank you, Neila. Thanks to Amma, too—she taught me how to prepare all these dishes in the traditional style," Chris said.

"You certainly are a good student," I said.

"And Amma was a terrific teacher," Chris said, sharing her credit with Amma.

What a wonderful relationship these two women must have had with each other; aside from the fact that they both loved Kris, they had nothing in common between them! Why did this not happen in every family in India? With this thought, I remembered my parents talking about a joint family where familial tension and stresses were rampant; my mother seemed to always put the blame on the mother-in-law, who, mother said, would take the charge of the entire household after the men left for work and abuse her powers, treating her daughter-in-law like a slave of the family, with a constant reminder that one day she would be able to take it out on *her* daughter-in-law. I remembered my mother saying that after many years of suffering at the hands of her mother-in-law, it would be no surprise if the daughter-in-law would take revenge for her sufferings on *her* daughter-in-law in the future. Ironically, I had actually witnessed encouragement for such behavior coming from *women themselves!*

Is that why, I had wondered at the time, most of the married women in India secretly wished for a son? Not for continuation of the family name or any such reasons given openly, but just so that one day, he would grow up, bring home a wife, a free slave to do all the hard work and also take all the abuse?

"You are very quiet, Neila—is everything okay?" I was brought out of my contemplation by Kris.

"Yes, yes, everything is okay. I am really enjoying the delicious food. The curry taste is such that I can almost swear it is made in some hotel of Bombay or Delhi. Are you sure it is not imported?" Everyone laughed at my joke. Just as we were finishing our dinner, Tatah came in the kitchen and said that he was leaving and would be back at the usual time.

"Tatah, I just ate the curry, and I know exactly what you meant," I said in Hindi, concurring with his earlier remarks about the curry being authentic and tasty. He looked pleased. He laughed with his quivering of moustache and lips, and waved 'good bye' to me as he left. We were eating and enjoying small talk for a while. Kris and I helped Chris do the cleaning up and then, as she put it, the kitchen was closed for the day.

It was getting late. I had a great dinner and even a greater evening in such warm family surroundings. When Chris excused herself to go and tuck her son in bed, I also got up, and after giving her a gentle hug, I bid a goodbye to her with sincere thanks. Kris drove me back to my place. I went to bed that night after having earned a good family friend!

I spent the entire weekend in the library. Monday was insane, with too many classes, along with my teaching assignment that started in the late afternoon. It was way past my dinner time, and was almost eight o' clock in the evening when I finally finished everything. I was walking home, feeling completely exhausted. I was very hungry, too, and while thinking of food, I remembered the great meal I had at Chris's home on the previous Friday. The food reminded me of the entire evening I had enjoyed with her family, especially her father-in-law, Tatah. He had made a wonderful, positive impression on me with his polite and helpful attitude towards his son and his family. To me, he seemed like a model father, a model grandfather, and a model *father-in-law* too! Tatah reminded me also of my own father, for no other reason than age, and brought my own father's memories to my heart.

I started thinking about Tatah, wondering what he must be doing right now, perhaps being at the park and playing bridge or something with his buddies. I reached my residence, and was almost floored to see both Kris and Chris standing at the door, waiting for me.

"Hey guys, what a pleasant surprise! What are you doing here?" I was very happy and equally surprised to see them there.

"Kris had a late lab today, so I decided to wait too, so that we both could drive home together. By the way, where were you in the afternoon? I didn't see you in the lab for the whole day," Chris said as I was unlocking the door of my apartment.

"You are right—I didn't go to the lab at all. For the whole day, I had classes all morning and a tutorial until now. Did you miss me?" I said smilingly while welcoming them inside.

"Yes, of course, sis!" Kris said with a wink and a smile and I liked that a lot.

"You know, it's funny but while I was walking home just now, I was just thinking of you all," I told them.

"And so were we, this morning, when I was wrapping up some leftover curry from last Friday, just for you." Chris held a plastic lunch box for me.

"Oh, bless you my friend, I am famished!" I didn't waste any time and grabbed the lunch box from her hands.

"Warm it up, because it has been sitting in our lab fridge since morning. Actually, first see what else is in the box, because Tatah is the one who packed it up while I was getting ready this morning," Chris said.

Tatah had packed the food for me? No wonder he reminded me of my father, I thought. I opened the box and was very happy to see a small plastic bag with two *roti*[21], a second small plastic bag with some rice, and a third plastic bag with some curry in it.

---

21 *Roti is an Indian bread made with whole wheat flour. It is flat, round and roasted dry on a fry*

"Oh my God, there is a complete meal in here!" I said.

"Is that what it has? It did seem a bit heavy to me when Tatah handed me the box," Chris said.

"What about your dinner?" I asked them.

"We already ate at the cafeteria, as we can't wait till this late," Chris said while pulling out a chair and getting comfortable on it. "Tatah was talking about you the whole weekend," she said.

"Really?"

"Yes, you should visit us as frequently as you can, really," Kris said. He was still standing, holding his car keys in his hands, as if to leave soon.

"Aren't you going to sit down, honey?" Chris asked him.

"Yes, but on what? There are only two chairs, and you two women are sitting on them already," he said, looking around in my room. He was right. I had a small kitchen table with only two chairs; anything bigger than that would be too big for my small, one-room studio apartment. The same room played many roles; it was my kitchen, my living room, my study room and my bedroom too, depending on the time of the day and what I was doing at that time.

"I am sorry, Kris, but you will have to sit on the sofa bed there." I pointed at the nearby sofa bed that was still in bed form. I rarely put it back into its sofa form because no one visited me, whereas I needed its bed form every night to sleep. Kris walked there, put it back to its sofa form, and sat on it. "This is not bad, quite comfortable too, as a matter of fact," he said. He looked comfortable on it.

I warmed the food on the stove, served it on just one plate, and started eating. It tasted as good as it did on the previous Friday, reminding me of that evening.

"Your father is truly a very congenial and friendly person, Kris," I said, starting some small talk with them about Tatah while enjoying the delicious meal.

"Yes, he is a very good and friendly person indeed!" Kris looked happy when I complimented his father.

"But he was not so, and not too long ago, either," Chris said, and quickly looked at Kris.

pan.

"You didn't have to say this. It is all over—all that is in the past, forgotten completely." Kris quieted his wife rather abruptly. He obviously did not like Chris passing a remark like that about his father. I personally had no desire to ask about what they were referring to, so I kept quiet. However, I saw them looking at each other, as if trying to decide whether to explain Chris's remark or not.

"Chris was right; Tatah was a 'gone case' after my mother died. Can you believe that?" Kris said looking at me. I guess they had decided to share with me after all.

"That's hard to believe." I was genuinely surprised to hear what he said about Tatah.

"But I suppose it can happen to anyone when he or she loses a spouse of almost forty years, and suddenly, too," Kris said.

"That's true. Losing anyone suddenly—especially your life partner, and after so many years of association—must be a very hard pill to swallow." I concurred with his general comment without knowing what exactly he was referring to about Tatah. Perhaps he was a little reluctant to talk about him.

"Yes, I suppose so, too," Chris said. She was about to wrap up the subject when Kris started talking. "I was in the lab helping a graduate student with some experimentation when the telephone rang," Kris said as he started telling me Tatah's story. His initial reluctance seemed to have vanished completely. "It was Tatah on the telephone. He sounded very excited, with a funny shake in his voice. 'Something has gone wrong with your Amma, come home right away,' he was trying to say. I tried to calm him down, grabbed my jacket, and left the lab immediately. Before leaving my lab, I informed Chris. She almost ran to my lab, and we both drove home as fast as we could."

"I had gone back to work after Rishi turned one year old, because Amma was there to look after him," Chris said.

"Amma was lying down on her back on the bed with her eyes shut, looking pale white, and Tatah was sitting next to her. He was still like a statue, saying nothing, just staring at her. I telephoned the emergency, and as soon as the ambulance arrived, we all went to the hospital. But it was too late. The doctors declared Amma dead on our arrival to the hospital. Nobody could diagnose what happened exactly to her, except that it could be a sudden massive heart attack that had killed Amma. I was speechless, and so was Chris. Tatah looked inert and completely expressionless. I was more worried about him than grieved by Amma's passing away. He was just staring at her body, not crying, not uttering a single word, nothing. I put my hands on his shoulders but he was still like a statue. I was crying, and Chris was crying, but this man who was married to my mother for more than forty years looked totally inert. He was totally frozen. I was calling him continuously, saying 'Tatah, Tatah, are you okay? Say something!' He just looked at me with two blank eyes and then looked away." Kris became suddenly quiet and looked at Chris.

"The sudden passing away of Amma must have shocked him," I said.

"Yes, it was just too much for him. We were all shaken badly by Amma's sudden death, but we were more concerned about Tatah. He had become like a robot. We went home with Amma's body. Kris looked after the cremation procedures, and everything else as required by the Hindu rituals, but Tatah was completely speechless all through the rituals. We thought that it was due to the sudden shock, but even after many days, he was doing nothing, saying nothing at all, always sitting still in one place for hours, going through his daily requirements like a robot. Kris's sister, Neila, came from India and extended her stay especially for him, but nothing mattered to him. We both needed to go back to work, so we arranged a daytime baby-sitter for Rishi, but Tatah was the same, like a robot." Chris looked at Kris. He was looking like he had his emotions under control and could continue the story.

"It was just terrible to see Tatah like that. We had lost Amma to death, and now it seemed like we were losing Tatah to something unknown," Kris said.

"*Another* unknown," Chris said.

"What do you mean by another unknown?" I asked.

"Well, death is unknown too, right? Life's biggest unknown!" Chris said.

"Slowly, I would say after many months, Tatah started coming back to life, very slowly, but, but…"

"But what?"

"But we couldn't recognize who he was?"

"What do you mean?"

"Whoever that was, that was *not* Tatah, that's for sure."

I had a questioning expression on my face while listening.

"He was so unfriendly and curt, so impolite and rude, that even I, his own son, had a difficult time adjusting to him; it was as though there was a totally different man residing within him, someone we never knew or met, and someone who *despised* us," Kris said.

"Did you say *despised?*"

"Yes, despised. We would come home after picking up Rishi from the babysitter and go upstairs, but the door to his room would be locked tight. *Perhaps he is sleeping,* we would think, and leave him alone. For days we didn't go in his room, because the door would always be shut tight when we three went home at the end of the day. We almost never saw him for days at a time. He would put a note on the outside of his door, telling us to send his food to his room. It was so strange, you see. I personally would take his food upstairs to his room and inform him about it, but he would just say 'Hmm' and not open the door for me. I would wait outside his closed door, hoping he would open it, but he never did, not even once. Before our bedtime, when Chris or I would go near his room to check on him, there would be an empty plate outside his closed door. We would silently take it downstairs for washing. This went on for days." Kris looked a bit serious.

"Oh my good God, really?" It was very hard for me to believe all this about Tatah.

"I tell you Neila, Tatah had become a phantom. Except for the food that we kept for him outside his closed doors, and the empty dish every night, there was absolutely no mark of his existence in the house. We would never hear anything from his room, any sound at all—not even the sound of him taking a shower or flushing a toilet or his coughing or something, nor anything else that revealed human existence. It was horrible," Chris said.

"Oh, there was one more mark of his existence, remember?" Kris reminded Chris.

"Oh yes, late at nights, I mean really late, we would hear the sound of Tatah reading some hymn-like thing. Eventually, the sound got louder and louder, to a point that even Rishi would wake up from his deep sleep occasionally, due to his loud reading of the hymns. They were *shloka*[22] from the *Bhagvat Geeta*[23], Kris told me," Chris said.

"We took it as his effort to console himself, his effort to reconcile himself to Amma's death. After all, her demise was very sudden. So we kept quiet and silently put up with what he was doing. If only things would remain thus, it would still be okay."

"Why, what happened?"

"Things started going from bad to worse, day by day. He started coming out of his room eventually, which was good, but he was very rude and offensive, almost intolerable. We just couldn't figure out what had happened to the loving, amicable Tatah we knew. It was as if this new ill-bred person had totally taken over our genteel Tatah."

"Oh my, that is hard to believe." I could not believe what I had heard.

"We tried different things to bring him back to the original self, even sending Rishi to his room to play with him, but nothing helped. I gave up. It was causing a lot of tension at home, even between Kris and me. We tried to talk to him or go somewhere with him, but all our efforts were in vain. We finally decided to let it go and leave him alone. When Amma was there, occasionally, we would go to a movie or dinner in a restaurant in the evenings, and leave Rishi with her. We decided to resume this by having someone look after Rishi. I have my aunt living here, I told you—my Aunt Martha who raised me. I would request her to come home and sit for Rishi occasionally. She gladly agreed and came. I felt good that there was somebody from the family for us, and for little Rishi, too." Chris sounded slightly relieved.

"And then one day, Aunt Martha asked me, 'Why is your father-in-law giving me a dirty look every time I come to your place, Chrissie?' I was really surprised to hear that. She told me that Tatah always gave

---

22 *Shloka* is a couplet.

23 *Bhagvat Geeta* is a shortened name of *Shri Mad Bhagvat Geeta*, a book on philosophy that is universally regarded as the highest form of Hindu philosophy. It is originally written in Sanskrit and entails about 700 *shloka* covering the entire Hindu philosophy.

her a look of utter hatred. My Aunt Martha is a real sweetheart of a person, so why would Tatah, or anybody for that matter, give her a dirty look? I told her that she was mistaken. The next time the same thing happened, she told me that he was downright rude to her. So finally I told Kris about it and requested him to talk to Tatah about it."

"And then?"

"Well, I did try to talk to him about it. See, it all happened this way," and Kris narrated to me exactly the way it transpired.

"One day I went upstairs and knocked on his closed door rather hard. After knocking for a few minutes, he reluctantly opened the door. I went inside and sat on the bed, Amma's bed. This was after a fairly long time, and perhaps for the very first time after my mother's death, that I had entered his room. I saw a small photograph of my mother laid out on his dresser. She looked so sweet in that picture, exactly the way she was. Looking at that picture, and thinking of her, I was overcome by grief again. I looked at Tatah. He seemed so sad and so lonely, I was about to give up my purpose of going in his room, but then I controlled my own emotions and decided to ask him directly why he was so rude to everyone in the house, including our guest, Aunt Martha. I was feeling a little awkward to ask him all these questions, but somehow I pulled my courage and managed to ask him all that. But, instead of answering, he asked me, 'Who the hell is this Aunt Martha?'

"'Tatah, that is Chris's aunt, her mother's sister.' I was stunned to hear him swear like that, but I answered patiently.

"'I never saw her here before. Where the hell was she all these days?' he asked me again in the same rude and rough tone, using a swear word again.

"'She was out of the country for many years. Her husband was in the Canadian Peace Corps and was stationed elsewhere. She was with him, naturally.' I was trying my best to be patient and ignore his unnecessary rude behavior.

"'So is he transferred here now?' he asked.

"'No, Tatah, he died, just a few days before Amma died.' I saw some changes on his face after I told him. I waited for a few minutes, thinking he might get a little soft now, express his sympathy, but nothing like that happened. Instead, he asked me with sarcasm,

'So, is this Martha woman trying to trap another man for herself?'

"'Why do you assume that, Tatah?' I asked him, barely able to hold my patience.

"'Why would anybody dress up so much, wear make-up and lipstick, and wear pearl strings and all that glitter so soon after the death of a spouse?' Even amidst that tension, I was a bit amused to see that Tatah had observed her attire. I stayed quiet for a minute. Then he said, 'She didn't stop at that, Krishna—she even asked me to come downstairs and play cards with her while you two were out and Rishi was sleeping. Why would she do such a mischief?'

"'Is that what happened, Tatah?' I asked him and he nodded.

"'And is that why, you think, she wants to trap someone, you in particular, Tatah?' I asked him again.

"'Well of course. These white folks don't have any depth whatsoever like we Hindus do, Krishna, especially white women! As soon as one spouse is dead, they are after another. They have no respect for the dead spouse, I tell you, Krishna! They just like to enjoy and have fun in life, especially white women. Look at our Hindu widows, so pious and so very sorrowful! They don't indulge in dressing up or wearing jewelry or any such things, and they never talk to any one stranger—they don't even eat properly. That's the way it should be with all those who lose their spouses, especially the widows.' I knew he was stretching my patience almost to a breaking point.

"'So what our Hindu widows do—remain depressed and distressed all their lives after their husbands die—is the right way, and what these white women do—come to terms with their husbands' death and go on with life—is the wrong way. Is that it Tatah?' I asked him facetiously. He nodded with full agreement to what I said.

"'Absolutely! That's the way it should be. Look at their philosophy, Krishna. They do not believe in the concept of reincarnation. They have no idea of *paap*[24] or *punya*,[25] and they give too much importance

---

24 **Paap** *in Sanskrit means sin.*
25 **Punya** *is something like merit, which can be accumulated by virtuous behavior and good deeds.*

to *this life*, as though there is no life after this one.' I could see that this was going to be a long evening.

"'What are you saying, Tatah, that all white folks are superficial, and by 'living this life,' they are violating something that is pious and real?'

"'Yes—now, look at that woman!'

"'Her name is Martha'

"'Okay, look at that Martha woman. Barely a few days into widowhood, and what is she doing? She is already out there in the world, all dressed up in glitter and having fun. Where is the *piety* of a widow? Where is the *misery* of a grieving widow. Where is the *real* widowhood?'

"'So, if you lock up yourself in a room, stay miserable, and be rude to everybody—in short, *miss life*, as you are doing after Amma's death—then you are *deep, pious, and real*. Is that what you think, Tatah?'

Tatah didn't say anything.

"'Tatah, don't get me wrong, I certainly didn't mean to insult you or show any disrespect to your philosophy, but I do want you to meet Aunt Martha face to face. Try to get to know her before passing any judgment about her or the white folks and their philosophy.' I was really angry by then, but I tried to control myself. Tatah had forgotten that I was married to a white girl myself, who was Aunt Martha's niece; she had made not just me but my whole family, including him, very happy with her nature and behavior. Tatah looked a bit perturbed after what I said to him, for I had pointed a finger right at him. He gestured me to leave his room immediately. I did."

Kris took a long breath, and so did Chris. I could not believe he had this kind of conversation with his father.

He continued. "Aunt Martha informed us that she was going on a long vacation with a few of her buddies, so Chris and I invited her for dinner one day. When she came, we both insisted Tatah join us at the table for dinner. After a lot of pleading, he finally came downstairs, albeit begrudgingly, and sat on a chair, mute and stiff as a pole, looking down at his feet the whole time.

"Aunt Martha was sitting across from him, wearing beautiful clothes and a sweet smile. She was looking her usual charming self.

"'Good to see that you finally decided to step outside your room, Yadavaaah,' Aunt Martha said to Tatah in her usual high-pitched voice. She always addressed him by his last name, saying it in a peculiar way. Tatah just mumbled something and continued staring at his own feet.

"'So where are you all heading to, Aunt Martha?' Chris asked her.

"'To Glacial national park, my dear. I am so excited,' she said

"'Who are all coming with you?' Chris asked her again.

"'My whole group, all eight of us, who volunteer at the *hospice* every Tuesday.'

"Tatah looked at Aunt Martha the moment she mentioned *hospice*.

"'Tell me about your volunteer work, Aunt Martha,' I asked her.

"'Well, there isn't much to tell really. I go to this particular hospice on Queen Street and help the terminally ill patients, what they call palliative care. I volunteer there with anything they need me to do. Sometimes I talk to them. I feel good to be with these people—more importantly, I feel stronger and wiser every time I visit them, because I get an opportunity to witness that *certainty* of life, we call death! Strange as it may sound, every single time I am back from there, I feel some kind of an inner calm which needs no validation from the outside world.' Aunt Martha became suddenly very quiet for a few seconds after having said this, but then she regained herself and continued,

"'You know how my Jack died, suddenly and unexpectedly, right Chrissie?' Chris nodded and held Aunt Martha's hand gently. Aunt Martha continued. 'He was a planner and a scheduler. The only time that man gave me a surprise in our forty-two years of married life was with his last action—his death! He hadn't planned that one. Then again, perhaps that's how it was planned *for* him and *he* didn't know of it ahead of time, that's all!'

"'Otherwise, Uncle Jack would have planned for his death also in his usual way,' Chris said to Aunt Martha, and smiled. We all indulged in a mild laugh. So did Tatah. He looked amused and a little touched. A faint smile had wiped away the hard lines of remorse and hatred from his face. At least I imagined so. He was listening to Aunt Martha intently.

"'Jack had given me wonderful company for forty-two long years, and silly me, I thought it was going to be a lifelong one. How ignorant of me! He made me feel *complete* when we were a couple. How stupid of me to assume that this could continue forever! He died suddenly and left me alone. I felt betrayed by him—how selfish of me! I kept on thinking and thinking about his demise. Why did he leave me alone, why did he die before me? Too many questions and too much thinking! But when all that thinking stopped, a simple thing dawned upon me.'

"'And what was that, Aunt Martha?' Chris asked her gently.

"'That I was not alone. That I had *me*. That I was not *incomplete* without him, that I *myself* was a complete person! I did not need any validation from outside, not even from my dear Jack to make me feel complete. He followed his path, and I had mine to follow. It was as simple as that,' Aunt Martha said with a firm voice.

"''That is so beautiful, and so very true, Aunt Martha,' I said to her. Suddenly we heard Tatah say, 'I didn't know that you were interested in Hindu philosophy.'

"Chris and I were almost thunderstruck to see Tatah show interest in what Aunt Martha was saying—or interest in anyone or anything after Amma's death, for that matter.

"'What Hindu philosophy? This is no Hindu philosophy! I don't know *any* philosophy, Hindu or whatever. This is a general, everyday rule of *practicing life,* my dear Yadavaaah! A rule based on a simple, uncomplicated philosophy of life,' Aunt Martha said with a smile.

"'You mean to say you don't know the concepts of reincarnation or *paap* or *punya*?' said Tatah. I saw Tatah's demeanor alter immediately from that of an interested listener to a spiritual being.

"'Reincarnation and all those other things you mentioned, I don't know any of that, Yadavaaah. Never heard of it. I don't even know whether any such concept exists in Christianity or Christian philosophy or in any other books in the West. I am actually two times a Christian. I have been baptized into the Methodist and the Baptist churches.'

"'Oh my, really, Aunt Martha?' Chris said. Aunt Martha just nodded.

"'Yes, really, but it doesn't matter! The impulse to *behave* in life, in what they call a spiritual way, comes to each and every one of us from beyond the five senses, whether one believes in God or not, whether one lives by any particular philosophy or not. And to me, that is living! How I *behave* is living, and what I *know* of my behavior is my philosophy of living, and that's all I can do and I do.'

"Tatah was quiet for a while.

"'Tatah, ask her how she feels about *her* loss,' I prompted Tatah in Hindi in a low volume, but he waved it negatively. I was determined to make Tatah hear what she had to say, so I asked her about how she felt after Uncle Jack's death.

"'Oh, Kris my child, you ask me about my darling Jack, may his soul rest in peace! Not a single day passes without me remembering him, my dear! When he died suddenly, that almost killed me, too. I went in mourning for days wearing only black, never talking to anyone, never returning anybody's telephone calls, never meeting even my dear children and friends whom I always considered to be the *wealth* of my life! I wanted to end my life too, but then, after a lot of contemplation, I reached a conclusion. My Jack is gone somewhere beyond the horizon, never to return to his Martha, but his Martha is still here, alive and well, in this beautiful world, so she must *celebrate* life!'

"I saw Tatah looking at her with his quietly observant glance. Aunt Martha had to be very perceptive for, she added further, 'Yadavaaah, you see me dressing up in all these wonderful clothes and wearing pearls and all that, but that is a part of my way of celebrating life! I refuse to die with the dead. I simply refuse to end my life with my dead beloved. My Jack's path came to an end suddenly one day, but mine didn't! Not yet, anyway. I firmly believe that the experience of living should be received with wonder and gratitude by one and all! If I am to live, I must go somewhere, do something, experience *life* with all my five senses. And that's precisely what I am doing, Yadavaaah.'

"Aunt Martha was quiet for a while. We were all quiet. I looked at Tatah. He was looking at something with his eyes fixed on it. I didn't know what he was thinking, but I knew my father very well—he was thinking of something for sure!"

After Kris had narrated this whole incident, he became very quiet. Chris and I could feel that he was overcome by emotion. Chris got up from her chair and walked towards him. She gently held him, gave him a light kiss on his cheek, and took over telling me about that evening.

"'What have you made for our dinner tonight, Chrissie?' Aunt Martha asked as she finally broke the long silence that evening.

"'Oh, dinner tonight is pasta with a homemade sauce that you taught me how to make, Aunt Martha. That's Tatah's favorite too, right Tatah?'

"Tatah looked startled as if he had just come out of a deep sleep, when he heard me address him.

"'Yes, yes, that is my favorite too, something I ate only after I came here to Canada,' Tatah answered with a big smile on his face. His moustache was quivering as he smiled. It had been such a long time that we had seen him smiling like that. It was simply..."

"...wonderful to see that my old father was back," Kris said as he completed Chris's sentence. His glasses looked fogged. We silently watched him take off his glasses and wipe them.

"Hey, have you finished eating already?" Chris asked me when she noticed I was sitting with an empty dish in front of me.

I just nodded and said, "Yes, a long time ago."

She could guess that I was intently listening to their story. I thanked her heartily for bringing me a delicious meal and took the dirty dish to the sink.

"Shall we go for a brief walk? It looks beautiful outside, and it's not that late," Chris asked Kris and me, and we agreed. I locked my apartment and we stepped outside.

We were strolling in complete silence, looking around the campus area. There was a beautiful full moon in the sky. In that moonlight, the whole campus area looked as though it was covered by a thin layer of white ash, making the scene absolutely mesmerizing! We got busy soaking in the magnificence of the scene.

Personally, I was equally awed by what I had just heard from Chris and Kris.

Epilogue

Nature has taken away the vital force from Aunt Martha, the life practitioner, as well as from Tatah, her devoted 'pupil.' However, they have taught us all by setting a beautiful example of how not to just exist when alive but 'practice' life.

Kris, Chris and their son Rishi are truly following their teaching, for besides being full-time professors in one of the most renowned universities in Canada, Kris and Chris are quite involved in local community activities.

Rishi heads the local swimming team and aims to be a swimming coach for the Canadian Olympic team in future!

The Unchanged Visage

My course work at the graduate school was in full bloom. I was up to my neck in my studies and was swamped with assignments and term papers. Although understanding the English language was not a problem for me (being from India and having learnt English from teachers who were educated by the British during the British Raj), understanding Canadian accents did pose some problems for me in the first few classes. That required me to be much more attentive in the class work and a lot more diligent in studying.

One of the full credit courses I had taken for the semester was clinical biochemistry. This course entailed a specific research project that required me to collect blood, do a blood chemistry analysis, and then submit the report as a weekly assignment to my professor. For the collection of blood, I had to go to the university hospital every week. When I saw this hospital for the first time, I felt very lucky, as it was one of Canada's best and most reputable hospitals, and had very sophisticated laboratory equipment. I loved working there and found much fulfillment in it, so much so that even though I put in a good fifteen hours of work every time I was there, I never felt fatigued.

One fine morning, just as I was pouring a reagent in a beaker, my colleague walked into the laboratory in the hospital and presented me with a big, expensive-looking bouquet of long stemmed red roses.

"Oh my God, Ryan, what a beautiful bouquet!" I said, surprised. I hurriedly put away the stuff, took off my plastic gloves, and walked towards him. "Did you rob a bank or something?" There was just no way that Ryan—a full-time student living on a paltry scholarship, just like me—could afford a bouquet like that, not even for his beloved.

"I didn't buy it." He stood there holding the bouquet and smiling.

"Oh? Then where did it come from?"

"Don't know, but looks like it is for you, Neila." He was still holding it and smiling.

"What? For me?" My mouth was half-open. I must have looked like a dork! Why would anybody send such an expensive bouquet to *me*, someone who spent most of her time either in a laboratory or in a library, wore only jeans and a cheap tee shirt with a long laboratory coat over it, and made no efforts to look beautiful by any make-up or visits to a hair salon?

"It's from an admirer of yours." Ryan's mischievous explanation was even more stunning.

"Get out, an admirer? I don't have any admirers. No way."

"I see a card here." Ryan pointed to a card that was neatly tucked in the plastic wrapping of the bouquet. "Read it, then you'll know who your admirer is." Ryan's smile looked a bit mischievous, too.

Ryan handed me the bouquet and I laid it gently on the counter. He waited with blatant curiosity for me to open the envelope. The impish twinkle in his eye made me hesitate a little. I carefully removed the card from the bouquet and opened the envelope, wondering who my generous admirer could be. There was a "Get Well" card inside, which I was surprised to see, as I was perfectly healthy. There was some mix-up, I was sure of it. This was a hospital after all, so someone must have sent it to some patient there. In the corner of the card, I read the inscription: *To N. S. from your admirer.* The handwriting was small and peculiar looking. The envelope did not bear any room number or any other details except the initials of the intended person. I figured that the intended person must obviously have been a patient at the hospital, with the same initials as mine. That must have prompted the front desk to send the bouquet upstairs to my laboratory. I tucked back the card in the bouquet and left it on the counter without opening its plastic wrapping. When Ryan saw me do all this, he left with a bit of a disappointment as there was not much fun in this episode.

I got busy with my work, but the thought of that bouquet never left me even for a minute. It seemed a pity that the sender should spend a small fortune on such a beautiful bouquet and not have it reach the intended recipient. Finally, I decided to find the patient through the hospital registry. My own curiosity was triggered as well. I wanted to see who the admired one was, and how she (for she definitely had to be a 'she') looked.

I took the card to the nursing station on each floor, and with some help from the attending nurse, checked every patient's initials. Finally, I found a patient whose initials matched those on the card, N. S., same as mine—it was Natalie Smith! She had checked into the hospital the previous week on the seventeenth floor. I paused. The seventeenth floor? It was the psychiatric ward, with both open and closed sections.

I could have had the bouquet sent to the patient just with the help of the hospital staff, but I was compelled to do it myself. I picked up the beautiful bouquet, which had adorned my laboratory counter for a few hours by now, and went up to the seventeenth floor, the psychiatric ward, a place where almost everyone feels quite apprehensive and nervous to visit.

I went straight to the chief of the ward and explained my reason of being there. He led me inside and pointed at one patient.

"That's Natalie Smith," the ward chief said. Sitting at an upright piano, a young, frail looking woman was lost in her song. Her sweet voice, the lyrics and the tinkling piano filled the air with melancholy. I waited and listened to her for a few minutes.

"Day and night she sits there singing and playing the piano, with no thoughts for meals or bedtime or her medication," The ward chief said, waving indulgently in her direction with a mild contempt.

"Hmm..." I said. I was still listening to her sweet music, intently focused on every detail of her as she sang and played. She had very short, auburn colored hair that she obviously had not cared for in a very long time. Her hands and fingers were long and delicate, and her fingernails were painted in bright red color, the same color as the roses in the bouquet I was holding. I was mesmerized by the splashes of her red nails jumping and darting among the black and white keys of the piano.

"She must be really enjoying singing and playing the piano," I said to the ward chief, my eyes still fixed on her fingers.

"Yes, that's all she does." The ward chief hadn't left my side yet. "It's a pain in the neck to give her any medication or even to get her to say something." He was complaining about her.

"Why is she here?" I asked him.

"Since you are like one of our hospital staff members, I don't mind telling you a little bit about her." The ward chief told me briefly that she was suffering from acute depression and suicidal tendencies. Her husband had brought her there only a week earlier and her doctor had judged hospitalization as the only viable recourse to give her the help she needed.

I looked around. She was still engrossed in her music. No one was listening to her music, but she appeared totally oblivious to everything.

"May I?" I looked at the ward chief to see if he agreed to let me approach her alone with the bouquet. He nodded. I walked over to the piano.

"How sweetly you sing and play," I said. "Where did you learn to perform so well?"

Her bubble seemed to burst with my question. She rose, appearing flustered, and quickly moved away towards the hall. I quickly followed her and touched her arm. She stopped and looked at me. We held eye contact for barely a second or so, but her glance struck me rather intensely. She had big, deep blue eyes with long lashes.

"An admirer has sent this for you, Natalie. I thought I should personally bring it to you." I held the beautiful bouquet of flowers in front of her.

She accepted the bouquet hesitantly. She opened the envelope and, seeing the handwriting on the card, inhaled deeply of the flowers. I heard her murmuring to herself, "Oh, my darling, Mike. That Natalie is dead, but this Natalie is alive still."

"How did you get these?" she asked.

"The flowers were delivered to me by mistake. My name is Neila Singh, so I have the same initials as yours." She nodded and looked at me with her big eyes. From this close, I could see her eyes filled with sadness.

"But I am glad this happened. That way I had a chance to be introduced to you, a talented singer and piano player, right?" The words sprung to my lips on their own accord. I had an immediate affinity with her. She must have felt the same, for she smiled openly and said, "Now that we have been introduced to each other, and since you seem to like my music, why don't you come and meet me whenever you can?" She looked at me intently.

"Well, I will see." I wasn't sure I wanted to commit myself.

"As you can easily guess, I can't leave this place and meet you, not for a while at least." She smiled very sweetly at me.

For whatever reason, I ended up giving her my word that I would visit her. I thanked the ward chief and returned to my laboratory.

I found out later that afternoon that the technicians in the service laboratory did not like to go to the psychiatric ward to take blood samples from the patients. This was especially true of uncooperative patients, and Natalie was one among them. I volunteered to go to the ward and take Natalie's blood samples as required by her doctors. Surprisingly, I found her very cooperative. I started going there regularly and our friendship began rather quickly.

"Did you come from India?" she asked me one day while I was taking her blood sample. She was staring at my face and hair, both dark brown, looking even darker in the hospital environment.

"Yes." I finished taking her blood sample and put it on an ice pack in my caddy. "I was born and raised in India, but I have made Canada my home now."

"You left everything behind? Your parents, your family and friends, your home? Don't you ever feel homesick?" she asked me innocently.

"Yes, I do. As a matter of fact, I feel homesick very acutely at times. My *tambura* helps me through all this homesickness, though." I told her.

"Tambura … that is a musical instrument, right?" she asked me.

"That's right." I was impressed that she knew what a Tambura was. "It's a long-stemmed lute used as a drone for singing. I play it and sing the classical music of my homeland."

"You sing?" she said. Her eyes lit up.

"Yes, I do. When I sing, it doesn't even occur to me that I am so far away from India."

"Did you get formal training in classical music?"

"Yes, my parents noticed my musical talents and nurtured it with excellent training. Now, even after my immigration to Canada and going through these graduate studies, I have been able to put some serious time into the traditional classical music." I got a little carried away in answering her question. She listened intently.

"Do you have plans of getting married?"

This question came to me as a total surprise, but I collected myself and said, "Yes, one day for sure." I was tempted to tell her that almost all Indian women, myself included, *needed* to get married if they wished to be accepted by the Indian community, whether we were in India, Canada, or on the moon.

"Will you marry an Indian man?"

"Probably, yes. I don't know that for sure, though," I answered nonchalantly.

"And what will happen to your music when you get married, let's say to an Indian, same like you?" she asked me.

"Well, nothing will happen to my music, I am sure. Nothing *can* happen to my music whether I marry an Indian or not, Natalie, because, because..." I was searching for appropriate words when she interrupted me again.

"When you sit with your *tambura* and sing, won't your husband object to that?"

"No, of course not! I won't allow it, simple as that. If I get married to an Indian man, then this question may not arise, because I know most of the Indian men are fond of music. Many among them like classical music too, so why would he prevent me from practicing music, right?"

"Hmm," she said. She was intently listening to me.

"Besides, Natalie, suppose he objects to it—why would I submit to his whims?" I said with a smirk on my face.

"Why? Because if you don't give in, he will divorce you." She was very serious.

"No." I looked at her with wide eyes. "Natalie, what you are predicting is totally wrong. My sisters sing, as do many of my girlfriends and cousins, and they are all married women. My guru in India is a renowned musician who is also a married woman. Chances are that I will also marry someone who will encourage me in my music, right?" She didn't answer. She was sitting still, like a statue. *Had she gotten divorced because of music?* I wondered.

"You Indians believe in reincarnation and rebirth, don't you?" Out of nowhere, and totally irrelevant to the topic of music, she came up with this question.

I tried to stay as cool as I could and answered, "Yes, we do. That is not just a belief, by the way—that is the basis of Indian philosophy." The glow in her eyes that was so obvious when I talked about my musical endeavors had disappeared completely. She looked almost disappointed. "How does that relate to music, though?" I asked her.

"Maybe it does relate to it, or maybe not. But one thing is for sure: from now on, Neila, I shall pray that God grants me my next birth in India, where I shall be married to an Indian man who will care for my music just like the husbands of all those women you just mentioned," she said with a sad tone.

It now became clear to me what she was trying to say. I felt a little uneasy. Natalie was such an innocent and delicate woman.

"Natalie, this is Canada, a liberated society! The freedom women enjoy here is incomparable. The orthodoxy still flourishes in India, and in that orthodox thinking, females are at the bottom of the society. Daughters are considered to be a heavy burden, sometimes worse, by many families, even today. Seldom have you seen such families who express joy when a girl is born in their family. The birth of a female baby is seen as a punishment from God by some. Some consider it as a result of committing sins in the past life. Do you know that in many families, especially in the rural areas, female babies are smothered to death as soon as they are born? It is called 'female infanticide,' do you know that?" I saw extreme fear on her face after hearing this. I didn't intend to scare her, I just wanted to share some dark facts about India.

I continued: "Not only in rural areas, but many affluent families living in cities and big towns are not too different, either. They have money and modern technology at their disposal. As soon as a girl gets pregnant, the elders in the families try to find out the gender of the fetus by employing the modern techniques. And if it happens to be a female, abortion is advised right away."

"That's horrible," she said, managing to respond with a little stammer.

"Yes, it is. Also, when men marry women, the wives are considered to be the property of their husbands. In many instances, they are beaten regularly to keep them in their place. Mental, spiritual, and physical abuse seems to be the daily regimen of many women in the villages of India. You wouldn't believe this, but ironically even the most natural and necessary occurrence in women's lives—their monthly menstrual periods—carry a big taboo in that orthodoxy, assigning women a status of inferiority and ungodliness. The society has attached a stigma to menstruation, to a point where women have been removed from all the worshipping and religious rituals. Women are not allowed to pray, or worship God, or enter a temple during their unholy days, meaning menstrual periods. And this is not a tale of the olden times; this practice is followed even today." I took a long breath. Natalie was listening intently, her finely-arched eyebrows raised questioningly.

"Millions of women spend their entire lives within the ancient traditional boundaries. They can't cross these boundaries because of the fear of being outcast. That is too big a threat to bear. So what choices do they have, really?" I looked at her and then answered my own question, as though I was making a brilliant statement. "None whatsoever. They forsake their own longings and bear the injustice quietly. But here in Canada, in this free world, women are free, just like the men. Here, *women are persons!* They strike at even the slightest injustice or inequality." My voice swelled. I argued on, citing the principal accomplishments of women in the field of basic civil rights.

I even mentioned the 'women's lib' movement. I was simply eloquent, gloating in my own brilliance.

"All that you said about India, I didn't know, but everything you have said about Canada and her liberated society and women being persons and all that comes from what you see on the television or read in those glossy fashionable magazines, right?" she asked me with an icy gleam in her eye. I was startled and had to admit she was right, actually.

"Neila, Indian women like yourself who attend Canadian universities or settle here in Canada are usually from the good and educated families of India. Once settled here, you tend to communicate with the same class of Canadians who are also educated and affluent. The Canadians you are likely to know are of the liberated and free thinking set. The freedom of the women from this class enthralls you. You admire these women, but unfortunately you imagine all of us to be of their class. You gauge Canadian society by your own sheltered experiences."

She looked directly into my eyes and said, "Please don't get me wrong when I ask you this, but how much exposure do you get to other Canadians? You are a graduate student here, studying in one of the best universities in Canada. Tell me something, Neila; do you know any of the Canadian high school dropouts?"

I shook my head and just sat back, agog!

"You are living in a graduate residence, you told me. How much contact do you have with those who have dropped out of high school or have barely finished their high school but have no desire for post-secondary education? There is a very large population of such people in Canada. To tell you honestly, at least in my opinion, that would be half of the people of Canada. Do you ever get a chance to hear how *they* think?"

She went on and on, firing questions for a few minutes, continuing to look directly into my eyes. I felt the dense air of uneasiness around me and got extremely nervous. My earlier brilliance had vanished completely in that heavy air.

"They may have the trappings of the typical free-thinking class of Canadians, perhaps, but do you know that many Canadian wives have the same status as any household appliance?" She stressed the last word with more than a little contempt in her voice. "Do you know that these women have no roles or value outside of being mates to their husbands and mothers to their children? Do you?"

She had completely turned the tables on me. I could almost feel my extremities slowly turning to stone with every question she posed.

"The men in such homes can't even imagine that their wives could have potential of their own, potential to be somebody or do something beyond housekeeping, mothering, and keeping their beds warm whenever they want. And these men are right here in Canada, in this very liberated society, as you think of it." Now she was the eloquent one, with her voice rising periodically and her hands flying.

"You talk of the orthodoxy in India; I don't dispute that since I trust what you tell me. The old traditional values are rampant in India; that may be true too. The poverty in India I don't dispute that either, but I see tremendous wealth of culture in that country. I have read a lot about India and her culture." She looked at me intently. "You know what? While reading something about India, I came across a photograph of a human body, half man and half woman. The caption underneath explained it as God with two essential parts! I simply love that concept, that of a complete human being with its two essential parts, that of a man and a woman!"

"Was that *Ardha-Nari-Nateshwara*[26] from the Indian mythology?" I asked.

"I think so; I don't quite remember the exact name now. Tell me now, Neila, how many other civilizations can boast of such a beautiful perception of humanity?" She had a faint smile on her face.

I was intently listening to every word she said. I was quite surprised, and mildly impressed too, to see that she actually had seen a photograph of this famous Indian mythological creation. I doubted if many Indians knew of it or thought of it from this perspective.

"I genuinely think that India is really a rich country. Do you know of Canada's moral conditions? Only a slim portion of her men view women in more than one way. Most of the men here refuse to

---

26 *Ardha-Nari-Nateshwara is a mythological figurine considered to be that of Lord Shiv, with half male and half-female body depicting a whole human form.*

recognize the true caliber of women and show no trust in women. You call this a liberated society? How many women do you see in top executive positions in corporate Canada? Or in the Canadian Parliament, for that matter? Canada hasn't had a powerful woman prime minister yet, which India has already accomplished.[27]"

I was stunned. I knew all of this but had never realized. My head started spinning with new, incomplete thoughts.

"You must have been brought up in a very cultured home," I said.

"Well, not really. My parents were poor and uneducated. My father was a dockworker," she replied. "His work was seasonal and subject to the country's economic ups and downs. He did not complete his high school diploma, not even grade ten, so he never had a chance for any steady work. And yet he never let my mother go out to work because of his traditional mind-set. They broke up when I was seven years old. After the divorce, my mother was unable to care for me, so I was sent to a foster home. I grew up in a foster home. That is another of Canada's ironies, in my judgment. Single mothers are often below the country's poverty line, and out of sheer economic necessity, they have to part with their children. Fortunately, my foster home proved to be a good place. That is where I was exposed to reading many interesting books and to music. This home had a beautiful piano, and my foster parents taught me how to play the piano and sing. They were gentle folks, both retired and spending all their time in fostering and raising children like me. I took to the music like wild fire, singing and playing the piano for hours, dreaming of becoming a classical musician one day."

I was enjoying listening to her background story.

"A few months after I arrived, my fosters took in a young boy. His name was Mike. He was fond of music too. We both were crazy, I think. He would listen to me for hours. My truest fan! He was sure that I was going to be a wonderful classical musician one day. He used to talk about it all the time, reassuring me to continue dreaming and encouraging me to seek my dream. He was only five years younger than I was."

---

27 While countries such as India, Israel, Sri Lanka, were led by women prime ministers, there was no woman prime minister in Canada when Neila met Natalie, and had this conversation.

She sighed a little, looked at the ceiling for a few seconds, and continued. In spite of my presence, she seemed as though she was talking just to herself.

"Unfortunately our paths separated later on. Mike was sent to another foster home for whatever reason and when I reached the age of eighteen years, I was turned out of the foster home altogether. I was a year short of my high school diploma, so I started working as a waitress in a small restaurant and attended night school. Then I met Bob."

She seemed to come back to this world again, aware of my presence.

"Bob was a butcher who delivered meat to the restaurant. He seemed so different from all the others, so poised. Bob would drive me to night school and to music lessons after work in his truck. We started going steady, and eventually we got married. No sooner were we married than he turned into a typical chauvinistic husband. The typical male chauvinistic pig! He made me quit my job at the restaurant."

"What about your night school?"

"I barely managed to complete my high school diploma," she said.

"And music?"

"That's where the whole thing went sour. Bob made me stop my music lessons. We couldn't afford it anymore, with me not having any income, as he explained. Even if I hummed in the kitchen, his jaw set in a way that meant he could lash out any minute. I guess he felt insecure."

"Insecure? Because of music?"

"Yes. I had made such wonderful progress in music all those years that if I pushed it and devoted myself exclusively to it, there would be wonderful prospects for me. That made him uncomfortable. In his judgment, my opportunities in music meant that I would leave him. His feeling of insecurity worsened every day. He became fearful. Trapped in his own fear and insecurity, how could he support my music?"

"Oh my God, really?"

"Yes. And as if this was not enough, one day, Mike came looking for me. I remembered some time during our courting days, I had told Bob about Mike being a true fan of my music. To make it worse, Mike had done much better than me. He had completed a community college diploma in commercial art and photography. A college graduate coming to meet me? That did it! Bob became the declared staunch enemy of my music. I can't take it anymore, Neila, I really can't." Tears started to flow.

"I have tried many, many times to explain to Bob about my sincere desire to pursue music, but he won't hear of it. He does not understand that I *need* my music. I need it to overcome my ordinary humdrum existence. He doesn't realize that music gives me a complete boost of strength, both physically and mentally. He just doesn't get it." She waited for a few seconds and then said, "I know Bob loves me. I never doubt his love for me, but he loves me to be his bedmate and a housekeeper, and a mother of his future children, but that's all. He simply doesn't allow me any role beyond that."

Her speech came in shorter and shorter emotional bursts. I wondered about our common denominator, and I found it very easily. She was a woman and she was a musician, just like me. Music touched me with the overwhelming, beautiful pathos of life. I could relate to her state of mind with no effort.

"I really can't take this anymore. I tried to break out of this situation many times, but the only way out of that I could find was to end it all. Surrender to death! I tried to kill myself a couple of times. Since then, Bob has become very suspicious of all my activities, closely watching my every move and continuously screening my mood for any suicidal tendency. He and my doctor have agreed to put me here. They both think that with the right psychiatric treatment, I may be healed of my mental illness. Bob thinks that with proper medical attention, I will no longer insist to pursue classical music, which he believe is the root cause of my suicidal urges. Poor Bob! Ignorant too! He just doesn't understand what I want in life. Why can't he?" She covered her face and started sobbing. All I could do was gently pat her back.

Almost three months after this incident, Natalie was pronounced cured and granted permission to return home. Before leaving the hospital, she came to my laboratory to say goodbye. I was delighted. During those three months, we had met regularly and enjoyed a rich give and take of beautiful thoughts. We had become friends. She kissed me sweetly on my cheeks and said, "Neila, promise me now that you will pray to God that I shall be reborn into a rich culture, like that of India, so that in my next life I may get a chance to live like a person, and fulfill my dreams of pursuing music."

I held her hand and without saying anything else, promised her. She looked happy and hugged me tight for a moment.

We kept in touch by telephone, calling each other from time to time. Although she sounded a little depressed sometimes, her overall mental health seemed improved to me and I was happy for her.

One day, I was surprised to find a letter from Bob in my mailbox at the hospital laboratory. I opened it in a hurry. It was an invitation to Natalie's funeral.

Natalie's funeral? Energy drained out from my legs. I felt a tremor developing in my whole body. My knees convulsed. I somehow managed to pull a chair and sit on it before I fell down. With shaky hands, I dialed Natalie's number. Bob answered my call. I asked him how Natalie had died. "She emptied a whole bottle of sleeping pills and succumbed to death long before any medical help could arrive," he told me.

Totally incredulous, I hung up the receiver and stared at the telephone. There was a steady flow of tears down my cheeks, and I could feel extreme grief drilling a deep wound in my heart.

Years ago, I had borne another similar deep wound. It had slowly closed over the years, but with Natalie's news, it was harshly wrenched open again. I slipped backwards in time.

I was a little girl, growing up in India. Aunt Kamal always used to visit our home. She was a close childhood friend of my mother. My mother and Aunt Kamal were both bright and ambitious young women. They both finished their matriculation from the same school with excellent marks. In accordance with the Indian traditions of the time, they both got married promptly after matriculation. Indian tradition had also reserved strictly arranged matches for them.

My mother had the luck to marry a loving and encouraging partner, my father. Broad-minded men, who would allow their wives to pursue their goals, like my father, were extremely rare in every social stratum in India in those days. My father was behind my mother in her every endeavor. My bright dynamic mother soon enrolled in college. She completed her undergraduate degree and then pursued graduate studies, completing her master's degree in language arts. She became a full-fledged tenured college lecturer.

Aunt Kamal proved to be less fortunate. She was married into a family where all the members were old fashioned and staunchly orthodox. Worse still, her husband was as resistant to change as was his father or grandfather. He was a clerk with the Indian railways with no intention of moving upwards or forwards. He understood his wife to be an assistant caretaker of his family and the means of providing his heirs. This, of course, did not mar Aunt Kamal's friendship with my mother.

Aunt Kamal was a mild-mannered, average-looking Indian woman with a loving face and a headful of thick, black, curly hair that would always look shiny. She would smear lots of coconut oil on her head every day before weaving her hair into one plait. "That keeps my head cool," she would joke, and then she would laugh heartily. She was a hit with all the other children and myself. She lit up the room with humor and teasing, with one gold tooth sparkling in her full mouth whenever she laughed. Best of all, she was a master storyteller. Many times, she would act out her stories, using her *palloo*[28] and plait as her props.

Aunt Kamal spent a lot of time in her kitchen cooking and serving spicy dishes for her family. Whenever she entered our house, we children had to only sniff to know she was visiting. She carried a characteristic smell about her, that of coconut oil and *masala*[29] mixed together.

---

28 *That part of a sari, which hangs down from the left shoulder.*
29 **Masala** *means curry spice in Hindi.*

Aunt Kamal was also an ardent reader. When she would read any literary periodical, she would take her views to my mother in a great haste, debating and analyzing it at length. In literary discussions, she would make quite a few impressive references and quotations. I remember my mother always saying to her, "Kamal, why don't you go to the college and do a degree in literature? A smart person like you must do much more than mere household drudgery."

Her answers, in a peculiar tone that I still remember, were always the same. "Education? You must be joking! Vimal, you know how it is in my home. If I take just a book in my hand, the atmosphere at home becomes very poisonous. My husband thinks I am ignoring the children, my mother-in-law thinks I am avoiding the household work, my sister-in-law thinks I am showing off. They all treat me as if I am committing a crime and disgracing the family. And all this over what? My liking and fondness for reading a good piece of literature. Any reading I do is always in the middle of the night when everyone, including my husband, is sound asleep." When she spoke in this tone, it was my mother who would get more depressed.

After a few years, Aunt Kamal's husband got transferred to another city in India, and the entire clan left with him to resettle in the new place. Aunt Kamal came to say goodbye to all of us, and cried with my mother. I still remember their conversation quite clearly. They were sitting in the living room of our house. When I took a tray bearing two cups of tea and some snacks for them, my mother told me to sit right there in the room in case they needed something. I guess I was allowed to be there because I was considered to be grown up enough.

"Kamal, please be happy, and do continue your reading," my mother said to her.

"I don't think so, Vimal. I had you here. Even coming here took a lot of wrangling, because my husband knows you are a college professor and he is sure you were contaminating my mind. But you were also my childhood friend, so it was still possible. I never felt listened to or valued in my own house, so who will befriend me now in the new place? Where will I meet another lady college professor that I will be allowed to meet for literary talks? Now I must spend the rest of my life just like any other unfortunate woman, no reading or literary discussions or anything wonderful like that." Aunt Kamal looked so sad that she almost had to wait for a few seconds to control her emotions.

"What do you mean by saying 'the rest of your life'? Why are you talking like an old woman? You are barely forty years of age." My mother tried to put hope in her heart.

"Vimal, it seems to me that even you don't understand. No one ever will! I was so eager for something higher, something wonderful in life, like college education, some deep learning! That seemed to be the right way for me. That was the only thing that I felt would be bliss in my life! I totally forgot that I was married to an Indian railway worker who himself never finished high school. When I passed in the first division with my matriculation diploma, I was so excited, I was flying high, but then what happened? I was brought down flat on my face. I was married to a stranger who had no liking for education at all. I was made to serve in a home where no one cared for anything but the routine housework and where women's studying was completely looked down upon. To me, it was a strange home, more like a prison where people imprisoned themselves in their prejudices. Still I held on to my hope. After the whole day's drudgery and struggle and despair, I would open a book in the middle of the night and sit with the book for hours. It was like heaven. Like a small access to that bliss! The only tools I required were my two eyes and a hope in my heart, hope of someday pursuing my dream." With her lips quivering and eyes filled with tears, Aunt Kamal looked like she was going to break down any moment. Her usual laugh, with its sparkling gold tooth, was buried somewhere deep in that face. I saw my mother swallow a lump in her throat too.

"Vimal, when you enrolled in the college after your marriage, I began to beg my husband to allow me to go to the college also. With my marks, it was quite easy to gain admission in college. I promised to work very hard to make sure neither his parents, his sister, nor he and our children would be neglected. I became utterly submissive to him and even told him that I would remain his humble servant and never assume the part of a master ever in our married life, even if I get my degree. He just scoffed. When I insisted, he grew very angry and spoke abusively to me in front of his parents. He talked ill of my parents and friends too, you included, of course! I was so badly hurt; I decided never to bring this topic up again. But I still kept my dreams alive."

She started crying silently. I had never seen her that way before. My mother intently listened to her, she herself being on the verge of crying. After a few moments, Aunt Kamal pulled her courage, stopped crying and stared talking again.

"When I would be in the kitchen cooking for the family or in the bathroom doing the family laundry, I would daydream about being in the college, enrolled in the B.A. class, reviewing difficult topics, basking in the professor's look of approval. I would imagine the professor's congratulations for my mastery of the subject. Oh, I would be so very happy, the happiness coming out of me naturally like the thread out of a spider. But alas! Someone, my mother-in-law mostly, would see me in this joyous state and yell harshly at me, bringing me back to cruel reality, as though a storm or an earthquake had struck me. Anytime I indulged in this innocent passion of mine, I would be snapped out of my joyful state with cruelty and indifference. The same dreadful thing would happen every single time. I felt destroyed and horribly defeated."

Aunt Kamal looked at my mother and started sobbing, and my mother started crying silently with her, too. They both got up from the sofa in the living room and went into the bedroom. I presumed Mother wanted Aunt Kamal to lie down on the bed for a few minutes, because she was looking quite exhausted. I was disappointed that I was going to miss their further conversation. But soon after, my mother called me to take some fruits and a glass of water for Aunt Kamal. I jumped at the opportunity to be with them and hear their conversation again.

"My husband never relaxed his position," I heard Aunt Kamal telling my mother when I entered with a couple of *musombies*[30] and a glass of water as mother had asked me. "He was too insecure in his manhood to allow me to pursue my education or any of my dreams

---

30 *Green in color and similar to oranges in size and shape, musombies are tropical citrus fruits, usually given to a weak or sick person for gaining strength.*

I had. I stopped requesting his permission to pursue education, or to at least understand my aspirations, but still, my desire must have been expressed in some way, on my face or in my behavior, because he said to me one day, "I wish you were not my wife—I wish I had a *normal* woman as my wife." I could not believe what I heard. At the first impact of it, I thought he meant he hated me and wished he never married me. But after much thought, I realized that he felt that way because of his own limitations. And to hide them, he was exercising his superiority over me that he had gained by being my husband. He is a sorry man, protecting his false self-image of power. Vimal, I became so fearful for a while thinking that my marriage was at stake. My husband had a great facility for living illusions; being a man, he could justify it all. What if he and his parents sent me back to my parents, disowning me altogether? What would I do? How would I face society? Worse still, how would my parents face society? What would they do?"

Aunt Kamal started crying again, in bouts. My mother gently stroked her forehead and asked her to sit up and have some water. Aunt Kamal had a few sips of water and continued. "My fear turned into depression. I have given up hope now, completely given up. I have stopped talking, or even thinking, about my education. There is no desire left in me for anything that I want in this life, really. This life is going to be one long journey of total drudgery and depression for me. But I am still hanging on to my dreams though. Who knows, my dreams may just come true in my next life, right, Vimal?"

Aunt Kamal looked so innocent at that point, almost like a child asking for some assurance. Mother nodded to her and gestured me to peel the *musombies* for Aunt Kamal. After a minute or two, when she ate a few pieces of the fruit, Aunt Kamal looked a little better. It was hard to say if it was the fruit or her dream of the next life that had done the trick. She finished the fruit, and after giving my mother a long hug, left.

Aunt Kamal and her whole family left the city soon after. Aunt Kamal used to send us letters from her new city regularly. They were very beautifully written, with skillful narrations about anything that she came across in her new city. The letters were a source of delight to our family. There were group readings of these letters. Sometimes Aunt Kamal used to draw really funny and descriptive sketches. My father would tease my mother, saying, "Vimal, looks like your friend has entered her second childhood."

"Well, at least she is trying to be happy..." A slight annoyance from my mother was expected. "You know that this letter writing is a sort of therapy for her, don't you?" Then, with a deep sigh and her eyes rolled to the sky, she would say, "Only if Kamal were in an advanced country like America or Canada, she wouldn't have to resort to such crude methods of therapy. She would get expert psychiatric care for her depression."

Before my departure for Canada, my parents had arranged a big send-off party with all our friends and extended family. It was a big event. Their daughter was flying to a far-off country in the Western Hemisphere for advanced education, and that too with immigration papers. 'My daughter is going to Canada, a country of liberty and opportunity', as my father told with pride to everybody who came to meet me prior to leaving. I could feel his pride.

My mother wrote about my leaving for Canada to Aunt Kamal, insisting on her presence at the party. My mother had to beg Aunt Kamal's husband and other members in her family to let her go for just a day. They must have given in to my mother's insistence because Aunt Kamal did come. When she saw me, she almost suffocated me in her loving hug. In her hug, I got a lungful of her characteristic smell, that of coconut oil and masala, and I felt very good.

"Neila, you have really grown now! Looking like a young and con-fident woman! And now, you are flying to Canada! How wonderful!" She gave her usual, hearty laugh. I saw her gold tooth sparkle, and that made me feel very good too. "You are bright and you are well raised by my friend here. I am sure you will pursue further education and make a name for yourself and your family. I am so happy for you, my love!"

She went on and on, constantly reminding me to focus on edu-cation and pursue further studies in Canada. Her enthusiasm had remained the same, and so had her loving nature, and a hearty laugh that went with her nature. But her physical appearance had changed drastically. We saw that her thick black hair was all grayed and thinned out, and her loving face was all wrinkled. She looked prematurely old. We couldn't believe our eyes; however, no one said anything, not even my mother. We were happy that she could come and see us.

I flew to Canada almost immediately after the sendoff party, as planned. The sudden transition from my home in India to a new place with its totally different culture and ways of life proved to be a tremendous shock to me. The excitement and thrill of flying to a new country wore out rather too quickly, and reality struck hard. It took me some time to recover from the culture shock. It took a lot of effort on my part to assimilate in the new lifestyle of the new country, and I felt homesick all the time. I wanted to quit everything in Canada and fly back to India. It was a trying time indeed.

However, slowly and steadily, my new lifestyle started becoming a routine. I felt that it was time to look forward to some planning and preparation for the pursuit of my dreams. All this intense activity and emotion of getting adjusted to the new environment, had left no room for thoughts of Aunt Kamal, until I received her letter in my mail one day. It was a very long and beautiful letter. She wrote,

"After you flew to Canada, I smuggled in some literature on Canada and read it. I took special interest in reading about the social structure and conditions of women there. Personal independence and freedom are the main priorities there, aren't they? No citizen of that country ever faces repression. I was fascinated to read about freedom for all human beings, women included."

She wrote in detail about what she read in the brochures and other pieces of literature she had found on Canada. Then the mood of the letter seemed to change. She wrote,

"Lately, I had become a little suspicious of my own self, thinking I was abnormal in wanting to be free, but after reading about Canada and her free society, I realized that wanting to be free is intrinsic to *all* human beings; and that being forever repressed and denied is actually what is abnormal. I felt good that Canada lets her people be free, all of them, not just men. I felt bad that India does not. If only I were to be born in Canada. My dreams wouldn't have been trampled beneath the oppression of our old ways."

She continued further, writing, "No traditions are waiting to kill the personalities of women in Canada. I was awed to read about women's forcefulness. The basic right to freedom allows even the *women* citizens to blossom and bear fruit there. I shall pray to God that I may be reborn in Canada in my next life, where all my dreams will be fulfilled and I shall live like a person and not like a mere two-legged, faceless mammal of a female kind."

Her letter deeply disturbed me. I could feel her pain so acutely. I had every desire to reply to her, and give additional information about the life in Canada and a few other things that she would have liked to read. But I never did write to her. Instead, I sent her a couple of post-cards of Canada's grandeur, like the beautiful Niagara Falls and the Canadian Rockies, with brief notes. Eventually Aunt Kamal's letter went to the back of my mind. And so did any thoughts about her.

A year or so later, a letter came from my mother that struck me to my soul. The letter said, "Having no strength left to bear her husband's sarcasm and being badgered in her own home by her in-laws, and worst of all, despairing over the loss of her hopes to pursue education and the passion of literature, your Aunt Kamal finally gave up and took her own life by setting herself on fire."

My mother had become very emotional towards the end of this letter. "My childhood friend, a friend of almost fifty years, with her simple love for the luminous beauty of education and literature, who struggled all her life to remain close to her field of interest, finally found a way out, the only way she could find, and that was to end her life! She surrendered to death."

I was holding the invitation to Natalie's funeral in my hand. Aunt Kamal's life was almost a mirror image of Natalie's life. Natalie had even used the same words my mother used to describe Aunt Kamal's death. They were resounding loudly in my ears, to a point of almost deafening me.

I put the card under my desk phone, held my head with my hands, and shook it rather hard. Any attempt to regain my physical or mental balance was in vain. I sat there, completely numb.

The day was practically over, and dim orange light was coming in through the window. I propped my head on my left hand and absent-mindedly started spinning the small globe I kept on my desk. My own reflection shone clearly on its glossy surface.

However, it was not *my* profile, nor was it *my* face that I saw. It was the profile and face of a plain, non-descript woman. From the Old World of India to this New World of Canada, the reflection of this woman and her unsmiling visage was one and the same, absolutely unchanged.

I don't remember how long I sat there, in that position, alone, spinning the globe endlessly and looking at that unchanged visage of a woman.

Epilogue

Both Natalie and Aunt Kamal, as we know, are in Heaven.

Perhaps they are waiting for an answer to their genuine question, one that tortured them and made them terminate their lives prematurely; they had both posed a question that I heard from them many-a-time: when God creates all humans to be equal and withholds love from no one, why do some people, especially men, think they are superior to others, especially women?

Wouldn't this be ignorance of the biggest kind?

In a Promised Land

Her full name is Akkinini Kondai Arathi Luckshmi Rao. It is a customary practice in her village in India to have a long list of names, she tells everyone. Fortunately in Canada, she goes by only the last two of her series of names, making Luckshmi the first name and Rao the last one. Some playfully call her "A.K.A. Luckshmi Rao." She didn't get it at first, but once she became familiar with English the *Canadian* way, she got the joke.

Luckshmi is of average Indian height, about five feet tall, with a shiny, dark brown complexion. She has big, beautiful eyes with long lashes and thin eyebrows that line the shape of her eyes. Bright white teeth complement her full mouth, and they seem to sparkle when she laughs heartily. One glance at her reveals that she is a charming young woman with a pretty face.

I met Luckshmi Rao when I was teaching English to the new immigrants through the Indian Immigrant Aid Society in Toronto, during my graduate study days at the university. All the students in my class were immigrant women from India (usually referred to as 'women' rather than students), and knew only Hindi, the national language of India. I would do most of the explanation in Hindi, and then try to translate everything slowly in English. Occasionally I would come across someone who didn't know Hindi either, which could cause some problems in communication. Fortunately, I was functionally fluent in a few regional languages of India, which helped me in teaching English as well as creating a friendly and congenial environment in the class. It also helped in encouraging many of them to open up and talk about their personal lives in Canada as new immigrants.

One such woman was Luckshmi, who was enrolled in my class for learning English. I read about her in the application form. The form said that she came from a small village in India, and knew only her mother tongue. The name of her mother tongue was not mentioned in the form. When I read this, I was a bit concerned about how I would communicate with her, but the problem was solved immediately when I found out that she came from a village in a province called Andhra Pradesh; her mother tongue was Telugu, the official language of that province. As luck would have it, I was born and raised in Hyderabad, the capital city of the same province.

Hyderabad was one of the major education and business centers in South India for many decades, with people from all regions of India coming there for higher studies and better prospects. Many of them had made Hyderabad their settling place, and had developed knowledge about each other's cultures and regional languages since historical times. My parents also came from North India and settled in Hyderabad for better opportunities; we children picked up many languages from other regions of India while growing up there. Telugu was not my mother tongue, but being the official language of that province, I learnt it through my schooling. My fluency in Telugu made Luckshmi feel comfortable in the English classes, and with my help, she started participating in the open discussions with others.

It was during such *opening up* sessions that Luckshmi developed a kinship with me, eventually sharing her entire personal story with me. It was then that I came to know that she had faced horrific situation when she had newly landed in Canada. However, she had faced it with strength and a positive attitude, and conquered it. I found her story bizarre, and quite sad too, but fortunately it ended on a happy note, mainly because of her abilities and boundless mental strength which I observed in her over a short time. Her personal encounters in the first few years after landing in Canada had made her a little defiant and formidable, but at the same time, she was very hard working and well-focused. As she herself had put it later, "That period gave me reason enough to have a strong determination to set high goals in my life, and to work hard to reach them."

I heard her full story when I visited her one evening at her request. Her husband, who was fluent in English, was also present, and together they narrated it to me. Their earnest narration during that evening was so touching that their story remained with me for a long time.

One evening, after finishing the English class, I started walking home. It was not really late, but it seemed so as it got darker than usual because of the clouds gathering in the sky. I could see the rain on the horizon, and the clouds looked like they would burst and empty themselves any minute. So, instead of indulging in small talk with the women after the class, which was my usual habit, I hurriedly gathered my stuff and started rushing home. I was walking really fast when I heard a faint holler of my name. I didn't turn around, although I could very well recognize that it was Luckshmi calling me. I should have stopped, but instead I blatantly ignored her calling and raised my own speed of walking. She must have started running, for she caught up with me in a few minutes. I had no choice but to stop and pretend that I didn't hear her.

"I have brought some *upma*[31] for you, ma'am. You left immediately after our class so I couldn't give it to you there." Luckshmi said in her broken English mixed with Telugu, while trying to catch her breath. She was holding a small plastic box.

"Oh, you didn't have to do that." I looked at her and then at the plastic box.

"Please take it. I prepared it this afternoon. It is freshly made." She reverted back to Telugu, while handing me the plastic box.

"No really. It's alright. I really don't want it." And I started walking again. I didn't know why I was so incredibly rude to her.

"Remember when you were talking to me about Hyderabad? You said that you loved upma made in the Hyderabad style, so I prepared

---

31 *Upma is a spicy dish prepared with cream of wheat as the base. It is a favorite breakfast food for the people of South India.*

it in that style and brought some for you." She sounded so innocent. She had started walking side by side with me.

"Oh, alright! Thank you." She looked quite happy when I, although reluctantly, took that little box of upma from her hands.

"Yes, I do remember telling you once that eating upma and then sipping a good cup of strong coffee was almost like a rule in Hyderabad." I said. I had to say something to cover up my initial rudeness.

"Yes, and you can follow that rule here too," she said with a smile.

"What do you mean?"

"Here, here in Canada, at my place," she said.

"Oh no, no, no thanks, I was only joking." I wasn't aware at all that this is how she would respond to my casual remark.

"No really, ma'am, please come to my place for upma and coffee now," she said again.

"Now? But, but, it is so late now, how can I come to your place now?" I was surprised at her invitation.

"If you have some spare time now, please come right now, I will make a fresh pot of coffee in Hyderabad style to go with this upma, and after our coffee, Narayan will walk you home." It looked like she had already made a plan for my visit to her home that evening.

"Narayan, who is he?" I knew that Narayan was a man's name in India.

"Narayan is my husband. We live very close from here, very close to the university, just like you do. He is taking some night courses there. This night is his night off. Actually, every week he does that so that I could enroll in the English class at the Society. So, please come home for coffee right now, ma'am." Looking very honest, she spoke very fast in Telugu, except for the last sentence, which she said in English—or the *Canadian* language, as the women called English, making me smile at her attempt!

I thought for a minute. A plate of spicy upma with a hot cup of coffee in Hyderabad style was tempting, no doubt. However, I wasn't sure if I should accept her invitation. That meant getting a little too close to the students whom I taught at the Society. But then, this woman was a little different from the rest, as she was from the same province as I was in India. Whatever the reason, I honored her request and started walking with her to her home.

The drizzle had started already and it was raining the whole time we were walking to Luckshmi's place. It wasn't the tropical monsoon rain that I was used to in India. The rain in India was warm, dense and it would come down like thick drapes, drenching you in seconds with not just water but with its warmth as well. It would make you feel that nature has embraced you yet one more time. This rain, a typical Canadian rain, was more like a sprinkle, a sprinkle of chilling, cold water with almost no personality of its own. I always questioned if this rain could ever feed the trees or wash the lush green grass adequately.

It didn't wet us much when we arrived at her doorstep. The door was unlocked. Obviously Narayan was expecting her. She opened the door and let both of us in. She took my jacket, shook it to get rid of the rain droplets, and hung it neatly on a small rack kept near the door.

"Narayan, we are home," she called out in Telugu. The *we* part must have made him curious because he came into the front room immediately.

"Please meet my English teacher from the Society." She introduced me to him. He smiled and held his both hands at his chest, joining the palms in a *Namaste* position, and so did I, with a smile. Narayan looked very pleasant and almost similar to Luckshmi in his looks. He had the same type of skin color and complexion, the same type of facial structure, and his height must be a little more than five feet to match hers. He was wearing a typical white Indian suit made of cotton, called *jhabba-pajama*. I was used to seeing men wearing that suit all the time in India, since it was not necessarily a nighttime dress meant only for sleeping.

"She is also from Hyderabad, *your* city in India. And she is a graduate student in science at the university. Can you believe it?" Luckshmi sounded like she was quite proud of me. And I felt happy to learn that Narayan was also from Hyderabad, same like me.

"Where in Hyderabad did you live?" I asked him.

"In the Sultan Bazaar area. And where did you live, ma'am?" he asked me politely.

"In Barkat Pura; my parents still live there," I answered.

The moment he heard the area's name, he said, "That's a wonderful area, with only bungalows surrounded by tall trees, not like the concrete jungle of tall apartment buildings you see in the Sultan Bazaar area. And it is very close to the university too, right?"

I nodded with a smile.

"Please, have a seat, ma'am." Narayan pointed to a sofa chair. I took a couple of steps to the sofa chair and sat down. I looked around. It was a small room with two sofa chairs facing each other, a small coffee table in between them, and a huge desk and a chair in one corner of the room. The desk was holding a big stack of papers, an old manual typewriter, and some pens and pencils. I saw a couple of engineering books lying on one side of the table. A small black-and-white television set was placed on a small table at an angle to the two sofa chairs. Obviously this room was meant to be their living room, family room and study room, too. I could see, from where I was sitting, a small passage leading inside, perhaps to the kitchen or to the bedroom. The walls of the front room were decorated with wall hangings, pictures, family photographs, and an Indian calendar, cumulatively all creating a very homey atmosphere.

"How is Damini?" Luckshmi asked Narayan in Telugu.

"She is alright, fast asleep now." Narayan answered her in Telugu and then looked at me and said, in English, "That's our daughter, she is two years old."

"Oh, you have a daughter, how nice." I looked at Luckshmi and said it with a smile. She just nodded with a smile.

"Damini means lightning, right?" I asked.

"Yes, that's right. Like we say in South India, lightning is a 'goodwill gesture' straight from the heavens! Damini is our happiness and bliss. We found out about Luckshmi's conception just as we entered Canada for better life. That's when we decided, if it's a girl, we would name her Damini! She was born to us at a time when we were…" Narayan started saying something in a rather serious tone, when Luckshmi interrupted him.

"Not right now, right now, only upma and hot coffee." Perhaps she could guess from his serious tone what he was going to say, and did not want him to talk about it. She made an attempt to ask him in English, "Narayan, you want coffee?" He nodded with a smile. I could see a streak of admiration in his smile for her attempt at speaking in English.

"Do you need my help?" he asked her. I was impressed with his attitude and his offer to help his wife, something that was rare amongst Indian husbands. She gestured *no* and went inside. He sat on the chair in front of me and started a conversation.

"Which college did you attend in Hyderabad, ma'am?"

"I went to the Nizam College for my undergraduate degree. How about you?"

"I went to the engineering college in Warangal; five years I was there," he answered politely.

"So you are a graduate of Warangal Engineering College! That's excellent."

He looked pleased that I had heard of that college and its reputation. He nodded happily.

"What branch of engineering did you study there, if I may ask?" I asked him.

"Yes, yes, of course. I was in the faculty of Chemical Engineering there. That makes me a chemical engineer by training, but I wish to develop skills in engineering management here in Canada. I am currently taking some night courses in the management faculty at the university here." His voice was full of politeness when he was speaking.

"Luckshmi told me about you," I said.

"Luckshmi told me about you too, ma'am. She feels so proud of you that, in spite of you being an immigrant woman from India, you are single and a full time graduate student here in Canada. That sure is something." I could see some admiration on his face.

"What do you mean, 'an immigrant woman?'" I found that intriguing.

"Well, I have never seen single women from good Indian families coming here alone and enrolling in the graduate schools, or for any other higher studies. All of them come here as wives. Plus, you are an *immigrant,* unlike most of the Indian students at the university, who are here on student visas." What he said was absolutely true.

"Well, my good fortune, I suppose." I was genuinely thankful for the opportunities and for the tremendous parental support I had. As Narayan put it rightly, women came to Canada only as young brides of men, who were either immigrants of Canada and had gone back for a quick trip to get married to them, or occasionally, who were about to get their immigration. Seldom did women of my generation have the opportunity to immigrate to a foreign land by themselves; and even rarer was any of them joining the graduate school for advanced degrees in a Canadian university.

"Did you have to write any qualifying examinations for getting into the graduate school here, ma'am?" he asked me.

"Yes, of course! No university or college in Canada admits foreign students unless they write the required exams and qualify themselves. As a rule, nothing ever is available for you unless you pay its full price, isn't it?" I threw a general, somewhat motherly statement at him, and he nodded with a smile. Just then, Luckshmi walked in with three cups of hot coffee, and three plates filled with upma. The room was filled with the delicious aroma of the food. She offered Narayan and me a plate of upma and a cup of coffee each, and took the third plate and cup for herself. She pulled a chair that was next to the desk and sat on it. We started eating right away without much talk. The only sound in the room was that of our chewing.

"This is absolutely delicious! Straight from the kitchen in Hyderabad—wow!" I said a few minutes later.

"Luckshmi is a good cook. I really enjoy her cooking." Narayan complimented her immediately after my compliment, and repeated it in Telugu for her to understand.

"Thank you, thank you very much." Luckshmi felt good.

"She is a very smart woman." Narayan started praising his wife, without bothering to translate in Telugu. "However, she didn't get an opportunity to study after high school. She grew up in a village and there was no provision for secondary education there."

"Hmm," I said. I was busy eating.

"When the matchmaker brought her proposal to my parents, they really liked her, but it was me who wasn't sure of it. This was a village girl who didn't know the urban style of living, and didn't know any other language besides Telugu. She wasn't very educated, either. I wasn't thrilled with this proposal at all. But my father was a very good judge of character. He assured me that I would be very happy with her. He was the one who told me that she was very smart; it's just that she needed an opportunity. I trusted his judgment fully. His prediction in my older brother's case had come out one hundred percent true. So I took his advice and married Luckshmi."

"And you have been very happy ever since, right?" I asked.

"Yes, yes indeed! Initially I had this fear that we didn't have much compatibility between us, and we did face a few problems because of it. But I tell you, they were nothing compared to what we faced when we were newly arrived in Canada. It was like huge waves of problems were drowning us, some of them of a gross nature, but no problem ever became too big to handle. Thank God for Luckshmi—because of her complete support, we overcame them. My fear of incompatibility vanished in no time."

It was good to see Narayan being so honest and straightforward in talking about his wife. However, I felt a little awkward to hear him talk so frankly with me on the very first day of our meeting. I requested him to speak in English, and if needed, also to translate some of it in Telugu, so that Luckshmi can participate in our conversation. That was my effort in minimizing my own feeling of embarrassment.

"Okay ma'am. I must say, you are a good and caring teacher. No wonder she praises you all the time." I saw an expression of appreciation on his face.

"Oh, one more thing, now that we all are in Canada, will you please call me by my first name? Let's cut that Indian custom of addressing women with ma'am, shall we?"

"Ok, ma'am, I mean Neila. You are right." He smiled.

"So, how did you come to Canada?" I asked casually, looking at Luckshmi.

"Sponsorship!" she said, displaying pride that she understood what I had asked in English.

"My older brother sponsored me, and I sponsored Luckshmi as my wife," Narayan started explaining, "My brother lives in another province in Canada."

"Oh, so he is not here inOntario" I asked, looking at Luckshmi, trying to pull her into our conversation.

"No, Quebec." Luckshmi answered.

"Where in Quebec, in Montreal?" This was the only place I knew of in that province.

"Very close to Montreal, in Lachine. But within a year, we moved here. No one knows us here, we know no one. And I feel that that's good, for that is helping us know more about Canada, and assimilate better into the Canadian society." Narayan looked at me with anticipation, and when I smiled at him, he smiled back as though I had given him an approval for such a feeling. He continued: "When I finished my Engineering studies, I expressed my desire to immigrate to Canada. My father was reluctant and didn't like the idea of both his sons living outside India, but then I convinced him. Finally he agreed, but also requested that I get married first before immigrating to Canada."

"Your father *requested* this of you?"

"Yes, he requested"

"What a good man." I knew that Indian men and women in that age group always *demanded* their children get married whenever *they* desired, especially if the children were to leave their hometowns.

"Yes! My father was a sensitive man. He was not very well educated, but he was a wise man. He was instrumental in selecting Luckshmi for me." Narayan then looked at his wife and said, "He was the one who judged her and assured me that she would be a great life partner for me." Narayan explained all this to Luckshmi in Telugu. She obviously liked it, because she was smiling.

"Yes, I remember you saying earlier that he was a good judge of character." I actually wanted to ask him about his brother who lived in Quebec, but this would have been too soon.

"Yes, my father was a very good judge of character! Look at the girl he selected for me. In just two and a half years, Luckshmi has managed to know everything about this city—and without knowing the local language. Just give her a couple more years with training in English, and she will do even better." I saw Narayan looking at his wife with a proud face.

"Initially I thought of teaching English to her myself, but then I changed my mind. It would be better if she learnt it in a methodical way. That is why I encouraged her to enroll with the Society. There, she could learn not just the language, but everything about Canada too. That way, she could assimilate with this society and be a part of this culture."

"Yes, yes indeed!" How true it was! How true it is so, even today! Once you know the language of any given place, it gets so much easier to move around and connect with the local people and develop an affinity to that place. And once that happens, you automatically develop a *sense of belonging* to that place. I was genuinely happy to see Narayan's positive approach towards Canada.

"That is why I arranged my night courses so that I am there to babysit Damini. This way, Luckshmi can go to the Society to learn English," he said.

"Oh, I see. Yes, Luckshmi told me so."

"Once Luckshmi knows English, she can learn to do something else too, like take some vocational courses to make herself employable and all that, right?"

I nodded.

"She is emotionally quite strong; I am going to encourage her to be financially strong and independent too."

"Yes, absolutely, how thoughtful of you." He liked my compliment and immediately translated this to Luckshmi.

"Narayan is a good man," Luckshmi said. It was refreshing to see a young couple from India—a couple who had an arranged marriage—being so supportive of each other.

"You mentioned Luckshmi being *emotionally* strong, but I think Luckshmi is genuinely a happy person."

"Yes, she is happy. She is a happy and loving person with a very positive attitude towards life. But we went through hell when we arrived here, ma'am, as I told you earlier." Narayan said this and turned to Luckshmi to translate all this to her, but she just waved with her right hand and said, "I know, I know what you want to say." Then she quickly gestured to him and started sipping her coffee quietly. He was quiet for a minute, and then turned to me and said, "Luckshmi doesn't wish to bother you with our personal story. Besides, you may not have that much time either."

"Well, time may not be the concern here. The real concern would be *you* feeling comfortable sharing it with me." Having said this, I started sipping my coffee slowly. The coffee felt really good. With the cold winds howling outside and the drizzle of the rain, hot coffee was the most welcome thing at the moment. Everyone was quiet, sipping their coffee silently.

Luckshmi and Narayan looked at each other and said something fast, and then laughed at the coincidence of talking at the same time. Whatever I got from their fast talk, they had decided to share their personal story with me that evening. Narayan looked at me and said, "We would like to tell you what happened to us, Neila, because we have never told it to anyone thus far. Not even to my parents or her parents in India. It would be like unloading a big burden from our shoulders. Is that okay with you?"

I just nodded.

"It is too much, just too much." I noticed Luckshmi put her plate and mug down on the table, and then cross her arms across her chest, lightly slapping both her cheeks with opposite hands, a few times. As I observed her doing this, I knew exactly what type of sentiments she was expressing. During my childhood in India, I had observed it occasionally among many elderly people, especially women, and even among servants in my parent's house; whenever they wished to express disgust or fear or extreme repugnance for something very offensive, they would do such an action. Watching Luckshmi do that, I got an idea of what sort of personal story I was going to hear from Narayan. I kept quiet as intrigue clouded my thoughts. Narayan started telling their story.

"The first two years after our arrival in Canada were absolutely horrible, as I mentioned earlier, it was pure hell. We don't wish such times upon anyone. You see, it so happened that after my graduation from the Engineering college—which I did with excellent marks—I wanted to start working, but my father suggested I should pursue further studies. He was very proud of me, for I was the first one from my entire family to get a degree in engineering. 'You are still quite young Narayan. Don't join the work force as yet,' he said. 'Pursue further studies, get some advanced degree, and then look for employment,' he said. I thought that was a very good idea, so I started applying to every good school in India as well as abroad."

"I used to call it 'abroad' too when I was applying to schools in Canada and the US," I inadvertently said to Narayan. I suddenly got quiet, realizing my interruption. He nodded with a smile and continued. "My older brother was already in Canada. He had barely managed to finish his high school graduation when he ended up marrying a, uh… marrying a, uh…woman. I really don't know what to call her." He faltered a bit.

"Why, what's wrong with her?"

"I think everything. She was the type that I don't think any man from a respectable family would marry."

"Oh, wow."

"Yes. She's much older than him, and to add to it, I don't know what is uglier, her physical appearance or her inner self."

"Oh my God."

"I don't wish to describe her, for it is so wrong of me to do so to another man's wife, even if that man is my older brother. But when Ram, that's my older brother, declared his intentions of marrying this woman, my whole family, especially my parents, were completely devastated. Just imagine, a very docile man, my brother, barely in his twenties, wanting to marry a woman who must be closer to forty years of age and very rough in behavior. She held absolutely no dignity or respect in society. Obviously, many people knew about her background, because relatives from my extended family started calling my parents, asking about the news of my brother marrying this Surpanakha[32], as some referred to her. Her name is Surekha."

---

32 *Surpanakha is a character in India's famous epic called* **Ramayana**. *Surpanakha was an ugly, demonic female character who approached prince Ram for his hand in marriage; since he was already married, he refused her proposal and directed her to his younger brother Lakshman.*

"Oh my God, really?" I knew the story of Surpanakha from the Ramayana epic quite well. Most of the Indians did. Prince Ram had directed this female to his younger brother as per the epic. Quoting that, I asked him with a jest, "Then why didn't Ram direct this Surpanakha to you, his younger brother?"

"Thank God for that. I am Ram's younger brother, yes, but I'm not Lakshman, I am Narayan," he answered back with a smile. He quickly turned serious and said, "Besides, in this case, Ram himself was interested in marrying her. My parents were simple people. Although totally flabbergasted with this news, they never uttered a 'boo' against it to Ram; if anything, they tried to speak well of her to all our relatives, but I knew very well that, deep down, they were full of grief when Ram married her. I overheard my mother telling someone, just once, that it was Ram's big *paap* in his last life that made him marry a woman like Surekha in this life. Mother totally believed in karma and reincarnation. My father also never uttered a word about this marriage, except just once to me in privacy that Ram would never be happy and would never have a peaceful life with this woman as his wife. They held their silence ever since."

Narayan waited for a few minutes, quietly looking at Luckshmi.

"It was not just her age, unfavorable physical appearance, or rough behavior, but her family background, too. Ours was a small community, and everyone in that community was suspicious about it. They would frequently gossip about it with all kinds of allegations. She was, according to them, a woman of easy virtue, and had many regular 'clients,' if you know what I mean. In that 'work,' she trapped my brother, who was obviously one of her 'clients,' into marrying her." Under the pretense of wiping his forehead, Narayan turned his head downward and held it there for a few seconds. It became clear that he was feeling awkward to say so about his brother.

From what I heard so far about his brother's wife, not only was she much older than Ram (almost twice his age, which could not fly well with his family, nor could it with any other traditional family in

---

However, Lakshman knew that she was a demon incarnate, so he cut her nose and sent her away. Known to be an ugly demonic woman, she stands for all such characteristics in females, according to Indian people.

India), she was also a woman of dubious character. This was a much more serious matter especially when the principles governing behavior and thoughts about morality were fairly rigidly defined. There was no room for acceptance or accommodation of women like her in respectable families who had their values (which were prevalent at the time in Indian society) unquestioned or unchallenged. Even in the forward-thinking West, I could say with certainly that a match between two such people would be almost non-existent; such a union would not fit into the 'norm' of the society. It was not a question of any one particular family's values or traditions; it was true for all in the society.

"Everyone that we knew was puzzled about this marriage. I am really sorry I am giving you an unnecessary account of Ram's life here, but believe me, all this bears a valid context to our personal story as to what happened after we came to Canada," he said in an apologetic tone.

Narayan looked at me for a minute and continued. "Hardly a month must have passed after their wedding when Ram received a letter from the Canadian embassy saying that his application for immigration had been approved and that he was to leave for Canada with his wife. This was news to everybody. No one had the slightest idea of his intentions of going to Canada until then. I still remember the day when he walked in my father's room and gave him the news. I was talking with my father about something. Ram walked in the room and said that he wanted to talk to my father privately. I was about to leave the room when my father gestured me to stay back.

"Ram had no choice but to talk to father in my presence. 'Appa, I am leaving for Canada,' he said with his face down, in a tone as if he had committed some crime. Appa, that's what we called our father, looked startled.

"'When?' Appa asked Ram while trying to conceal his surprise.

"'Next week,' Ram said, his face still downward.

"'Next week? So soon?' Appa looked even more surprised.

"'Yes.' Ram answered.

"Appa was quiet for a moment, as though he was gathering his thoughts to put them together articulately. Then he said, 'Tell me the truth now, Rami. Did you know about all this *before* you got married?'

"Appa was looking calmer now, for some strange reason.

"'Yes...' Ram said. He looked flustered.

"'Look at me Rami—is that *why* you married Surekha?'

"Ram just nodded.

"Then Appa asked him, 'Did you visit her any time before you decided to marry her, Rami? And you know exactly what I mean...'

"Ram nodded.

"'And did she make an offer to you, Rami, that should you marry her, she would help you go outside the country, somewhere in the West? Is that it?'

"Ram nodded again.

"And then Appa said, 'Tell me everything, Rami,' and just sat quietly with his eyes fixed on him.

"Ram, after a few nervous moments, said, 'She told me that she knew someone.'

"'In her clientele, is that it?' Appa abruptly asked him and became quiet again, listening.

"'Uh...yes, I guess. So, she knew someone who could help both of us to go to Canada. But that offer would be there only if I married her.' Ram was talking to Appa, looking down and continuously wiping his forehead with a handkerchief. He looked extremely nervous. I shall never forget this conversation for as long as I live. It must be so very difficult for a father to hear his son telling him directly that the son went to a prostitute and took some favors from her for his benefit.

"'So, in essence, you sold yourself so that you could go to Canada, is that it Rami? Tell me the truth.'

"This was like a blow to Ram, I could see, but it must be a bigger blow to Appa in my judgment.

"Ram nodded again, and he looked like being almost on the verge of tears.

"I was feeling very uncomfortable to be standing there, but I had no choice. Appa didn't say anything for a few moments. The room was filled with thick air and dead silence. Then Appa removed a gold ring with a huge yellow stone from his finger, gave it to Ram and said, 'My father gave me this ring for eternal happiness, and now I give it to you. Be happy, my son; never forget your family values that we raised you with.'

"He turned his head and gestured Ram to leave the room. He then asked me to give him his towel that was lying on the headboard of his bed, and gestured to me to leave the room also, and to close the door behind me. While giving the towel to him, I saw tears running down both his cheeks. I knew why he needed a towel—it was soon going to be drenched with his tears. While closing the door behind me gently, I heard him mumble to himself, '*Panduranga*[33], I failed him as a father, but you look after him now,' followed by a deep, pain-filled sob.

"Ram and his wife left for Canada within a week. He never wrote to any of us, nor did he keep in touch with any of us. Appa never even once mentioned Ram's name after he left for Canada. My mother, who was especially fond of my older brother, used to say, 'Ram was like a passing dream for twenty-two years, and then the dream suddenly turned into a nightmare and then vanished forever.' I used to feel very sad for both my parents."

Narayan took a long sigh, and became very quiet. Luckshmi and I also became very quiet, just staring at him.

"How did you manage to get Ram's sponsorship with this kind of background?" I asked, breaking the silence.

"I am sorry, I get so emotional anytime I think of all this. I am really sorry, but let me continue. I decided to pursue further studies in Canada and went to my father for his blessings and encouragement, when he voluntarily told me, 'Narayan, get me Ram's address and I will write to him for calling you there.' I wanted to negate him on this, but I knew my father very well. I managed to locate Ram's address in Canada. You won't believe this, Neila, but I honestly cannot imagine, to this very day, what made Ram sponsor me to come to Canada. It has been a mystery to me, even today. Equally intriguing was what Appa must have written to him in his letter that forced Ram to sponsor me. Anyways, I got the sponsorship from

---

33 *Name of a Hindu Deity.*

Ram, and as soon as I got it, I applied for immigration, and decided to leave immediately for Canada."

"I marry you first," Luckshmi said with a smile. She was obviously able to follow him so far, although he was narrating the story in English.

"Yes, you are right, Luckie." Narayan looked at her, smiled and then turned his head towards me to continue the story.

"When I decided to leave for Canada, my parents requested me that I get married first. I agreed. My parents were extremely hurt with Ram's marriage, so I had decided to marry a girl of their choice. As I told you earlier, my father chose Luckshmi for me as the suitable girl; we got married and came together to Canada."

"And, where was that, initially?" I asked him.

"We landed in Montreal, and then took a cab to my brother's house in Lachine, Quebec. We were his responsibility, as per the immigration laws. In short, we went from my parent's home to..."

"Surpanakha's house." Luckshmi completed Narayan's sentence with an emphasis on the distorted name of Ram's wife and giggled.

"Luckie, don't be childish, okay?" Narayan, suddenly angry, yelled at her in a voice that startled her and made her nervous. This was more in reaction to her remark, but she felt insulted. She hastily got up from her chair, picked up her plate and coffee mug, and marched inside. He also picked up his plate and mug and started following her. I could overhear their heated conversation; she sounded quite upset and he was trying to pacify her.

I didn't know what to do while they were inside. *This must be a typical husband-wife thing,* I concluded, and got up and walked to the window with coffee mug in my hand. I looked outside. It was dark. I definitely needed someone to walk with me to the residence. So I waited patiently, sipping coffee and hoping they would end their 'tiff' soon so that Narayan could walk me home as promised.

A little while later, they both came outside, profusely apologizing for leaving me alone in the front room. Luckshmi looked like she had shed a few tears.

"We both get very edgy when we think of all this. It invariably leads to those memories of the gruesome experiences we both had to face at that time," Narayan said.

"It is getting quite late now, so I suggest we should talk about all this some other time, if you don't mind," I said to Narayan.

"No ma'am. I'll finish up the story shortly. I just want to get it out of my system, if you will. I promise you, I'll never again bring it up to anyone as long as I live. Really."

Narayan sounded like he really wanted to unload the past in that evening with me as his audience, so I concurred. "Luckshmi, can you please put another pot of fresh coffee?" he said. Then he turned to me and said, "Thanks ma'am, for being patient with us. So, as I was saying, I shudder to think of those gruesome experiences we had."

"*Gruesome* experiences? Why, what happened?" I asked.

"Quite honestly, I don't know where to begin or how to tell you, ma'am," Narayan said. He had gone back to his original way of addressing me. This was perhaps the extension of his apology for leaving me alone in the front room for few minutes, or perhaps his appreciation for my patience for agreeing to listen to his story. Whatever it was for, I didn't bother to correct him.

"Actually, that's where our gruesome experience started, in my brother's house in Lachine. It so happened that we all traveled from Hyderabad to Bombay first, and then went to the international airport. Both our mothers cried a lot at the airport. They just couldn't bear to say goodbye to us. Luckshmi herself was very sad to leave India and to travel so far away to another country. But I assured everyone that everything would be alright and that we were going to be alright. We boarded the plane to go to a totally new country, totally unaware of everything in the new country of our destination."

"Not seen a white person before," Luckshmi said, interrupting Narayan.

"What?" I looked at Luckshmi.

"Luckshmi is right. Not only was Canada new to us, but neither of us had ever seen a white person before in our lives, until we landed in one of the European airports. Luckshmi and I were sitting in the transit lounge to catch our connecting flight to Montreal. There were whole bunch of people, white people, surrounding us. We got a little apprehensive, I must admit, for we both were seeing white people for the very first time in our lives. And quite honestly, ma'am, they all looked the same to us. Now when I think of it, I feel so amused at my own folly. Luckshmi was especially interested in looking at the women, as you can guess. She was literally staring at their faces. I poked her a couple of times telling her, 'It's not polite to stare at them like that,' but honestly, so was I myself, quite bewildered to see all those white folks!" Narayan stopped and laughed at his own lack of experience of seeing white people. He continued, saying, "Luckshmi was wearing a sari, and was completely covered, whereas most of the white women in the lounge were wearing skirts or short dresses, which meant one could see their legs. I think Luckshmi had turned her gaze from their faces to their legs by now." Narayan then turned to Luckshmi and said, "Luckshmi, tell ma'am what you said to me after noticing their legs."

"No I can't…" she hesitated.

"Don't worry. Do tell, I won't laugh at you Luckshmi," I assured her, but she still shook her head and looked down at her own feet.

"Okay then, I will tell her whatever I remember. After staring at those women's legs for a long time, she turned to me and said in a low voice, 'How is it that these women have white faces and white hands, but brown or black legs?'

"Huh? What do you mean?"

"That's exactly what I said to Luckshmi when she whispered her silly question in my ears. Then I also started looking at the women's legs and wondering about their darker pigment," Narayan said.

"The nylons and stockings ma'am." Luckshmi pointed to her own legs and showed me the brown nylons she was wearing. That gave me an instant answer to my confusion. I chuckled, and so did Narayan.

He said, "We feel amused at our own ignorance now, but at that time, we didn't know anything about these things." We started laughing, and Luckshmi joined us with her hearty laugh. The earlier strain had disappeared completely with our laughter.

Narayan continued his story: "We boarded another plane and landed in Montreal. That was the very first place to touch the

Canadian soil for us. That was also the very first place for us to go through the Canadian immigration and customs. I was told that in most countries, experience with the immigration and customs officers was a formidable one, and also that the visitor or new immigrants were usually hit with a volley of questions, which many times seemed almost like an interrogation. I tell you, with all this hearsay knowledge, we were very nervous in the beginning. I knew nothing of how to answer any such questions, as I had never set my foot outside India before. Luckshmi's help was out of the question as she didn't know any foreign language. We were quite scared and we were wondering what kind of questions the officer is going to ask us. However, I must say that our experience with these Canadian authorities was excellent."

"How so?"

Narayan cleared his throat at this point and continued. "The Canadian immigration and customs officer started his questioning with a pad of papers and pencil in his hands. However, prior to asking us any questions, he pulled out a couple of chairs and told us to sit down, and offered coffee. That was our first pleasant surprise. We nervously accepted his offer and felt a little relieved. This cordiality on part of a government official, quite contrary to what I had heard earlier, was a new experience to us. Imagine a customs officer doing all this to new immigrants before the questioning process starts. I liked it a lot. I quickly turned to Luckshmi and said, 'You see, Luckie, the civility and decency of these countrymen starts right here at the border,' and she nodded, fully agreeing with me. When all the official work was completed, he stamped our passports and said, 'Welcome to Canada.' We were so happy and pleased; our hearts were filled with hope and joy. Nothing was ever going to stand in our way to happiness and prosperity, I told myself. I had brought my young wife with me and had come here with dreams in my heart and hopes in my eyes. After such a pleasant welcome, I felt sure that we were going to have wonderful prospects in this newly adopted land. I took her hands in mine and said, 'Luckie, this is what I promised you in our wedding vows, happiness and prosperity; this is what I shall deliver, in this beautiful country, Canada.'"

Narayan stopped talking and looked at his wife with a smile. She smiled back.

However, within seconds, he got a little serious and made a funny murmuring sound that resembled a laugh. I felt a sad overtone in that laugh, so I looked at Luckshmi, and saw tears in her eyes. I was puzzled.

"How little did I know, and how very wrong of me to promise this to Luckshmi!" Narayan said.

"Why do you say that?"

He was quiet for a few seconds and then said, "After the border work was over, we picked up our luggage and came outside, officially entering Canada, the first-rate nation, the envy of the world! We were very happy and ready to start our lives. We waited for my brother to meet us at the airport and take us to his place. We waited and waited for almost two hours, but my brother never showed up. Finally, I managed to make a telephone call to him. He said he was too busy to come to the airport and told us to go to his house on our own. I had no choice but to agree. We had only sixteen Canadian dollars with us because they allowed us only eight dollars per person at that time. I didn't know how much could a taxi cost, so I went to the information counter and inquired about transportation to my brother's house in Lachine, and also telling them about my difficulty. Fortunately they arranged a cab for us for only ten dollars to reach the address that I had given them. All along the cab ride, I was getting a funny feeling, almost like a bad knot in my stomach, that things were not okay, but I didn't say anything to Luckshmi.

We reached his place. It was a small, two-bedroom apartment on the third floor, and the building had no elevators. Lugging our huge suitcases all the way to the third floor was almost like an ordeal. But we did it. We stood in front of his door, took a long breath, and I gently knocked on his closed door. We were nervous like anything, a hundred times more than we were with the Canadian Customs officer. After a little while, I saw my brother opening the door. I was excited to see him after a long time, so I rushed in with a desire to give him a big hug, when I heard a command in a very dry, harsh voice,

'Get their luggage inside and close the doors first.' It was my brother's wife commanding him. I felt a bit alarmed but obeyed her command. Luckshmi and I placed our suitcases inside. My brother was just standing there while we were struggling to get the luggage inside. His wife came outside and shut the door without giving even a glance at us. I changed my mind about hugging my brother. Instead, Luckshmi and I bent down to do a *Namaskar*[34] to him and his wife, as it was a custom in my family. We could clearly see that their faces didn't look pleased at all, and there wasn't even the slightest warmth on their faces. The civility and decency we had experienced at the Canadian border had ended right there, with no trace of it in my brother's house. There was no welcome or anything even remotely close to it in their house for us. Instead, in the next few minutes, we found out that there were strict rules and regulations already set up for us. As soon as we did the Namaskar, she called us inside the kitchen and showed us the groceries kept, ready to do the cooking. She was expecting us to cook for seven people—their family of five, and we two. My brother had become a father of three children, two daughters and a son, but he had never informed anybody in my family, not even my parents. Totally perplexed and confused, Luckshmi and I just looked at each other. Ram didn't say anything at all when his wife was giving us these orders. I could see that he had absolutely no say about any-thing in his house. The reins were in his wife's hands. I came to know in just few minutes of reaching their house that she was very angry with Ram for sponsoring us to Canada, something he had never told her; and in doing so, he had clearly defied her authority. I still can recite the conversation that took place between Ram and his wife within minutes of our reaching their house from the airport. Can you believe it? The conversation went like this, 'Happy, now that your brother and his wife are here?' Surekha said to Ram, adding further, 'the expenses will soon go through the roof now. How are you plan-ning on supporting them? By selling my gold jewelry? And how long do you intend to keep them in my house?'

---

34 *In some parts of India, it is a custom to bend down and touch the feet of the elder family members when meeting for the first time. This gesture is to express utmost respect to the elders in the family.*

"'This is my house, too,' I heard Ram say as he mustered up his courage.

"'Oh, so now that your family is here, you are giving me the lip, are you?' After saying this, Surekha darted straight into their bedroom and locked the door from inside. Ram followed her and started gently knocking on the door, imploring her to open the door in a very apologetic tone. We were speechless, witnessing the whole drama in a way that we couldn't believe."

"Oh my God! Are you serious?" It was hard for me to believe what Narayan just told me. To me, even a casual guest (or even someone just a that casual guest) would get better treatment than what these two young people, a younger brother and his new bride, got from his older brother and his wife. Even more shocking was that they received this poor treatment right after they had arrived for the very first time from a far-off land, and after a very long flight.

"Yes, and the story gets worse as it goes further." Narayan cleared his throat and continued. "Luckshmi and myself didn't know what to do—should we cook as ordered or not? We had never expected any such thing to happen, not in the very first hour of our arrival, anyway. I didn't know how to cook, and although Luckshmi knew it, a Canadian kitchen was completely new to her."

"Yes, I can very well imagine." I remembered my own experiences when I saw the well-equipped kitchen in my apartment for the first time. The unfamiliarity of the whole place had confused me so much that I couldn't make simple steamed rice on my first day.

"We had never seen an electrical stove before, so we just stood there, totally dumbfounded and frustrated. We heard Surekha finally opening the door of her bedroom and coming out. She darted straight into the kitchen where we were just standing still in our frustration. She looked very angry to see that nothing was done in the kitchen. Without so much as even looking at us, she started cutting some vegetables and angrily mumbling something. When Luckshmi and I approached her with the intention of helping, she yelled at us and told us to get out of the kitchen. So we did. What else could we do anyway? Ram also came into the kitchen and just sat on a chair without uttering a single word. He didn't say anything at all, not even simple inquiry about our parents or other family members. Surekha cooked something, and as soon as their three children came home from school, we all ate quietly. There was no introduction of the children to us, or of us to the children, as though we didn't count at all. We felt like beggars in their house the entire time, begging for food and shelter." Narayan was quiet for a minute during which I heard him swallow a lump in his throat. Was he swallowing his pride too, while telling me his story?

"As soon as dinner was over, it was time for washing the dishes. Surekha yelled out my name, 'Narayan, come here!' There was such an authority in her voice, I obediently went to her. She slapped a sponge in my hands and, pointing to a bottle of dishwashing liquid, said, 'Use the soap and do the dishes. I hope you can do at least that much for us. And do not use hot water; it costs money to heat the water.' I was stunned! And I was angry, absolutely livid. Not because we didn't want to do the dishes, although we had never done dishes before in our lives; you know how it is in India—most of the educated class of people have a servant or two in their homes.

"I was angry at my brother because he had not expressed any kinship whatsoever towards me as my older brother, let alone any hospitality. Why the hell did he even sponsor me then? Especially when he knew very well how things were in his life? Sorry ma'am, I don't mean to swear like this, but I get angry even as I think of it. I looked at Ram, but he was sitting quietly on the chair, looking down at his own feet the whole time."

"That is incredible," I said. I was shaking my head in disbelief.

"Luckshmi came forward, took the sponge from my hands and approached the wash basin. Even the plumbing system with one faucet and two knobs, one for cold and another for hot water, was new to us, but she managed to start the tap water, making sure the hot water knob was not opened. With ice cold water, Luckshmi started washing all the dishes, pots and pans, and I tried helping her with it."

"And all through this, Ram was just sitting there, saying nothing?"

Narayan just nodded and said, "He may have been feeling bad, I am sure, but he looked helpless and didn't say anything, anything at all! That's when I realized what kind of life *he* was having. Poor

Ram! That's when I also realized what was going to befall *us* if we stayed there."

"Hell," Luckshmi said spontaneously. I felt slightly amused at her blurting this word at such an appropriate time, making me reinforce my belief that people develop vocabulary of any new language not necessarily only through training but also through swear words placed in their apt times. "Our life started in Canada in such a wretched way, I tell you—it was an absolutely lousy beginning. But I was not prepared to give up my hopes, because this terrible experience had nothing to do with Canada. As a matter of fact, my first experience at the Canadian border was excellent, and that's what I wanted to cling on to. This ugly episode with Ram and his wife was just a bad patch on my road to prosperity, I told myself. That meant a lot of patience and hard work on our part until we could stand on our own feet. We both were ready for it. Finding a job and earning some dollars became the top priority. I was tempted to ask Ram for his help in finding a job, any job, but I knew he wouldn't help. In order to please his wife, he became completely indifferent to us, and I didn't want to ruffle any feathers unnecessarily, either. I put some papers together, my résumé and testimonials that I had brought from India, and started what they call in Canada *pounding the pavement* of the city for a job."

"Every day, he goes out," Luckshmi interjected.

"Yes, I went out every single day in search of a job. First I tried to look for something in the engineering field, but everywhere I went, I was asked if I had any Canadian experience."

"Canadian experience?" I asked.

"Yes, Canadian experience! I never worked here, so naturally I had none."

"That's right."

"And because I didn't have it, I didn't get work. I got stuck. No Canadian experience, so *no* job, and *no* job, so *no* Canadian experience! I was at a dead end, feeling totally hopeless and frustrated. To make matters worse, many prospective employers inquired about my knowledge in French language. I was fluent in English but I didn't know French at all. That transpired into another big hurdle on my path. And as if this was not enough of a hurdle, situation in Quebec was worsening day by day; local people strongly feeling like they were living in a police state, the Prime Minister invoking the War Measures Act and the civil liberties being suspended for the nation. I couldn't believe that this was happening in Canada; Canada, a peaceful and most liberal country of the world. I had lost all my hopes. Situation on the home front was getting equally worse - my brother was getting impatient with us and his wife was getting rougher on him because of us. We offered ourselves as free labor to them for all the household chores including looking after their children in return for food and shelter."

"Could *no one* help you?" I asked. He shook his head.

"No, no one could help us. I went to the Canadian Immigration Office for some help, but I was told that they did not provide any help to a family-sponsored immigrant as it became the responsibility of the sponsor to look after the sponsored immigrant. They were right in refusing help, but where would I, or anyone like me for that matter, go if the family disowns them?" Narayan's face looked red. I didn't know if it was anger or extreme repentance.

"Ma'am, I honestly don't know how many immigrants are out there who have faced such punishing experiences like ours, after landing in Canada. New immigrants' lives can be quite hard in the beginning in this country, no doubt. When you are sponsored by your relatives, you are completely at the mercy of these sponsoring families. If they feed you, you eat, if they don't, you don't eat, tough luck! The Canadian government assigns that responsibility solely to the sponsor!"

"Can you complain against them to the authorities?"

"I don't know, perhaps yes, or maybe not! But even if you can, who would actually do such a thing? Since the sponsor is usually a close relative, who would want to complain against them to the authorities, right?"

"You are right."

"Our situation was this: we were in a new country with no money and no roof over our head; we couldn't complain against my brother to anyone although he had sponsored me, and therefore, technically responsible for my welfare. And to make it worse, I had no Canadian experience to find work and provide for ourselves. So there we were, completely stuck with nowhere to go."

"What about Government welfare? Can a new immigrant get that?" I asked.

"I don't know, but I don't think so. Let me ask you, ma'am, how many new immigrants do you think have heard of a system called 'Government welfare'? Did you ever hear about such a thing in India? And how many countries are there in the world which have such a system for their citizens, like they do here in Canada?"

I shook my head to all his questions. Narayan was right. I had never heard of the social welfare system until I arrived in Canada, where the government took care of citizens in their need. I even heard of some people getting this help for a few years, and in some cases, for their entire lives. This system was completely new to me, and occasionally I had wondered about its merit, for I had heard on the radio or seen on television many debates and talk-shows expressing strong negative views about it. I remembered, during one such talk show, hearing the new Canadian expression, "From cradle to coffin" in context to this system.

In India, everyone had to pull their own weight. They did it through their own hard work; the onus was on *them* to prosper or remain poor, and the government had very little to do with it. I was sure this was true for people in many other countries.

"I hadn't heard of the welfare system either," Narayan continued. "Besides, do you think all immigrants are willing to procure help from the social welfare system? I don't think so; some of us are almost *averse* to take help from the government. Do you agree, ma'am?"

I nodded, agreeing with him completely.

"We came to this country to work hard and prosper! You don't travel halfway across the globe to collect a few dollars from the government, right?"

"Oh, you are absolutely right, it's not an option. I personally don't know any immigrants who have exercised this option," I concurred with Narayan.

"Welfare is a good system, no doubt, but it is there only as the last resort. It is, after all, an assistance given *until* you can provide for yourself."

"So what did you do finally?" I didn't realize my simple question about going to welfare would strike such a negative chord in him. I managed to bring him back to his personal story.

"Well, things were getting worse by the day, as you can imagine. We were feeling like two wounded young animals living in a cage with no escape nor hope for tomorrow. Surekha was good at rubbing salt on our wounds by suggesting jobs that she knew we would never accept."

"Such as what? There is no dignity attached to any work in this country."

"Not in this country, I agree, but when you are new here and the values that you carry with you from your originating country are still fresh in your mind, it does matter." Narayan said this with quite an emphasis. I just looked at him with a questioning face.

"One day, Surekha approached me when I was alone in the room and said, 'Narayan, you have no money or job, but you cannot live here free forever, right? So I suggest that you send your wife to work in a bar as a cocktail bunny. They make a lot of money in tips, and who knows, a young, charming thing like her can get some more money for some work on the sidelines too, if you know what I mean.' She then winked at me with a wicked smile and started approaching the door."

"Oh my God!" I couldn't help but exclaim in disbelief.

"I was livid, completely stiff with anger. Quite honestly, at that time I didn't know what a cocktail bunny was, I didn't even *know* that word! But the way that witch smiled and winked at me, I knew right away what she had meant? 'You *chudel*[35], do you think all women are *rundis*[36] like you were?' I yelled at her in extreme anger. Ram came running into the room. He started inquiring, but before even I had a chance to say anything, Surekha said that she had only suggested Luckshmi also start looking for work, which had made me angry, and

35 *A wicked witch.*
36 *A prostitute.*

then hurriedly she left the room with a sad face as though terribly hurt by me. I was stunned! I didn't realize until then that Surekha was so cunning and such an expert liar. She had skillfully avoided telling Ram *what* job she had suggested for Luckshmi. I was too damn dumbfounded. Was this real?"

Narayan got up from his chair and started pacing the floor. He looked terribly upset even thinking of that incident. I could not believe what I had heard. I looked at Luckshmi and she just gestured me to stay quiet, explaining in Telugu how riled up and disturbed he got every time he recalled that incident. What a blow to a man's dignity! We all kept quiet for a few minutes.

Narayan collected himself and started apologizing. "I am sorry, I am really sorry that I got upset in front of you, ma'am. My wife invited you to our house for the first time, and I made you uneasy with my emotional display. Please, please do forgive me."

"That's alright. Obviously you still get disturbed with that memory," I said.

"Yes, yes I do. I have tried my best to forget it, but I think it will take a long time to erase it from my memory." He seemed to calm down a little. He said further, "I certainly don't mean to undermine any of those professions, please don't get me wrong. My Luckshmi was a charming young woman with feminine grace, I knew that too. Everyone could see that, but the way Surekha said and winked with a dirty smile, it meant nothing but something very dirty. She damn well knew that it did not fit into my old-fashioned values of dignity, and that I would get riled up. And that's exactly what she wanted, to prove to Ram that I was an impatient, short-tempered man with too much pride in me. Ma'am, I was born in a typical, educated, middle-class family where my opinions were formulated in traditional ways about some professions of this world; these professions did not fall within the framework of those traditional ways. Do you know what I mean?"

"Oh, absolutely," I said to him.

"I agree—you see no labels or *taboo* or dignity attached to any honest work in Canada, unlike in India; here, hard work is hard work. And I really like that aspect of Canada, believe me. But some professions still carry that taboo, even in this free and liberal society, don't you think?"

"Yes," I said. I had to reluctantly agree with him. Even in a free and liberated country like Canada, I knew that the world's oldest profession was not legalized, nor accepted by the general populace! A call girl, for example, could be in that profession out of sheer necessity; she could be supporting her education or she could be a single mother supporting her child. However, society still looked down upon her for her means rather than the intent of working!

"Did Ram come to know about it finally?" I asked Narayan. He shook his head.

"No?" I was surprised.

"No, I never told him, and he never bothered to find out why I had yelled at her with such anger. But since that day, things went downhill rather fast. Ram told me, in no uncertain terms, that I had two weeks to stay in their house, after which time we were to get out of his house, even if I didn't find a job."

"And where would you live or how would you support yourselves?"

"Well, that was not *his* problem, he said. Where we would go or what could we do was totally *our* problem. That was 'not his lookout' as he bluntly put it. We were to get out of his house in two weeks, as he demanded. The older brother had served an ultimatum to his younger brother within days after arriving from a faraway country into this foreign land."

Narayan became suddenly very quiet. It seemed like he was trying to control his emotions. And like the clouds that gather during the monsoon season in India, deep sympathy and tenderness were gathering in my heart. All kinds of questions and answers about the whole immigration system were crowding in my head after listening to his exasperating experience.

How many new immigrants have gone through such gruesome experiences after landing in Canada? I wondered. At least Narayan knew English, the language of the new land, but how many were there like him? Not too many. Most of them were like Luckshmi, who didn't know even the language of the land. I could say this with some authority, for I was an English instructor and had the first-hand experience of meeting such people, and observing their lives from up close. Things were especially tough for women, who were coming out of the sheltered cocoons of their homelands, finding themselves in impersonal surroundings with no means of communication with others due to this language barrier.

Everyone in the room was quiet, looking absorbed in their own thoughts. Narayan finally collected himself and started talking again.

"With the ultimatum served to me that way, I decided to get aggressive. I suppose extreme frustration gave me some kind of courage, as I had nothing to lose anyway. I went to Canada Manpower the very next day with Luckshmi. We had brought sixteen dollars from India when we came here—that's all that was allowed by the Indian government, out of which I had already spent ten dollars for cab fare on the day I arrived. When my turn came to see the counselor at the Manpower center, I literally begged him to find me some job, any job, not necessarily in the engineering related field, but just about any field. I took out my wallet from my pocket and opened it in front of him, showing him the last three dollars that were left in it. I told him that that's all the money I had, and that it was a question of our survival, mine and my wife's. I didn't know what he thought, but he looked at me with an inquisitive eye for a minute and then asked me, 'Can you sell insurance?' I said, 'Yes.' He made a couple of telephone calls and then directed me to an agency to meet someone there. I immediately went to the agency with Luckshmi and again put my cards completely on the table. I talked with the man, convincing him about my capability of selling insurance, and then showed him the three dollars I had. I told him the truth that it was all the money I had, and that it was a question of our survival, mine and my wife's. He was an astute business man. He saw my fluency in English, and more importantly, my dire need to work and make some money, so he gave me a job offer and I took it."

"Well, good for you," I said. Besides breeding invention, does necessity also bring out courage in people to face dire situations? Perhaps, yes!

"Then I went straight to the bank, and asked to see the loans officer." Narayan said.

"The loans officer?" I was surprised to hear that.

"Yes. I was fortunate to meet one. The Loans officer was a friendly lady with a compassionate face and voice. I think she believed in me and agreed to give me a loan of three hundred dollars, which I would return in small installments every week from my new job earnings. Can you believe all this? A whole three hundred dollars loan to a man who had absolutely nothing, except a job offer in hand and an honest desire to work at it. I used a few dollars to immediately open an account there. Ma'am, I have been doing all my bank business, to this day, only with that bank. That's how I felt and feel about that bank even today. With those three hundred dollars, I felt like a millionaire. I took the money and went to a cheap residential area, knocked on many doors that had a 'for rent' sign on them, and finalized a very small, inexpensive, furnished place for us. Luckshmi looked excited, although the place was like a dump, and quite shabby too, but it was going to be *our* place, with no one to harass us or strike at our self-respect. We decided to move into our place the very next day." Narayan looked happy now, and so did Luckshmi.

"Ram had given us two weeks. We thought we would move out in one day. I gave the owner some money as a deposit and left. It was a long day, a very long one, but a very productive one. We had not eaten anything for the whole day. However our hearts, and stomachs too, were filled with joy, as it was like getting a release from prison. We went back to my brother's place. We told him that we were moving out the following day. Surekha was stunned, and so was Ram, but they didn't ask any questions at all. I thought at least he might show some curiosity about where we were moving to or how we were going to manage financially. But he didn't, and at that point, I wasn't surprised to see Ram's cold response either. Strange, isn't it?"

"Yes, he should at least have asked something." It was odd that even Ram showed no interest.

"Surekha did do something before our move, though. She made sure that we packed everything in front of her," Narayan said.

"Why?"

"She wanted to make sure that we didn't take anything from her house."

"You are kidding, right?"

"No I am not. In spite of packing everything in front of her, she still inspected every little thing we packed."

"Oh, my good Lord!"

"But honestly, it didn't matter to us, as we were too happy to feel insulted or bad about it. There was one more reason why we were very happy to get out of there as soon as we could, which I haven't told you yet."

"What is it?"

"Well, our honeymoon had resulted in Luckshmi getting pregnant, and we found out about her pregnancy just as when we landed here."

"Oh my, did you tell this news to your folks?" I asked Narayan, while looking at Luckshmi.

"Yes, unfortunately we had to, as Luckie started having morning sickness. Let alone being happy for us, do you know what the first thing she said when we told her this news?"

"What?" After hearing their story so far, anything was possible.

"'Abort the baby, first abort the baby immediately. This was what she said to us."

"Oh my God, why?" I thought any young couple having their first baby would be an exciting news.

"She thought that now they would have to bear even more expenses, especially when we found out that the Canadian health care services did not cover maternity in the first year of immigration at the time in Canada."

"Oh my God! That's another reason you had such a sense of urgency to find a job soon and move out of your brother's place, right?"

"Yes, that's right. All that excitement of being pregnant quickly disappeared because of the worry and anxiety associated with the additional financial burden. We needed all the help we could get after this discovery. We needed God to help us!" Narayan looked at Luckshmi with keen eyes and said, "Tell her, Luckie, tell her what *you* were going through when I used to go out job hunting, every single day." She just nodded, and I saw that her big brown eyes were filled with tears.

"She wanted to kill my baby." Luckshmi barely managed to say this much and stopped abruptly.

"What?" I couldn't help but get a little excited.

"She is right," Narayan said. "Afraid of all the possible expenses with the coming of our baby, Surekha started trying her damnedest to get our baby aborted."

"Oh my…" Was this woman a monster incarnate or something?

"Yes. In the first few days, she made sure Luckie didn't get any food. This way, out of weakness or something, she thought Luckie would lose the baby. Well, nothing like that happened, and Luckie and the baby remained strong and healthy."

"Oh my good God! Are you serious, I mean really?" I could not believe what I was hearing.

"Yes, I am serious. It sounds far-fetched, but it is true. My wife and the baby remained strong and healthy. That was, also because of a beautiful blessing bestowed on us straight from the heavens."

"What do you mean?"

"Apples, the tonic…" Luckshmi said. She was a little excited but couldn't explain.

"What apples, what tonic?" I was intrigued.

"Ma'am, you won't believe this—no one would ever believe this even if I told them while swearing on my own mother's name."

"What, what? Tell me!"

"While I was out the whole day looking for employment, Luckie would finish all the housework and then get about half an hour break every afternoon when she would go outside for a walk, I had encouraged her to do so. At a ten-minute distance from Ram's house, she had located a single apple tree, a tree that somehow didn't seem to belong to anyone; it was standing in the middle of nowhere, in a meadow, bearing sweet fruit. When we arrived in Canada, it was autumn; there would be plenty of apples falling from this tree, but no one to pick them up. Luckie would walk there every single day, pick up those sweet fruits, wipe them clean with her *palloo*, and eat them up in a hurry. She used to call these delicious apples 'sweetmeats straight from heaven.'"

"God is great, really!" I felt my own eyes slowly filling up with tears.

"Yes, that's for sure. When she told me about the apples, I advised her not to tell this to anyone, and to continue eating a few apples every day. It was a 'tonic' straight from God, for Luckie and our baby!"

I really didn't know what to say to Narayan. I had never heard of an un-owned apple tree in Canada. An apple tree was always either a part of an apple orchard or a part of someone's garden in the front or back yards. That was amazing! A baby is a gift from God, and in this case, the baby was *nurtured* also by God!

"Surekha was surprised to see nothing ill happened to the baby or my wife in spite of not giving her enough food, but little did she know what the secret behind their good health was. Surekha came up with many devious and barbaric ways for aborting our baby, especially when I would be out somewhere looking for employment. Some of her ways were so cruel and hideous, that I can't even mention them, but fortunately God was on our side." His voice was breaking down.

He covered his face and was about to cry. Luckshmi went near him, put her hand on his shoulder, and patted him gently, covering her own face with the other hand and crying silently.

I couldn't believe it. Nothing that I heard from Narayan about his wife's pregnancy or their baby's news fit in with the normal response that people give after receiving news of someone's pregnancy. The response to this news from his folks was far from simple decency. "Abort the baby first," they said. "First get rid of the baby," they commanded. What a cruel and grotesque response to a young mother-to-be, and what a blow to the dignity and self-respect of a young father-to-be! I just sat there in total disbelief, not knowing what to say.

"You must really hate this woman intensely, and perhaps your brother too," I commented after a few silent moments.

"No ma'am." He cleared his throat to regain momentarily his dignity and said, "You would be surprised, but no, we do not hate them." He emphasized the word hate. "They were given to us as an opportunity to learn from and grow, like having a lesson in school, and so we did."

"Indeed!" I exclaimed. Just then, we all heard the words "Mimi, Mimi..." being called in a child's soft voice, coming from inside.

"Damini, I am coming, sweetie." Luckshmi hurriedly wiped her tears and ran inside. A few minutes later, she brought the little toddler in the front room, all wrapped up in a small, pink blanket. She handed the bundle over to Narayan. He took the bundle, and quickly wiped his tears with his sleeves. While clearing away the blanket from his daughter's face, he said, "Ma'am, this is our Damini, a gift from heaven!"

Although half asleep, the little girl gave me the sweetest smile I could imagine. And that changed the mood of the whole room instantly! Her smile wiped away tears from her parents' faces, as they too were smiling, with their faces genuinely expressing happiness. Their little girl was like true bliss sent from heaven for that young couple. Up until this point in their story, I was afraid that they would have had to relinquish all their hopes and dreams; however, looking at the instant effect the little girl had on her parents made me believe that they were strong and determined enough to endure their predicament through any tough times. They would not surrender so easily, and were capable of giving themselves and this child an excellent life in Canada. Their dreams were indeed to come true in their newfound promised land!

Epilogue

This is truly a success story of an immigrant family from India.

When I met Narayan and Lakshmi many years later, I learned that Narayan had completed his MBA degree from the same university as mine. That opened many doors for him in the job market, and after working for almost twenty years with an engineering company, he had started his own engineering consulting firm, and had been busy with his work ever since.

Luckshmi had done quite well in her career, too. With diligence and hard work, she mastered her skills in the English language, and completed all the requirements of a certified teacher. She had been working as an ESL teacher in the local school board.

Their "bliss," Damini, a bright young lady, was studying in dental college. She was a 'Dentist-in-the-making'!

About The Author

Author Jayashree Thatte Bhat holds a Master of Chemistry from York University of Toronto, and Master's and PhD degrees in Classical Music of India. As a Graduate student in Toronto, and as an English teacher at the Immigrant Service Agency in Toronto for several years, Jayashree mingled very closely with immigrants from around the world living in Canada. That provided her with endless inspiration for her books, especially those immigrants, who were overcoming challenges and adversities in their lives in their native lands.

When she decided to write about some of the personalities, who had emigrated from India; the publishers in India overwhelmingly supported her by publishing her first book, titled, Mawalthichi Zadey meaning, "Personalities in the West." It was published in Marathi (her mother tongue), and earned Jayashree a literary award in India for her observation and perception of people. She has since published three more books in Marathi and two books in English. All of them have been very well received by the readership, with rave reviews.

Jayashree spends her time in writing books; and performing and teaching music at North American Universities. She is blessed with two children, Tejashree and Meghana, and five grandchildren, Amruta, Arjun, Vikram, Jahnavi and Nicholas.

Jayashree lives in Calgary with her husband, Suresh.

CPSIA information can be obtained at www.ICGtesting.com
Printed in the USA
LVOW08s0507160814

399377LV00002B/18/P